KRIMSON SPARK

KRIMSON EMPIRE BOOK 2

JULIA HUNI

KRIMSON SPARK

KRIMSON EMPIRE
BOOK 2

JULIA HUNI

Krimson Spark Copyright © 2020 by Julia Huni

All rights reserved

All names, settings, characters, and incidents in this book are fictional. Any resemblance to someone or something you know or have read about, living or dead, is purely coincidental. This is fiction. They're all made up.

The distribution of this book without permission is a theft of the author's intellectual property. If you would like permission to use material from the book (other than a short excerpt for review purposes), please contact info@juliahuni.com. Thank you for your support of the author's rights.

Cover by Deranged Doctor Designs

Originally published by Craig Martelle, Inc.

Published by
IPH Media, LLC
PO Box 62
Sisters, Oregon 97759

Second US edition, October, 2023

*For my husband David
who reads all of my books,
handles all of my advertising,
and gives me space to create new worlds.*

CHAPTER 1

WHEN THE STRIKING blonde walked into the coffee shop, heads turned. Her piercing blue eyes roved over each face, cataloging and dismissing. They finally settled on Quinn Templeton, seated against the back wall of the cafe. Quinn raised an eyebrow. The blonde glided between the tables, ignoring the hopeful looks.

"Hello, Quinn."

Quinn smiled. "Francine. What are you doing here?"

"Looking for you," Francine Zielinsky replied. "You weren't hard to find."

"I wasn't trying to be." Quinn ran a self-conscious hand over her wavy brown hair, wishing she'd taken a moment to brush it before pulling it back into a ponytail. Francine always made her feel so frumpy.

Francine's lips quirked. "May I?" She indicated the empty seat at Quinn's table.

"Be my guest," Quinn said. "I was looking for an excuse to stop reading this."

Francine picked up the tablet Quinn indicated and read the book title. "*Theories on Management*? Yeesh. Sounds deadly."

"It's for my new certification," Quinn said. "The tech-y stuff is fun, but jargon in this management module is making my eyes cross."

"Why are you doing it, then?" Francine dropped the tablet on the table.

Quinn didn't comment on Francine's lack of respect for government-issued equipment. "I need to get a job and getting recertified in the Commonwealth is key. They recognize my degree from the Federation, but it's out of date. I need to—"

"I get that. But why do you want to get a job? Why not work for Lou?"

Quinn's eyes narrowed. "What makes you think Lou would want me? And besides, if working for a family is so great, why aren't you back with the Zielinskys?" She sat up straighter. "Or are you?"

Francine shushed her. "No, I'm not. Don't say that name here. Look, I've heard Liz and Maerk left Lou. She's looking for people she can trust. Surely, you're one of them."

Quinn gasped. "How did you hear that?"

Francine shrugged one elegant shoulder. "I have my sources. Are you going?"

"How can I go?" Quinn asked. "You know why they left—because they worried about their kids. If Liz doesn't trust her mother with her own children, how can I trust her with mine? They're babies compared to Dareen and Ender."

Francine looked away. "I guess. I was hoping—"

"*You* want to work for Lou?!" Quinn laughed. "I'm sure she'd love to have you."

"Hey," Francine said. "You're supposed to be my friend. Friends don't mock each other."

"Actually, they do." Quinn frowned. "You consider me a friend? I thought we were two lonely outsiders who met for coffee once in a while."

"Isn't that what a friend is?" Francine asked.

Quinn shook her head. "If that's your definition of a friend, I feel sorry for you. But I would be honored to be considered your friend."

Francine rolled her eyes. "Don't get all dramatic on me."

"Now who's mocking?" Quinn waved her hand to stop Francine's response. "Never mind. Why would you want to work for Lou?"

"I need to get off this planet. And no, before you ask, I'm not in trouble. I'm tired of the staid life of a well-behaved citizen of the Commonwealth. I need a little more adventure, and it's out there." She looked toward the ceiling.

"You're tired already—after a whole month? Why don't you go back to your family? From what I've heard, they aren't staid, well-behaved citizens."

Francine shook her head and lowered her voice. "Too controlling. The Russosken is run by the *nachal'nik*, and what she says, goes."

"You think Lou would be any different?" Quinn asked.

"No..." Francine drew the word out thoughtfully. "Well, yes. Lou's family doesn't put up with any crap. If they don't like something she says or does, they argue. That would never happen in my family. No one questions the *nachal'nik*."

Quinn fiddled with her spoon. She wasn't sure she could trust Francine. The woman had helped her escape from Hadriana, and save the lives of Lou's family, but she didn't know enough about her background to feel comfortable. All this talk of the Russosken made her nervous. She glanced up at the other woman from under her lashes. "What do you want from me?"

Francine turned in her chair, so she was fully facing Quinn. She locked her blue eyes on Quinn's brown ones. "I know you have a way to contact Tony. I want you to put me in touch with him, so I can join Lou's crew."

QUINN STEPPED into her quiet apartment. The kids were still at school activities, so she had it to herself for a few minutes. She set her bag on the couch and scratched the ears of the caat stretched across the back. Sashelle, the Eliminator of Vermin, endured the attention with a bored look, but nudged Quinn's hand with her head when the human stopped scratching.

"Everybody wants something. Even you, eh, Sassy? I wish I knew—" she broke off. Heaving a sigh, she pulled up the saved message on her comtab.

Lou's voice sounded grim, even though the words were innocuous. "Hi, Quinn. We had a visitor last week. I wish you could have met them." Or maybe the grim tone was her imagination. The *idea* of a message from Lou made Quinn feel nervous. And, if she was honest with herself, a little bit excited. After the craziness of Hadriana, life on N'Avon was a little dull.

The message was the code she and Tony had set up when he left her on N'Avon. She hadn't realized he'd shared it with Lou. Did that mean Tony was in trouble? Or was Lou simply calling in the favor Quinn owed her? And how had Francine known Lou called yesterday? Was it a coincidence she'd come looking for Quinn this morning?

She closed the message and tossed the comtab on top of her bag. She couldn't do anything until Lou called again—the ship captain hadn't left any contact details. Crossing the small apartment, she went to the kitchen and pulled out snacks for the kids. They'd be home any minute.

"I SAW DAREEN TODAY." Ellianne grabbed an apple slice off her plate.

"Where?" Quinn demanded. Why were the Marconis coming out of the woodwork this week?

"At school," the eight-year-old said.

"I saw her, too," Lucas said through a mouthful of peanut butter crackers. "She was in the office."

"What was she doing there?" Quinn asked.

Lucas shrugged. "I dunno. She was talking to the secretary. I said, 'hi,' and she hugged me and said she'd see me later, but she was busy." He grinned. "My friends were like, 'how'd you meet such a hot girl,' and 'ooh, older woman!' I said, 'gross!' I mean, we're practically related!"

Quinn's eyebrows drew down. "Related? How do you figure?"

"Tony's kind of like an uncle, and she's his cousin. Whatever, she's not my type."

"I wasn't aware you had a type." Quinn bit her lips to hide a smile.

Lucas lifted his chin. "I don't tell you everything."

"True," she agreed gravely. "But can you tell me if you saw her later? Did you find out what she was doing?"

Lucas shook his head and jumped up from his stool. "Nope. Me an' the guys are playing soccer in the quad, okay?" Without waiting for a reply, he raced to his bedroom.

Quinn looked at Ellianne. "Did Dareen tell you why she was here?"

Ellianne stuck out her bottom lip in an exaggerated pout. "No. I was in lunch line. I couldn't talk to her."

"I guess we'll find out when we find out." Quinn filled Lucas's water bottle and tossed it to him as he streaked through the living room on his way to the door. "Don't forget this! Be home by six!"

QUINN WASN'T surprised when the doorbell rang. She checked through the peephole, then opened it. "I've been expecting you."

Dareen grinned. "I figured the kids would tell you. Can I come in?"

"Sure." She pulled the door wide. "I thought you might get here earlier, though. You want some coffee?"

Dareen made a face. "Ew. No. Ya got any FizzyPop?"

Quinn laughed and went to the fridge. "Of course. Have a seat. The kids are asleep."

The younger woman flopped down on the sofa. Sashelle strolled over and stepped into her lap. "Hey, Sassy." Dareen scratched the caat's ears. Sashelle purred and closed her eyes.

"Why does that caat like everyone else better than me?" Quinn handed a glass to Dareen and dropped into an armchair. "I'm the one who buys the tuna."

Sashelle opened one eye, looked at Quinn, then turned her head away.

"I swear she understands everything I say!"

Dareen nodded. "They do."

"I visited Hadriana—many times—over fifteen years," Quinn said. "No one ever suggested the caats were intelligent."

Dareen switched to a silly voice, cuddling the caat's face in her hands. "She doesn't mean that, Sassy. She doesn't know you're special." She looked at Quinn. "Most of the caats on Hadriana are a cross of Earth cats and the local feline species. They're just pets. But I think Sassy is a purebred Hadriana caat. They're smarter."

The caat sat up and laid her head on Dareen's chest.

Quinn gave them a sideways glance. "How do you know so much about caats?"

"Report for school," Dareen said with a shrug. Before Quinn could ask, she continued. "Homeschool. Kert makes sure the family doesn't produce any 'ignorant offspring'." She grinned as she said the last two words in a deeper voice.

With a nod, Quinn changed the subject. "Why are you here, Dareen? Not that I'm not happy to see you, but—"

Dareen held up the hand not stroking the caat. "I get it. Business. We need your help. Tony has gone silent."

"What do you mean?" Quinn's stomach twisted. "Is he all right?"

"We don't know." Dareen moved the caat from her lap to the couch, then pulled her comtab out of her pocket and swiped at it. "He sent this message." She held out the device.

Quinn took it and pressed the play button. Tony's voice sounded tinny through the cheap speakers.

"I need some help. Message Quinn." The recording ended with a string of numbers.

"What are the numbers?" Quinn asked, holding out the comtab.

"We don't know. We thought you might." Dareen looked at the device but made no move to retrieve it. "Keep that. It's a burner. That message is the only thing on it."

"Where is he?" Quinn asked.

"Romara."

"He went back into the Federation?!" Quinn's voice broke on the last word. "What was he thinking? If they catch him, they'll kill him!"

Dareen nodded, blinking hard. "We know. That's why we need you."

CHAPTER 2
TWO WEEKS EARLIER

TONY BERGEN SAT in a dark booth in the back of a small restaurant on the outskirts of Romara. The bowl of borscht on the table smelled as bad as it looked, but Tony dipped his spoon in anyway. Sending it back would draw attention he didn't want. Besides, if he put enough sour cream on top, it should be edible.

He suppressed a shudder when the soup hit his tongue and pretended it was the best borscht he'd ever tasted. A gulp of beer—passable—killed the taste and settled his stomach. Beer always made him think of spaceships and hyperjump, and that was usually a good thought.

A boxy woman of tank-like proportions slid into the seat opposite him. "I hope you know what you're doing, Tony," she said.

"I wouldn't order the borscht, if that's what you mean." Tony took in the sheen of sweat on the woman's upper lip and the tremor in her hands. "Take a deep breath, Evelyn. No one knows you're here."

"How do you know?" she demanded in a hoarse whisper. "I could have been followed. Or maybe I'm double-crossing you."

Tony smiled, and the woman across the table visibly relaxed. "You weren't followed." He tapped his comtab, laying on the table in the shadow of the soup bowl. "I've been watching. And if you double-crossed me, I guess I'll find out soon enough."

Evelyn Seraseek straightened her spine. "It may have taken a while for me to make this decision, but I don't renege on my promises. I said I'd help you. *They* claim you're a Krimson spy— Pah. I stand by my friends."

Guilt dropped into Tony's stomach and picked a fight with the sour borscht. He smiled, in what he hoped was a convincing mixture of relief and fear. "I appreciate that about you, Evelyn. You always did stand by your friends. But this is serious business. If they think you're connected to me, you could get arrested. Convicted even. Treason is kind of a big deal."

"The truth will out," Seraseek said. "I believe in the Federation—we stand for truth, justice, and the best for all."

Tony looked away.

"Besides, they wouldn't dare mess with a Seraseek. My family will protect me." The matter-of-fact way she said it—as if being a member of *her* family made her more important than anyone else—set Tony's teeth on edge. Generations of Seraseeks had pulled the strings of the Federation since its inception. Evelyn clearly believed it was her birthright to be treated differently from the common citizens. The sheer magnitude of her arrogance strengthened Tony's resolve.

He looked deep into her eyes. "I wish I were a Seraseek. Life would be so much better. For all of us."

Pink washed over her cheeks and disappeared. She smiled smugly and fluttered her eyelashes. "There are ways other than birth to join a family."

Yikes. Time to get back to business. "That's something I can't even think about until I've cleared my name," he said. "Did you get what I asked for?"

Seraseek looked around the room, but no one else had ventured inside. The ancient waitress had disappeared into the kitchen after delivering his soup, and the bartender must be on a break. "I have it." She reached into her bag and placed a thick envelope on the table.

She tapped it a couple times, as if making a decision, then slid it toward him.

Tony put out a finger to stop it before it slid into the puddle of spilled borscht. He set his comtab on top. "You're a lifesaver, Evelyn," he said.

She nodded and stood, hooking her fingers through her purse strap. "I'm going to powder my nose. I'll be right back."

As Tony watched her stroll across the small restaurant and into the dark hallway beside the kitchen, he reached into his boot and pulled out a mini-blaster. Seraseek had claimed she'd never been to this restaurant. How did she know where to find the bathroom?

With a faked start, he picked up his comtab and held it to his ear. "Hang on, my reception is terrible in here." As he spoke, he tucked the envelope into his pocket. Tossing his napkin onto the table, he stood, eyes roving over the empty booths and tables. "You're breaking up. I'm going to step outside." He turned toward the hallway Seraseek had disappeared down and came face-to-chest with a large man in dark clothing.

"Excuse me," Tony said, tucking his hand—and the mini blaster in it—into his pocket.

"No excuse," the man answered. "You will come with me."

"But my friend—"

"She will be fine," the man said. "Pay your bill. You're leaving." He wrapped his meaty hand around Tony's bicep and shook. Hard.

Tony pulled a handful of cash out of his pocket and threw it on the table. Then with a shrug, he picked up the beer and chugged it down. "Hate to waste good beer."

The big man shook him again, hard enough to rattle his teeth, and steered him toward the back door.

"What? Did you want some beer?" Tony asked. "I can get you one, if you like."

"Shut up." The big man kicked open the door. He drove Tony through, steering him effortlessly.

Outside, the man glowered at two even larger guys in black. "Got 'im. Where's the truck?"

"Put him in the back," the shorter of the two giants said. "Stay with him—he's supposed to be a tricky one." He snapped his fingers and the enormous one opened the rear door of a windowless van.

Tony and his captor climbed in. The door shut behind them and the big man pushed him down onto a bench along the side. Taking a seat across from Tony, he crossed his arms over his chest and glowered.

"Where are we going?" Tony asked as the truck rumbled to life and pulled out.

The man tucked his chin onto his chest and stared from beneath thick eyebrows.

Tony nodded. "You don't know and don't care. Fair enough. You don't look like Federation security, by the way. Contractor?"

The man did an excellent imitation of a statue.

"Got it, no answers from you. You don't mind if I talk, though, do you? I tend to chatter when I'm nervous."

"Shut up," the man said, his nostrils flaring.

The truck rumbled on, bouncing over the rough road. The man in black appeared to fall asleep, but Tony knew he wasn't. No one could stay balanced on that bench if they were asleep.

They hadn't searched him, which seemed odd. Stupid mistake for a Federation security contractor to make. Moving slowly, so he wouldn't alert his captor, Tony slid his hand into his pocket and wrapped his fingers around the mini blaster. He debated his options. He could stun this guy now and be ready for his companions when they stopped. Or he could wait and— Nope, always go with the gut.

"Not yet," the big guy said, cracking one eyelid.

Tony froze.

"Wait 'til we're farther out of town." The man shifted, his voice low over the growl of the truck engine. "Then you can escape."

CHAPTER 3

QUINN LEAPED up and strode across the room. Five strides took her to the kitchen, and she swung around. This apartment was not made for pacing. "I'll have to find somewhere for the kids to stay."

"Bring them along," Dareen said. "Kert will make sure they keep up on their schooling."

Quinn shook her head. "No. They've just gotten settled here. Besides, if I'm going to help Tony, I can't be worried about what Lou is making them do."

"I think Gramma's learned her lesson," Dareen pulled the caat back into her lap. "Mom and Dad left."

"Francine told me." Quinn frowned. "But you stayed? Wasn't getting *you* away from Lou the whole point?"

"How did Francine know?" Dareen cut across her words.

"She wouldn't tell me."

Dareen nodded. "Protecting her sources. But, yeah, they wanted me and End to go with them. I don't like to argue with my mom, but I can't leave Gramma in the lurch. She can't run the ship with only Tony and the uncles. She'd have to hire outsiders." Her voice dropped to a horrified whisper.

"Like me?"

"You aren't an outsider." Dareen shook her head. "Well, kinda, but not completely." She looked at the caat, then glanced at Quinn from under her lashes. "You're almost a cousin."

Quinn's eyebrows drew down. That was almost exactly what Lucas had said. "What d'ya mean?"

Dareen shrugged and looked away. "You came with Tony—kind of a package deal. That makes you a cousin."

Quinn paced across the room again. She and Tony weren't a package deal. That sounded like a couple, and they definitely weren't one of those. "We're just friends. He helped me. Then I came here. That hardly makes us a package."

The teen waved her hand. "Whatever. We need you now. Tony specifically asked for you. Pack your stuff." The caat batted Dareen's hand with her paw, demanding attention. The girl went back to stroking the furry head.

"Pack my stuff? You mean you want to leave now?" Quinn threw up her hands in disbelief. "I can't leave now! I have to make arrangements for the kids. And the caat."

"Sassy can come with us." Lucas stood in the doorway.

"What are you doing out of bed?" Quinn demanded.

"We heard Dareen and came to say hello." Ellianne bounded across the room to throw herself at the older girl. "Hi, Dareen!"

"Hey, Elli-belli!" Dareen squeezed the little girl. The caat, squished between them, let out an indignant meow.

"We're going on another mission!" Lucas's eyes lit up.

"You're not. You have school," Quinn said. "And I'm not leaving you alone on a ship with Lou!"

"They wouldn't be alone," Dareen put in. "End and I would be there. And Kert and Stene. And besides, no matter what kind of trouble End and I get into, you have to admit Tony turned out okay. He grew up on the *Peregrine*, too."

"That was a while ago," Quinn said. "And I imagine his mother had something to do with that."

Dareen's head shook. "Nope. She's never set foot on the *Pere-*

grine. I'm not sure Tony's even met her, to be honest. I mean, not since birth. I certainly haven't."

Quinn's eyes went wide. She and Tony had never talked about their childhoods, but she had no idea he'd grown up motherless on a spaceship. She filed that information away for later consideration.

"Come on, Mom," Lucas said. "Let's go!"

"I already said no." She pinned a glare on her son. "And you need to go back to bed."

"If I have to stay at school while you have all the fun, I may as well have stayed on Hadriana," Lucas muttered. "That was Dad's plan, too."

"Ouch." Quinn rolled her eyes. "You're going to have to try harder than that."

Lucas grinned. "I'll work on it. But really, Mom, we should do this. You get Tony out of trouble, and I'll take care of Elli."

"We'll do all our homework," Ellianne said. "And eat our veggies. And go to bed on time!"

"Maybe Dareen can stay here and watch you while I go rescue Tony," Quinn shot an evil grin at the teen.

"I— What now?" Dareen sputtered.

Quinn laughed. "Just kidding." She turned to the kids. "Go to bed. You've made your case—but continued wheedling will undermine your argument. I will take your suggestions under advisement." She glared at each of them in turn. "Go. To. Bed."

"Go on." Dareen made shooing motions. "Your mom and I need to talk."

Ellianne threw her arms around Dareen's neck. "Don't leave without saying good-bye."

Dareen winked. "Wouldn't think of it." She held out a fist to Lucas. "See you tomorrow."

Lucas bumped fists, then trudged back to his room, muttering under his breath.

With the kids safely out of the room, Quinn turned back to Dareen. "I can't take them aboard. They're settled here."

Dareen glanced at Quinn and away. "Have you met Lucas's friends?"

"A couple of them." Quinn's eyes narrowed. "Why?"

The girl shrugged. "I saw him in the park this evening. He was sitting alone, watching some kids play soccer."

"He must have been taking a break."

Dareen's head slowly wagged side-to-side. "He wasn't anywhere near the game. He was sitting on the far side, watching. And I'm not sure you'd want him hanging out with those kids, anyway. They were older—closer to my age."

Quinn dropped into the armchair again. "I thought he liked it here."

"It takes time," Dareen said. "Before we joined Gramma—when I was little—we moved around a lot. It's hard to make friends."

"He's a military brat," Quinn said. "They're used to moving and making new friends."

"Yeah, but the kids here aren't." Dareen stroked the caat. "They've got their social groups, and they aren't looking to add anyone. They don't know what it's like to be the new kid. Plus, your kids are from the Federation. That's another strike against them." She locked eyes with Quinn. "I was so much happier on the *Peregrine* than anywhere else we lived. And End would say the same."

The girl nudged the caat off her lap and stood. "Think about it. We want you back—all of you."

"Even if I was willing to take the kids on the *Peregrine*," Quinn said, "I wouldn't take them into the Federation. What if we got caught? They'd go back to Reggie, and I'd go to death row."

"Gramma is very careful," Dareen said. "That mess with the cloaking device was a one-off. She never takes the *Peregrine* into a Federation port or station. Space is big—lots of asteroids to hide behind, if you know where to look. She keeps the ship out of the way while the shuttles do the work. Think about it. I'll be back."

"Wait. Do you have a place to stay?"

Dareen nodded. "I'm good. I'll see you in the morning." She slipped out the door and shut it softly behind her.

Quinn rubbed her temples. When had Dareen gotten so mature? Should she take her kids on the *Peregrine*? Or was that whole discussion just a way to keep Quinn from asking more questions about the mission?

CHAPTER 4

"I WAS STARTING to wonder if I'd gotten in the wrong truck," Tony said, holding out a hand. "You must be one of Bruno's."

"You can call me Rafe." The big man shifted on the hard bench and glanced at his wrist device. "Bruno's got a car waiting for you about two klicks away. I'll start yelling and pounding on the wall for help. When they stop the truck, we'll take 'em down. Then you'll stun me and escape."

"Are you sure it's safe for you to stay?" Tony asked. "Won't they blame you for my escape?"

"I have a reputation for being a bit thick." Rafe smirked and shrugged. "I'm kind of surprised they left me alone with you. I wouldn't have." He laughed. "If you hit me with my own stunner, that'll be cover enough."

"Are you sure? They won't kill you for incompetence?"

Rafe shook his head. "They need brutes like me. The Federation isn't known for big men."

"True," Tony said. Federation citizens tended to be slender.

"Here we go." Rafe tapped his watch, then slapped a meaty hand against the cab of the truck. "Oy! This guy is getting—" He ended with a scream that curdled Tony's stomach.

The van skidded to a halt. Rafe handed his blaster to Tony and threw himself down on his side, facing the cab of the truck. Tony crouched, using Rafe's massive back as a shield. "I hope they don't shoot you," he whispered.

"I got my under-armor on," Rafe replied, knocking his fist against his shirt. The hard, hollow ring reassured Tony.

The back doors flew open and wild shots flew over Tony's head. He smirked. They were firing randomly from behind the truck's thick doors. He waited until a head popped around the right-side door to look.

Zap. Thunk. The first one collapsed on the grassy verge.

"Hey!" the other yelled. "Come out of there with your hands up! You got nowhere to go, and I got backup on the way."

Tony glanced down at Rafe, who rolled his eyes. "I thought you said *you* have a rep for being thick?" Tony whispered.

Rafe grinned but didn't say anything. Tony stepped over his massive companion and crept toward the back of the van. In a few seconds, the thug would peek around the doorframe. It was human nature, and these guys clearly hadn't been well trained.

A flicker on the right side. Surprisingly clever—he'd gone around, knowing Tony would expect him on the left. Too bad he hadn't kept his feet out of view. Three, two, one... There.

Zap. Thunk. Right on top of his friend.

Tony turned. "You sure I need to zap you?"

"Turn it down to minimum." Rafe rolled over. He propped himself up on his elbow and tapped his chest, below the neckline. "And hit me here. They'll test for residue and know if I wasn't zapped, but their equipment isn't high-end enough to detect levels or time lapse. Better get a move on. Bruno ain't gonna wait long. Here's the coordinates." He held out Tony's comtab.

Tony took the device, sliding it into his pocket without looking. He put his hand back out. "Thanks for your help."

"My pleasure." Rafe bumped Tony's fist hard enough to hurt. "Stay safe. *Semper libero.*"

"*Semper libero*," Tony repeated. He aimed carefully and hit Rafe with a minimum stun.

Rafe collapsed on the floor of the truck, rubbing his chest. "Damn, I always forget that's gonna sting."

Tony jumped out of the truck. He took a minute to relieve his erstwhile captors of their weapons, devices, and wallets, then fished the comtab out of his pocket. A quick glance at the screen and he wedged himself through the thick hedge lining the highway.

A field of tall plants stretched as far as he could see. Perfect cover for a short man. He pushed through the first two rows, then turned right and ran between the stocks. Pungent flowers waved over his head. At the end of the row, he leaped over an irrigation stream, then stopped in the shadow of the next row of flowers. Taking the cash out of the wallets he'd lifted, he dropped them in the water, followed by the blasters. They might have trackers.

Turning, he picked his way along the edge of the irrigation ditch, slipping in the mud twice. Then he turned right again and ran to the end of this field. Here a dirt road led away from the highway. Tony grinned and headed toward the rendezvous point.

His feet kicked up dust on the road, but it was faster than the irrigation stream. He increased his speed, keeping his ears peeled for drones or sirens. Nothing but the slap of his dress shoes on the dirt. When he paused at a crossroads to get his breath, he looked down. His polished leather Leroys would never be the same again. Tony was a city man—he could accomplish anything in a metropolis. All this dust and mud? Not his thing!

On the far side of the next field, a small black car waited on a paved road. Blaster in hand, Tony ran to the second-to-last row of plants and stopped in the shade of the tall flowers. He squinted at the car, but dark windows made it impossible to see inside. Fishing his comtab out again, he crept along the row until he was parallel to the car. Then he crouched and looked at the screen.

Rafe had added an app to his phone. The location of the car

blinked on a map, with coordinates listed below. A text box sat empty beneath the map. Tony tapped in some words.

```
                          Fish for dinner?
```

Then he waited. A few seconds later, the device vibrated.

```
    Ew. No.
```

```
                          How about chicken
```

The passenger door popped open as a new text popped up.

```
    I prefer pizza
```

Tony laughed and pushed between the stalks toward the road. He climbed into the car, closed the door, and fastened his seatbelt. The car zipped away.

"Good to see you, Tony." The gray-haired woman in the driver's seat tapped the screen and engaged the autopilot.

"Thanks for the assist, Bruno." Tony turned in his seat to shake the hand she extended. "Rafe did well."

"He was a handy asset. I hope using him was worth it. He's going to be useless to me for a while."

"History will be the judge," Tony said. "But from my perspective, it was worth it. I knew Seraseek would be tricky."

"Did you get what you wanted out of her?"

Tony pulled the envelope Seraseek had given him out of his pocket. His comtab had scanned for—and burned out—any tracking chips in the package. With a flick of his wrist, he opened his knife and slid it under the flap. "Five thousand credits. And the list." He pulled a piece of paper out of the sheaf of bills. He smiled.

It looked like a bank withdrawal receipt. The account numbers were listed across the top, with the cash withdrawal and balance below. Tony ran a finger over the numbers. "Exactly what I was looking for."

"What is it?"

Tony hesitated. He trusted Bruno, but their business was need-to-know. "Message from my banker."

"What would you have done if she'd replaced the whole thing with blank paper?"

"Plan B." Tony' lips twisted into a grimace. "But Seraseek considers herself an honorable woman. She wasn't going to do that."

"She turned you in—to the Federation! Why wouldn't she take your cash?"

Tony shrugged. "In her mind, they're two different things. Turning me in was for the good of society. Taking my money would be theft. I counted on her to take the moral high ground."

"If you say so." Bruno shook her head.

The car took an onramp and zipped onto the highway. Sirens and lights ahead made Tony's lungs constrict, but the cars sped past them, headed back the way they'd come.

"I think that was your ride." Bruno jutted a thumb over her shoulder.

"Sorry to disappoint them."

"The car is going to drop me at the next exit," Bruno said. "I've got a ride waiting. Send it back when you're done with it."

Tony nodded. "Who's is this?"

"University of Romara." Bruno chuckled. "I liberated it from their faculty parking."

"You rescued me in a car that belongs to the Federation?" A chill went through him.

"Well, the university might be owned by the Federation, but they're pretty lax with their vehicles. It's currently checked out to a Dr. Zerbinski-Wong. She never drives the damn thing but insists on having it available. It's a status thing. No one will notice it's been used until she trades it in for a new one at the end of the year."

The car changed lanes and drove down the next ramp. It pulled into a charging station and drifted to a stop near the maintenance bay. As Bruno opened the door, another car pulled up next to them.

"My ride." Bruno glanced at the other car, then stared into the distance for a moment.

Tony waited.

Bruno nodded to herself. "I can't believe the Commonwealth sent you back here. Take my advice and go home. The Feds are looking for you. If they catch you, you're dead."

"I know," Tony said. "But no one else can complete *this* mission."

"I hate to be the one to break it to you, Tony, but you aren't that unique," Bruno said sharply. "None of us are. We're cogs in the machine—highly specialized but replaceable. If you get caught, the Commonwealth ain't gonna do *futz* for you."

"I know," Tony repeated softly. *More than you realize*, he thought. "I'll have to make sure I don't get caught."

"Again."

"Again." Tony nodded. "*Semper libero*, Bruno. See you on the other side."

"*Semper libero*, Tony." Bruno climbed out and slammed the door shut. "And good luck."

CHAPTER 5

QUINN LAY awake half the night, mulling over the things Dareen had said. Ellianne was fine—she made friends quickly and easily. But Lucas was another matter. Fitting in wasn't fast or easy for a thirteen-year-old. And Dareen had been right about the military kids being more accepting. Even on Fort Sumpter, it had taken months for Lucas to find friends. But taking him away now wouldn't help. If they went back to the *Peregrine*, it would be permanent. And she wasn't sure she was ready to do that. Even if Lou asked.

When the alarm went off, she was no closer to an answer than she had been the night before. She rolled out of bed, exhausted, and stumbled into the shower.

Which didn't work.

"What the hell?!" Quinn pulled a robe on and stomped into the bedroom to look at her comtab. A message across the top, sent at oh-dark-thirty, announced an unplanned water outage for her apartment block. Estimated time for repair: unknown. Perfect.

She got dressed and shuffled to the kitchen, where she discovered the electricity was also out. "Bloody hell!"

"Hey, Mom," Lucas yelled. "The toilet won't flush!"

Quinn shut her eyes and pinched the bridge of her nose. "I

know." She pulled a carton of wet wipes out from under the kitchen and carried them to the bathroom. "Leave it. Use this for your hands and come get breakfast."

They ate dry cereal and fruit, because the milk was sour. Quinn checked the expiration date. "I'd swear I just bought this."

"I'm going to have cookies for breakfast," Ellianne declared.

"No, you aren't." Quinn handed her an apple. "Let's go. How can we be so late?" She grabbed her bag and herded the kids out the door.

The caat slipped between their legs and darted out. "Sashelle!" Ellianne pelted after the animal.

"This is *so* not what I needed today." Quinn chased after her daughter, her bag slapping against her side. "Lucas, go to school. Elli and I will get Sassy."

The caat stopped at the corner and looked back at them. Then she sauntered away and stepped onto the people mover.

As the little girl followed, Quinn put on a burst of speed and grabbed her hand.

"Mom! She'll get lost!" Ellianne cried. "She doesn't know this city."

"We'll catch her. Let's be smart about it, okay?" Quinn rummaged in her bag, looking for something to entice the creature, but mint gum and cough drops were not going to do the job.

The caat sat on the moving walkway about twenty meters ahead of them. She turned her back and raised a paw to lick.

Quinn held a finger to her lips and tiptoed closer. Fortunately, the people movers were mostly empty this morning. "Pardon me." She stepped around a woman with a shopping bag.

"Is that a Hadriana caat?" The woman pointed. "I've never seen one before. They're so much bigger than my Zazzles."

"They are," Quinn agreed as she moved forward. "And more independent."

Without a backward glance, the caat stood and strolled along the walkway, covering ground at surprising speed. She wove through the legs of a group of men in suits, leaving caat hair on their shiny pants.

Funny how she only seemed to shed on expensive clothing. Then she leaped off the walk, down several meters, landing on a faster, trans-city band.

"Mom, she's getting away!" Ellianne tugged her off the slideway and down a flight of stairs.

"How do you know where to go?" Quinn stumbled through the station behind her daughter.

"I can read, Mom." Ellianne pointed to the brightly-colored graphics painted on the walls. "That was a red line, and you get on the red line down here." She pulled her mother forward.

They ran out of the stairwell and across a platform marked with red. The trans-city belts required the rider to get on a slower feeder belt that ran parallel to the high-speed line. Then the rider stepped onto the faster one. If a rider didn't move onto the high-speed line before the end of the shorter belt, they were dumped back into the station.

Ellianne darted through the pedestrians getting off at this station and jumped onto the feeder belt. Quinn, still clinging to her wrist, stumbled behind. They stepped onto the trans-city belt and jolted into high speed. The caat strolled toward them along the belt, stopping a few meters away.

"It's almost like she's leading us somewhere." Quinn shook her head.

Ellianne nodded. "She is. What else would she be doing?"

"Uh, running away?"

The little girl shook her head vehemently. "Not Sashelle. She knows who feeds her. She's not going to run away."

"I thought you were worried about her getting lost?" Quinn took a couple steps closer to the caat. The caat loped a few meters away and sat again, tail twitching.

Ellianne looked up at her, shaking her head. "I was. A little. But mostly I wanted to make sure you let me follow her. She knows exactly where she's going."

"Then why don't we let her go and get you to school?"

"I don't wanna go to school," Ellianne said. "I wanna see where Sassy's going. Besides, I won't miss anything. They're doing times tables. Again. Ugh."

"Is the work too easy for you? We could move you to a more advanced class." As she said it, Quinn wondered if there was a more advanced class that would accept eight-year-olds. Ellianne was already well ahead of her peers. The Federation might be commanded by a bunch of greedy, power-hungry despots, but you couldn't fault their school system.

"You won't need to." Ellianne pointed. "Kert will take care of it."

Quinn's gaze followed Ellianne's pointing finger. The caat had strolled off the trans-city line at the shuttle port station. She sauntered across the deserted station and jumped up into Dareen's arms.

"Where's Lucas?" Dareen asked as they stepped off the belt. "And where's your stuff?"

"Lucas is at school," Quinn replied. "What are you doing here?"

Dareen shrugged. "I was coming to see you again. And there's no school today."

"What?"

"Today's a holiday." Dareen waved at the empty station. "You didn't know? Didn't you wonder about the lack of people?"

"I— What about those businessmen?" Quinn pulled her comtab out of her bag and pulled up the calendar app. Sure enough, Verheidegen Day. Whatever that was. No school, and government offices were closed.

"Work-a-holics?" Dareen shrugged. "You aren't here to join the good fight?"

"We need to get Lucas." Quinn avoided Dareen's eyes.

"Can I stay with Dareen?" Ellianne asked. "Sassy wants to stay, too."

Quinn raised an eyebrow at the older girl.

She shrugged. "Okay with me. We'll take a tour of the port. Maybe find some ice cream."

"It's nine o'clock in the morning!" Quinn said, but the girls had already started across the station.

QUINN STEPPED off the people mover in front of Lucas's school and found him on the front steps.

With a black eye.

"Fed Mommy came to save you!" a bigger boy sang as he and his friends disappeared around the corner of the school.

"What happened?" Anger burned in Quinn's chest, but the need to care for her son outweighed her desire to pummel the perpetrators into dust.

Lucas looked down. "I fell."

"Lucas, clearly someone hit you! What happened? Have those boys been bullying you?"

Lucas shook off his mother's concerned hands and shuffled toward the slide way. "Let's get out of here."

"I can talk to the school—"

"No!" Lucas said. "No, let's just go. Besides, school's closed."

"I know, I'm so sorry!"

"Mom, if you really want to help, take us with you." Lucas stopped, grabbing Quinn's arm. "On the *Peregrine*. I don't fit in here. They don't want a Federation kid in this school. I want to go back into space."

CHAPTER 6

WHEN THEY RETURNED to the shuttle, Quinn and Lucas dragged four duffle bags with them. "I didn't know if you had any pet food on the *Peregrine*," Quinn said. "I brought what we had. I can't believe Sassy has her own luggage."

Dareen grinned and grabbed the closest bag. "We don't carry pet food, but the synthesizer makes a reasonable tuna-like substance. Come on, Elli and I ran the launch checklists. We're ready to take off."

Ellianne grinned from the airlock. "I flipped the switches!"

"Drag this to the bunk, Elli." Dareen heaved the first bag into the lock. "Then come back for the next one."

"Aye-aye, sir!" Elli slapped her hand to her chest.

Quinn handed Dareen the next bag. "Well-trained crew."

The teen grinned. "Start 'em young! Lucas, take these two, will you?"

The boy stepped up into the airlock, imitating his sister's salute. "Yes, sir!" He grabbed the two bags.

"How'd you know we'd be coming along?" Quinn handed over the last duffle.

Dareen shrugged. "I didn't. Not for sure. But I need to get back to the *Peregrine*, so prepping for launch made sense." She paused. "You won't regret this."

Quinn took a deep breath. "I hope not."

THE SHUTTLE DOCKED to the *Millennium Peregrine* with a soft *chunk*. The ship's artificial gravity thumped them into their seats. "Clamps engaged." Dareen swiped through screens. "Engines powered down. Shuttle bay closed. Passenger access tube locked on." She turned in her seat to address the children. "You can unbuckle your restraints. Gravity is lower on board than dirtside, so watch your step. End is waiting to show you to your cabins."

Sashelle stood on Elli's lap, stretching slowly. She flicked her tail, twitched her nose, and jumped to the floor in a slow, graceful arc. Elli unlatched her belts and stood. "I love low-G!" She pushed off the ground, bounding out of the cockpit in long leaps.

"Grab your duffle!" Quinn hollered after her.

"Yes, sir!" Elli hollered back. She touched down, grabbing a handle to turn effortlessly toward the bunk. Lucas followed and helped his sister retract the webbing so they could reach the luggage.

"Before we go, let me see that message you got from Tony, again," Quinn said. "When you're done with the shutdown."

"I'm done now." Dareen swiped the final panel off the screen with a flourish. "All buttoned down tight and ready for the next run. Lemme grab my comtab." She grabbed the device and extended it to Quinn. "Here ya go."

"You know..." Quinn tapped the screen. "This set of numbers could be a comm address."

"You mean, like to call him? Like a normal person?" Dareen stared at her.

"That's exactly what I mean." Quinn copied the digits and opened the device's calling function.

"But comm addresses are twelve digits." Dareen flipped her

unlatched harness off her shoulders and pushed out of the pilot's chair. "Tony's message only has ten."

"They're twelve digits in the Commonwealth," Quinn said, pasting the numbers into the app. "In the Federation, they're ten. It's ringing."

They waited a few seconds, then a voice said, "Cartesian Travel Agency. This is Shirley, may I help you?"

Quinn slapped the disconnect button. "Cartesian Travel Agency? That can't be a coincidence. Cartesian Caviar was his cover job when we went to Hadriana. And Shirley was the name of the guard at the prison. What should I do?"

Dareen held up her hands. "Don't look at me, I'm just the shuttle driver. I don't know any of this secret agent-y stuff. Last time I helped with an op, I got into all kinds of trouble."

Quinn's lips twitched. "That wasn't all your fault. Speaking of that, are you recovered from your—" She waved her hand vaguely around the top of her head.

"Yeah, they gave me some mysterious med-pod treatment at the N'Avon Medical Center," Dareen said. "After a couple days, they scanned me and said I was fine. Don't worry, they checked the whole family."

"Good," Quinn said. Dareen's reaction to the untested tech Lou acquired had been frightening. Not to mention causing a rift in the family. "I'm going to try something." She pressed an icon on the screen. "Hi, Shirley. I'm looking for Tony."

Silence.

"I, uh—" Quinn started.

"Hold one moment please," Shirley said. A staticky jazz standard erupted.

"Fantastic hold music," Quinn muttered.

The music cut off. "Sorry for the wait," Shirley said. "May I have your account number, please?"

"My account number?" Quinn echoed. She made a face at Dareen. "I, uh—"

Dareen made wild motions at the comtab.

"Oh, yeah, hold on a sec." Quinn swiped at the screen and read the other sequence of numbers.

"Thank you." Shirley was silent for a moment. Then, "I have an itinerary and ticket for a Ms. Quinn Anthony. Where would you like them delivered?"

Dareen's fingers flew on her comtab, then she held it for Quinn to read.

"Can you deliver electronically?" Quinn asked.

Dareen gave a thumbs-up.

"Yes, of course. Give me an address."

Quinn read the one-time drop box address off Dareen's comtab and Shirley repeated it back. "Very good, I'm sending it, now. Will there be anything else?"

"No, I'm good." Quinn made a face at Dareen.

"Thank you for using Cartesian Travel. Have a nice day!" Shirley didn't wait for a response before clicking off.

Quinn stared at Dareen. "What did we do?"

"I think you started the mission," Dareen said with a satisfied smile.

LOU, Stene, Kert, Dareen, and Quinn gathered around the *Peregrine's* dining room table. Dareen had pulled the documents from her drop box, and they were exactly what Shirley had said: a ticket for Ms. Quinn Anthony.

"This is for a freighter going to Lunesco." Lou stared at the projection above the table. "Why would you take a freighter instead of the *Peregrine*?"

"I don't know," Quinn said for what felt like the nine hundredth time. "I only know what you see there. Since Tony's info got us this far, I have to assume I'm meant to follow this itinerary."

Lou harrumphed. "I don't like it. Doesn't give us any control."

"We can fly to Lunesco ourselves," Kert said. "Maybe pick up a cargo here. They must need lots of things out there on the fringe."

Stene swiped another document up on the display. "Fuel, livestock, specialists." He flicked each item off the display. "Supplements?"

Kert leaned forward, nodding. "Liz has a supplier here; we need to make contact. I hate calling these guys. I wish she was here."

"She isn't here, so suck it up," Lou said grumpily. "Put in the order. We'll make a spec run and take our time negotiating so we can extract you if necessary."

"I'm more worried about this end," Quinn said. "Romara Prime is crawling with Feds and cameras. I could get picked up before I get aboard the *Solar Wind*."

Lou nodded to Dareen. The girl pulled a small, flat cylinder from her coverall pocket and slid it across the table. Quinn picked up the little jar.

"Special makeup." Dareen nodded at the jar. "Celebrities use it to avoid paparazzi. There are reflective particles in the makeup that reflect light weirdly. You look normal to the naked eye—well, a little shiny—but cameras can't get a good fix on you. You appear blurry or pixelated, depending on the light. It's not common in the Federation, so you'll need to be careful. If the Feds have someone watching the cam feeds, they might come looking for you to find out why you're scrambled."

"This is illegal in the Federation," Quinn said. "It might be safer not to use it."

"Your choice." Lou shrugged and pushed back her chair. "Whatever you think will get you there."

Quinn nodded and slid the jar into her pocket. "I'll hang onto it, just in case."

CHAPTER 7

AFTER THE *PEREGRINE* had jumped to Romara, Dareen flew the shuttle to Prime, the major station orbiting the planet. They docked at the small shuttle berths, paying the exorbitant fees without comment.

Quinn checked the mirror in the tiny bunkroom one more time. Dark brown hair hung in a straight curtain around her shoulders. Deep tan skin, dark green contacts, nose ring, eyebrow studs, and a swirly tattoo on her cheekbone.

She wore ripped leggings, knee-high boots, and a tight T-shirt that emphasized her muffin top. The low-cut neckline made her squirm, and revealing her mom-bod to the world made her want to puke. But no one would recognize Quinn Templeton, convicted traitor, so she'd suck it up.

"You look, uh, wow. Different," Dareen spluttered.

Quinn laughed. "I know. Fabulous." She patted her tummy bulges. "I feel so sexy."

"Ya gotta own your curves, Quinn." Dareen smirked.

"Easy for you to say." She eyed Dareen's slim hips and narrow waist. "Let's talk again after you've had a couple kids."

Dareen shook her head and patted her flat belly. "I'm having mine via auto-womb."

"That's what you say now." She looked in the mirror again. "Anyway, you think I'll get through?"

"They aren't looking for you here," Dareen held out a pair of trendy glasses. "You were last seen on Hadriana—only an idiot would come back to Romara after escaping death row." She slapped her hands over her mouth when she realized what she'd said.

"Lucky for us, I'm an idiot." Quinn's lips twitched. She waved off Dareen's incoherent apology and slid on the specs. "Don't worry about it. You're absolutely right."

Dareen turned away and pulled out her comtab. "I got the closest berth to the freight docks. You'll leave the shuttle, hang a left down the access corridor, then take the elevator down two levels. Head spinward. The *Solar Wind* is the fifth ship. You'll pass fifteen cameras on the way, so keep your glasses on and your head down."

Quinn nodded, her stomach churning. She sucked in a deep breath and let it out slowly. "I can do this." With another nod to Dareen, she shouldered her bag and stepped into the airlock.

Although they were connected to the access tube, best practices required keeping the shuttle sealed. This worked in their favor, since it prevented random station employees—or nosy drones—from entering the ship. But the wait while Dareen cycled the lock gave Quinn plenty of time to regret her decision to come here.

Through the small port in the external hatch, a Federation flag hung front and center—a reminder that she was returning to the most dangerous place in the galaxy for a former death-row occupant. She pushed her glasses up her nose and did some more deep breathing.

The outer hatch popped. With a brief hesitation, Quinn stepped into the access tube. The incomprehensible babble of hundreds of people, with an underlayer of heavy machinery, assaulted her ears. Oil and body odor not quite covered by fake roses made her nose twitch. She ducked her head, pushed her glasses up again, and stepped out into the tumult.

Left to the elevator. She strode off to the left as if she'd done this a thousand times. Actually, she had passed through Romara Prime many times before, but almost exclusively in the military arms of the station. The last time she'd docked in the commercial sector, she'd been a cadet on her way to her last term at the academy.

She and some friends had spent their last break on a beach on Wakicki. They'd taken the cheapest flight they could find, which had taken twice as long as the regular flights. The last leg had been via a grain hauler. The captain of that ship made the best bread Quinn had ever tasted. She shook her head. She hadn't thought about that trip in years.

The elevator clunked and ground down two levels, moving Quinn and three dock employees from the slick PR-dream of the commercial terminal to the worn freight docks. When the doors creaked open, the loaders veered off to the left, leaving Quinn alone in the elevator lobby. She noticed the camera pointed at the doors and hurried to the walkway.

The floor gave way to open grating, and Quinn stared down. Level after level of open-grid flooring stacked below her, providing access to dozens of ships' berths. Up on the passenger levels, windows stretched the length of the dock, but down here were flat gray walls and utilitarian signage. She stumbled past the first hatch. Four to go.

A station official stepped out of the next access tube and stopped in the middle of the aisle. Quinn's heart went into overdrive and sweat broke out on her forehead. She ducked her head and kept walking. The man looked up from his comtab and stepped into her path.

"Papers," he said, his tone bored.

Quinn froze, visions of the solitary cell in the Justice Center flashing before her eyes.

"Papers." The man extended his hand.

She rummaged in her bag and pulled out her identification and ticket. Stene had taken a picture of Quinn in her guise and created realistic paperwork. End had a contact who was supposed to enter her data into the Federation database. Quinn swallowed. There had been no way to check. What if he hadn't done it? What if he'd done something wrong and the file was flagged?

The official yanked the papers out of her hand and scanned them with his device. He waited, his foot tapping impatiently on the gridwork floor. With a heavy sigh, he scanned them again.

Quinn slowly raised her head to look at the official. He was young—maybe late twenties. Military haircut, even though he was civilian security. Great. Those guys were usually out to prove they were as tough as their military counterparts. Just her luck.

He scowled at her and slapped his comtab against his leg. "Damn thing." He scanned her documents a third time. "Is this new?" He waved the ID card at her.

"I— Uh, yeah," Quinn said. "A couple months. Name change after the divorce."

"I've been having trouble with newer IDs all week." He shoved the ticket and card back at her. "I'm supposed to take you in, but you'd be the fifth one this morning. You don't look like a problem, and I don't want to do the paperwork." He gave her a once-over, dismissing her. "Don't make me regret my decision."

Quinn shoved her papers back into her bag. "I won't, sir. Thank you." She stepped past him, legs stretched to take her away as fast as she could without breaking into a run.

"Hey!"

Ice washed through Quinn's veins. She stopped, the metal grating biting into her feet through her thin boot soles. Slowly, she turned. "Yes?"

"You dropped this." He held out a piece of paper.

Quinn hurried back to him and practically snatched her itinerary away. "Thanks." Her throat eased a tiny bit. "I'd be lost without it."

He nodded and strode away.

Crap! She bit her lip to keep from swearing aloud. She dragged her eyes away from the departing official and turned. Forcing her legs to move, she took a step toward the *Solar Wind*'s berth. And another.

A little faster now. Her heart pounded, sure he'd call her back yet again and demand she go in for screening. Time stretched, panic dragging the minutes into hours.

She reached the fifth access tunnel and barely checked the name on the screen before waving her ticket at the reader. The device beeped. The display changed.

"Quinn Anthony, welcome to the *Solar Wind*. Please come aboard."

The hatch popped and Quinn hurried inside, pulling it closed so fast her bag almost got crushed. The airlock cycled, taking seconds that felt like days. Quinn watched through the viewport, sure the official would appear at any moment.

Finally, the internal hatch popped and hissed, and Quinn stepped aboard the freighter. She shoved the hatch closed, leaning against it. Eyes closed, she gulped air, trying to slow her heart and respiration. She swiped a hand across her face, knocking her glasses askew.

"You made it!"

At Tony's voice, Quinn's eyes popped open. She stared at him. He looked different, but she wasn't sure why.

"You cut it mighty fine, I must say, darling." He smiled gently and took her hand. He pulled her close and planted a kiss on her cheek. "If I'd known, I would never have left you to travel on your own." He spun around and pulled her forward. "The captain is dying to meet you. Come along."

"Ton—"

"You must learn to pay better attention to the time, darling." He hustled her through the grungy corridors of the ship. "I told you to be here two hours before departure, didn't I?" He gave her a sideways glance.

"I—I'm sorry, uh, dear," she stuttered. "The, uh, the shuttle to Prime was delayed. I would have caught the earlier one, but the caat got out and I had to track her down."

He patted her hand, a condescending smile on his face. "It's always something, isn't it?" Without waiting for a reply, he pulled her around a corner and through a hatch. "Captain! Here's my darling wife, finally. I'm so sorry if we held you up."

A tall, swarthy man looked down at Tony with hooded eyes. "You did not." His deep voice sounded loud in the tiny space. Then he turned to Quinn. "A pleasure to meet you, Mrs. Anthony. Welcome aboard. We depart in one hour."

Quinn yanked her hand away from Tony. "See, plenty of time."

Tony shook his head sadly. "We can't count on the kindness of strangers."

"What?" Quinn asked.

"What?" the captain echoed. "No kindness. Our scheduled departure is in one hour. If she hadn't made it, I would have left without her. The fees for late launch are astronomical. Reicher Wingard, at your service." He gave Quinn a half-bow. "And now, I must ask you to adjourn to your cabin for pre-departure checks."

"Come, my darling." Tony reached for Quinn's hand again.

Quinn pulled away again and slid the bag off her shoulder, dropping the strap into Tony's still outstretched hand. "Lead on, dear."

CHAPTER 8

TONY USHERED Quinn into the tiny cabin and shut the door. Before she could open her mouth, he held up a finger. He dropped Quinn's bag on the bed and pulled out his comtab. Holding up the device, he turned slowly in a full circle, watching the screen. Then he tapped an icon and set the device on a shelf. "Okay, we're good now. Sorry about all that."

Quinn sagged onto the bed. "What the heck is going on?"

"Nice adlibbing, by the way." Tony pushed the bag aside and sat next to her. "You definitely have the makings of a Krimson spy."

"Tony, tell me what I'm doing here." She crossed her arms over her chest and stared him down. "Where have you been? Why are we going to Lunesco? And why are you behaving like such an ass?"

Tony chuckled. "I'm behaving like an ass because Charles Anthony is one. He's a professor of comparative literature with special emphasis on early Federation morality plays. The other three guys who research that area are all sexist asses, too."

"You've met all three of them?"

"Oh, yeah. We're a tight-knit group. Although, they barely put up with me. I haven't been at it long enough to have earned their respect."

She snorted. "And Lunesco?"

"We're going there to meet Doug Parra."

"Doug Parra? *Our* Doug Parra? From Fort Sumpter? What's he doing on Lunesco? Isn't his wife still on active duty?"

Tony looked away. "She was killed in the evacuation."

"What?!" Quinn stared at him. "How did that happen? And why didn't I hear about it?"

He sighed. "You didn't hear about it because you were already in prison when Doug found out. The official word is 'a tragic accident.' She was crushed by one of the assault vehicles on the *Elrond*. It was badly secured, and when the ship took fire in a skirmish, it broke loose. Ironically—" His voice took on a harsh edge. "—it was Estelle Parra who secured the vehicle."

Quinn barked out a laugh. "Her own carelessness killed her?" She shook her head. "Yeah, right. No one was responsible for double-checking?"

"The report says she ordered her team to move on to other tasks." His look made clear he didn't believe that. "Did you know her?"

Quinn shook her head. "You?"

He nodded. "Met her once. She didn't strike me as the cavalier type. I've done a bit of nosing around. It seems she got wind that her husband had been left behind, and she refused a share of the gold that took his shuttle seat."

"Nice to know someone did." Her own husband had not. In fact, she suspected he'd been party to the plan from the beginning. "Hey, wait a minute. You said something about a skirmish? Why was the Elrond involved in fighting? They were carrying dependents!"

"Good catch. And good question." Tony raised an eyebrow. "There doesn't appear to be any other record of this skirmish."

"Hmm." Quinn tapped her finger against her lower lip. "If this skirmish occurred during the evacuation, Lucas and Ellianne would have mentioned it. Definitely fishy. And we're going to see Doug because..."

"I believe he has information that will help in my mission."

"What mission is that?"

"To take down Andretti," Tony said baldly.

"Andretti? Is this an official assignment? I thought you were retired."

"I am, and my handler knows nothing about this." Tony stood and paced around the edge of the bed that filled most of the tiny cabin. He turned, leaning against the miniscule dresser. "This is personal."

Quinn raised her eyebrows, waiting.

"Andretti abandoned us." He ticked the list off on his fingers. "He killed Estelle. He condemned you to death. He— He's not a nice guy. I'm going to take him down."

"There's something else," Quinn said, slowly, her eyes narrowing. "Those are terrible things, but it's not enough. I'm the last one to let him off, but is getting him worth risking our own lives? If this all goes wrong?"

"It won't go wrong," Tony said. "We're under the radar, and I've called in a lot of favors to make sure we stay that way. Once we get to Lunesco, we'll find Doug, learn what he knows and go on from there."

"Why do you think he knows anything we don't?"

"Someone has been digging. Through the same networks I've been using. I traced those questions back to Doug. I want to know what he's learned, and what he plans to do with that information."

"Why am I here?" Quinn gestured to herself. "This all seems like a bigger risk than it's worth. You know Doug—why not drop in on him yourself?"

"Doug trusts you. He trusted me on your say-so. Once he learned I was a Commonwealth agent, that trust evaporated."

"What makes you think he'll trust me now?" Quinn pulled off her glasses and rubbed her eyes. "According to the media, I'm as much a spy as you."

"But he's begun questioning the reports. If I had unlimited time, I might be able to bring him around. I have plenty of experience in recruiting informants. But I think he'll respond faster to you. And we don't have a lot of time to waste. Doug hasn't been particularly careful in his digging. Others besides me are tracing him. It's only a matter of time before he becomes Andretti's next target."

"You think Andretti is watching him?"

"Could be. But I don't think so—not yet. Soon. I think Andretti is spending his gold to shore up his political ambitions. If he gets wind of a leak, he'll go after it, but until that happens, he's busy."

"His political ambitions," Quinn echoed. "That's what this is about, isn't it? You said this wasn't an official mission but eliminating a political threat sounds like a very reasonable goal for a Krimson spy."

"It does, but it isn't," Tony said. "We can talk more when we get to Lunesco. For now, remember that unless this is turned on—" He snagged his comtab off the shelf and waved it at her. "Anything you say is likely being recorded and *could* be turned over to the Feds."

"Does that jam listening devices?" Quinn asked. When Tony nodded, she continued, "Won't Captain Wingard be suspicious if he hears nothing out of this cabin?"

"They're likely recording, but that doesn't mean anyone is listening." Tony smiled. "Besides, Charles Anthony hasn't seen his loving wife in weeks. Surely an ass like him wouldn't waste any time *talking* to her."

Quinn's face heated. "There would be *other* sounds."

Tony bit his lip then grinned and waved the device. "They made an app for that."

"Ew."

He laughed, but his face looked a little pink. "Speaking of which, I'm sorry for the close quarters." He gestured at the bed. "We can sleep opposite shifts if you prefer."

Quinn waved that away with a chuckle. "I promise not to attack you in the middle of the night."

His face went a little pinker. "Anyway, I'm a condescending ass, and you're my long-suffering wife. I've left my job—creative differences—and we're thinking about settling on Lunesco. Although I doubt we can afford a flight out on my pitiful savings, so this is probably a one-way trip. I don't think we talk a great deal. When we're outside the cabin, you can ignore me. I won't notice, because who could ignore all this?" He waved his hands up the sides of his body.

She snickered and rolled her eyes.

"Hey, that is hurtful."

"Don't worry, Charles won't even notice." Quinn waved a hand at her own *assets*. "Can I change out of this ridiculous outfit?"

"Sorry." Tony shook his head. "This is who you are now. When we get to Lunesco, you can change."

"Ugh, four days of this?" Quinn shuddered.

"Actually, it's ten," Tony said apologetically. "Three days to the Romara jump point, and then seven to Lunesco. They're a fringe colony—can't afford the more accurate jump beacons. The jump point is well outside the planet's orbital path. And this is a slow boat."

Quinn groaned again. "Say, what are you going to do about jump? Does this freighter carry beer?"

"The captain has assured me there is a full bar," Tony said. Hyper-jump made him deathly ill if he wasn't plastered. "I'm sure it's prohibitively expensive, though. I brought along my own supply of alcohol—cleared by the captain as long as it is used for medicinal purposes only." He reached into a drawer and withdrew a bottle of Sergeant Sinister's Spiced Rum.

Quinn laughed. She'd told him—weeks ago—about drinking that when she was a young ensign. "Have you ever tasted that stuff? It's not intended for a refined palate like Charles Anthony's."

Tony's face fell and he pouted. "I thought it was your favorite," he mock-whined.

"Not for a long time. Besides, I don't need to get drunk before jump, so it wouldn't be medicinal for me."

"Excellent point." Tony raised the bottle cheerfully. "More for me."

CHAPTER 9

DAREEN PUTTERED AROUND THE SHUTTLE. There was always something to do here—cleaning, routine maintenance, more cleaning. She sang loudly as she swiped a rag over the sparkling pilot's station, polishing imaginary fingerprints off the screen.

"What are *you* hiding from?" The voice cut through her song.

"Gah!" Dareen swung around, spray cleaner pointed at the source.

"It's me," Francine said. "Don't shoot."

"Francine?! What—how—what are you doing here?"

The elegant blonde lifted one shoulder. "N'Avon was boring. I can't believe I thought this would be more fun."

The girl stiffened. "Hey, I'm plenty fun!"

"Not you, this." Francine gestured to the ship. "I thought we'd be off on a clandestine delivery, or a secret extraction. You Marconis are known for your undercover government jobs."

"I hope not," Dareen said. "We wouldn't be very good at undercover if everyone knows about us."

Francine laughed. "Maybe not 'known' for it, but rumor—"

"How did you get here?" Dareen cut across her words.

"I snuck aboard when you were running your pre-flight at N'Avon."

Dareen stared. "You've been on the shuttle since N'Avon? That was days ago! What have you been doing?"

"Sleeping, exercising, pawing through your databanks," Francine wiggled her fingers as if typing, then laughed. "Just kidding. I didn't break into your systems. I did eat all the protein bars, though."

Dareen pushed past the other woman and opened the cupboard by the bunk. "You did! Those are for emergencies. What if I needed them?"

"You made one short jaunt to Romara Prime," Francine said. "You could have stopped in the food court."

Dareen spluttered for a moment, then stomped to the airlock. "I should leave you in here to starve!"

"No, I'm sorry! I'll buy new protein bars," Francine said, her voice strained. "I need to get out of here."

"Of course." Dareen gestured to the hatch. "Please, lead the way. You know I'm going to take you straight to Lou, and she's going to lock you in a cabin smaller than the shuttle."

"Yes, I know." Francine grumbled. "This was a bad idea all the way around."

"Not my problem. Why didn't you sneak off at Romara Prime?" Without waiting for a reply, she pushed past Francine and led the way to the crew lounge. "Sit."

Francine settled into the side chair like a queen to her throne. Dareen ground her teeth and hit the intercom. "Lou to the lounge, please. Intruder contained."

Francine cocked her head. "Contained? Did you know I was here?"

Dareen considered for a moment. "If I told you, I'd have to space you."

Before Francine could ask another question, the door opened. Ellianne bounced into the room. "Francine!" She threw herself at the blonde. "Finally!"

"Hi, Elli."

"Finally? What did she mean by that?" Dareen turned to the little girl. "Elli, did you know Francine was on the shuttle?"

Ellianne nodded. "I let her in when you were doing the pre-flight. She said it was a surprise."

"It was a surprise, all right." Lou stood in the doorway, fists on hips.

Francine leaped up from her chair, holding her hands up in surrender. "Hear me out. I came to help. I heard Liz had gone, and I thought I could, maybe, fill in?"

Lou's blank face grew still. "We don't need Liz, and we don't need you!"

"Please, I'm not cut out for civilian life," Francine said. "I have connections—"

"You have connections that are going to get us targeted by the Russosken." Lou stomped into the room and threw herself down on the couch. "We definitely don't need that!"

"I have other connections," Francine said. "And I've studied trade in the Federation. If you're trying to fly under their radar, you need someone who can help you make money without attracting attention. I can do that."

"And we should trust you why, exactly?" Lou demanded.

"Good question," Francine dropped back into her chair. "I—I've kept your secrets so far. I could have sold you out to the Russosken, but I didn't. You don't have to trust me—just give me a chance. Watch me like a—like a peregrine." She laughed. "I'll give you contact info for my family. If I try to double-cross you, you can ransom me back to them. Look, when you left me on N'Avon, you said I owed you. Let me work that off."

Lou's eyes narrowed to slits. "If I let you stay, everything you do—every breath you take, every protein bar you eat—" Her eyes flicked to Dareen and back. "—every contact you make will be tracked, recorded, and scrutinized. *If* I let you stay." She glared at Dareen.

"Take her to the cabin we had her in before and lock her in. We'll discuss this at dinner."

"WE GOT A MESSAGE FROM TONY." End pulled a serving bowl close and shoveled food onto his plate. "Quinn made it aboard, and they're on their way to the jump point. It's a slow freighter, so the Federation could waylay and board them on the way, but there aren't any red flags that I could find. The *Solar Wind* is as clean and boring as they get—a small freighter headed for a fringe world with a supply of electronics. They file all their paperwork, travel exactly the routes they filed, do business with legitimate traders on the surface."

"Sounds like a perfect cover for clandestine operations." Stene ripped a piece of bread off the loaf.

"But we would have heard something," End retorted. "I mean, the official logs are clean, but we would have heard through the net. I think they're exactly what they claim to be."

"Doesn't matter anyway," Lou said. "There's nothing we can do at this point except follow along. We've been granted a slot in the jump queue about three days after the *Solar Wind*. We'll catch up—we've got way more thrust than them." She pointed her fork at Kert. "What's the status on our cargo?"

"Located and waiting for pickup. Dareen can drop to Romara and get it at any time. If she picks it up tomorrow morning, we'll have plenty of time to reach our slot in the queue. Someone should go with her, though." He looked at his brother.

Stene nodded.

"I'll go," End said. "I haven't been off the *Peregrine* in ages."

"You went to the disco when we were on N'Avon!" Dareen said.

Her brother shrugged. "Yeah, but that was days ago!"

Lou glared. "Dareen, take both of them—and take Francine too. Maybe you can accidentally leave her there."

"No!" Ellianne cried. "Don't leave Francine here!"

Lou started. "Forgot you were there, kid." She scowled. "I was kidding. I wouldn't leave a caat on Romara."

Ellianne's eyes grew big.

"*Wouldn't*," Lou repeated. "The caat stays."

Ellianne relaxed.

"Can I go?" Lucas asked. "To the pickup? I can help load."

"It seems like a big risk for nothing," Dareen said. "LaRaine has got to be looking for her grandkids, right?"

End shook his head. "I've got crawlers running. Not a whisper of missing children. She seems to have given up."

Lou glowered. "That seems out of character."

"Not really." Dareen picked up her glass. "She cares about her reputation. Doesn't want anyone knowing Quinn bested her."

"More likely the Feds are squashing it," Kert said. "Makes me wonder why. You haven't heard any rumors on the dark net?"

End garbled something around the mouthful of food and shook his head.

"Are there cameras at the pickup site?" Lou asked Kert.

"There are cams everywhere on Romara," Kert said darkly. "But I'll check the field. If it's not too crazy, it might be okay. The kid will have to stay inside the shuttle."

Lucas started to protest, but Lou held up a hand. "Only way you're getting down there, my boy. Plenty of work stacking boxes inside the cargo hold. Or you can stay here. Your choice."

Lucas rolled his eyes. "Fine. I'll stay in the shuttle."

CHAPTER 10

THE SHUTTLE TOUCHED down at Romara Field Four about twenty klicks from the outskirts of Romara City. Neatly ordered fields spread out on each side, providing excellent visibility. Fluffy white clouds drifted overhead, and a pleasantly warm sun shone.

"Roger," End said into the mic. "The captain will release control of the shuttle to the tug-drone." He nodded at Dareen and waited for her to complete the sequence. "The tug has control."

The tug pulled the shuttle to their assigned cargo slot and backed them to a loading dock in front of a huge warehouse. The rear end of the shuttle slid under the loading dock roof.

"I've scanned the area." End waved a hand at the forward screen. "There are cameras watching the warehouse doors, but none inside. One on either end of the loading dock, but they're low resolution, and we're far enough away that facial recognition software shouldn't be a problem."

"You sure about that?" Dareen worked her way through her checklist.

"Yeah, but let's keep Lucas inside the shuttle anyway." He glanced back at his uncle and Francine sitting in the jump seats behind them. "They've got considerable drone coverage here."

The adults nodded.

"Francine should stay out of cam view, too," Stene said suddenly.

"You're right." Dareen looked up from her list. "It was no secret she was their tutor. That isn't a problem, is it?" She pinned the older woman with a look.

"I want to breathe some uncanned air," Francine said.

"Why did you sneak onto the *Peregrine*?" End unlatched his safety straps. "You've only been off-planet a few days and you're already anxious to get back. Are you a dirt hugger or a spacer?"

Francine raised her eyebrows. "I was trapped in this shuttle for most of that time. And then confined to a cabin. If I'd had free run of the ship, it would be different."

"Maybe." End watched as she sauntered toward the airlock.

"Stay inside the shuttle." Stene put an arm across the hatch, blocking her way. He nodded toward the cargo hold.

"Whatever you say, boss." With a sigh, Francine continued toward the rear. "I'll check in with Lucas."

Stene followed her through the shuttle.

"I don't trust her." Dareen finished the shutdown procedure and released the cargo hatch override.

"None of us do." End tapped his screen and flicked a few icons. "Stene'll watch her. And I've got a comms net running. If she tries to contact anyone, we'll know."

Dareen held up a hand. End slapped it with his own.

"Nice," she said. "Let's get this done."

When they reached the back of the shuttle, Stene stood at the rear control panel, lowering the back hatch to form a ramp to the loading dock. Huge doors rolled open, giving them access to the warehouse. Dareen handed coveralls to Francine and Lucas. "Put those over your clothes. You don't want to stand out." She gestured to her own coverall.

While they dressed, End crossed the cargo hold to the cabinet built into the front of the space. He ignored the empty bike-charging space and pulled two control tablets out of a drawer. He handed one to Lucas and one to Francine.

"Those are the loading plates." He pointed to two flat squares lying on the floor, then reached across to swipe Lucas's screen. "Maglev lifts. Virtual joystick to drive 'em. Move the plate to the square painted on the warehouse floor. Pallet drones will lift the cargo onto the plate, then you drive 'em back in here."

He turned to Francine. "You're running the lifters." He pointed to an arm hanging from the ceiling of the shuttle.

"Isn't that the drone scoop?" Francine asked.

End shook his head. "The drone and the scoop are on the *Peregrine*. They latch into that lifter when they're in use. But it's a multi-functional arm. We also use it for cargo loading." He tapped her screen. "It's pretty basic. Identify what you want to lift by tapping. The lifter will move to the right location and do its thing."

He led them across the hold to the open door. "I'll tell Lucas where to put the plate. You'll lift the cargo, and Lucas will move the plate out of the way, then you set the cargo down." He showed her the controls. "We tried automating everything, but humans are stupid and get in the way. Better to put us to work."

"I'm going to inspect the load," Dareen said when she was sure the new loading team was ready. She jogged into the warehouse, comtab in hand.

Each pallet had an ID tag, and she scanned them with the comtab. Then she randomly selected one box from each pallet and opened it. Big bags of powders and capsules filled the boxes. She pulled up her CargoScan app and waved it over the open box. "They're reading good," she called back to End. "I suppose they could have hidden something in the middle of one of these pallets, but my app isn't finding it if they did."

End nodded. "Run the InnerEye scan. I updated us to the top-of-the-line version."

"Looks good to me." Dareen held her device up for End to confirm. "I'm going to authorize payment, and you can load." She flicked a couple icons and pressed her thumb to the device. "That's it. Good to go!"

"Send the first one out, Lucas," End said. "Down the marked path—that's the only place the mag-lev works."

"Like Super Fretzoid!" Lucas scooted the plate across the warehouse to a bright orange square, then spun it in place.

"Not a toy." Stene glared at the boy.

"Sorry," Lucas muttered.

Loading went quickly once the new operators had learned their systems.

"Got it all." Dareen finished counting. "Fourteen pallets of assorted supplements. Let's get buttoned up and out of here. I'm doing the preflight checks." She trotted down the ramp and out of sight.

Francine stretched, handing the control tablet to End. "Is it safe for me to stretch my legs? Just a quick walk around the warehouse?"

End looked her up and down. "In a sec." He slotted the tablets into their charging drawer, then rummaged in a bin beside the bike locker. "Put this on." He yanked a hat over the woman's shining blond hair.

Francine scowled and adjusted the hat.

"You wanna go outside, too?" End called to Lucas.

The boy perched on a toolbox near the rear door, playing with his comtab. He didn't respond.

"Lucas! You wanna go outside?" End called louder, waving another cap.

Lucas looked up and shook his head, pointing to his device. "Playing a game. Damn, I'm dead!"

Francine shook her head as she passed. She carefully walked down the loading ramp. End wondered how she kept her spike-heeled shoes from getting caught in the tie-downs.

End strode across the cargo bay to Lucas. "Is that an online game?" He held out a hand.

The younger boy swiped something and handed the device to End. "Yeah, massive online survival game. I died."

End scowled. "What's your handle?"

Lucas sat up with a grin. "I'm T-Rexplode."

"How long have you had this handle?" He swiped through the game settings. "If anyone knows this is you, then connecting to the net tells them you're on planet."

Lucas's face went pale. "I—I'm sorry! I just wanted to play a game."

"Dude, next time, set up a new account!" End continued flicking through screens. "Better yet, don't connect to the net without asking me. I'm locking this comtab out." He handed the device back to the boy and jogged to the ramp. "Dar, we gotta go!"

"Where's Francine?" Stene asked.

End jerked his head toward the open hatch. "Out there. Get her, will you. And tell Dareen to step it up."

Stene nodded and jumped off the side of the ramp.

"I'm really sorry!" Lucas said.

"Not your fault. I should have checked your device." He put a hand on the boy's shoulder and gave him a little push. "Get strapped in."

Lucas pulled down the jump seat at the front of the cargo hold. End double checked the latches and tie down straps on the cargo pads.

"What's the hurry?" Dareen strode into the ship followed by Francine and Stene.

"Comms breach," End said in a low voice, jerking his head at Lucas. "Accident, but we need to move."

Dareen glanced at the boy. "Crap." She raced forward.

Stene closed the ramp. "I'll check on him and be up front in a sec." He locked the ramp and triple-checked the cargo ties then he made his way toward Lucas.

"Roger." End followed Francine to the cockpit.

"Why didn't your comms net catch it?" Dareen asked as she finished her pre-flight.

Francine looked up sharply from her seatbelt. "Comms net?"

End glanced back at the blonde. "I was monitoring communications in the area of the shuttle. In case you decided to contact anyone here. I didn't want to stop you, but I did want to track it if you did it."

Francine sighed, a mournful expression on her face.

Dareen rolled her eyes. "Please, you knew we'd be watching you. You'd do the same."

The older woman's lips twitched. "Yeah, you're right. Good thing I didn't call any of my secret underworld contacts."

Dareen fired up the taxi engines and eased the shuttle away from the warehouse. "Tower, this is shuttle x-ray-tee-seven-gee-four-six, the *Fluffy Kitten*, requesting permission to launch."

"Fluffy Kitten?" Francine whispered.

"One of many ridiculous names she uses," End said.

"*Fluffy Kitten*, Tower." The clipped voice came through the speakers. "We have a hold on your departure. Please turn right and proceed to the holding ramp."

"Tower, why are we being held?" Dareen increased the taxi speed. "Our transport has a slot in the jump queue."

"*Fluffy Kitten*, I have no information about the hold, just that one was issued twenty-three seconds ago. Did you forget to pay your bill?" A phony laugh followed the question.

"All payments are confirmed, Tower." Dareen ground her teeth. She flipped a few more switches and increased speed again. The metal launch shields closed over the front windows, and she put the external cam views on her screen. "Repeat, our transport has a slot in the jump queue." She hit the mute. "Could they have tracked him that quickly?"

End shrugged. "Probably a random cargo check."

"Probably." Stene came forward and settled into his seat. It didn't sound like he believed it.

"Whatever the reason, we don't want them coming aboard,"

Francine's voice sounded strained. "If they see Lucas, we're screwed. His face has got to be on milk cartons all over the sector."

The others looked at her blankly. "Milk cartons?" Dareen asked.

"Figure of speech." Francine waved a hand dismissively. "He's a missing kid. Law enforcement looks for them."

"Do we know if Reggie actually reported them missing?" Dareen countered. "Quinn seemed to think LaRaine might want to keep it under wraps."

"Is that a risk you're willing to take?" Francine asked.

"*Fluffy Kitten*, you've overshot the holding ramp," the voice from the tower said. "Please make a U-turn and proceed to holding ramp."

Dareen toggled the mute icon. "Sorry, Tower." She giggled, then muted again and looked at the others. "I say we make a run for it. What do you think?"

"This is Romara," Stene said. "Capital of the Federation. If we run, they'll chase us. Lots of fighters stationed here. We'll be dust before we reach low orbit."

Dareen nodded, decision made. "End, hide the kid. In fact, hide 'em both. I'm taking us to the holding ramp."

CHAPTER 11

END UNBUCKLED HIS STRAPS. "You sure about this?" He glanced at Francine. "Once she knows our hiding place, she can't unknow."

"What do you suggest?" Dareen pulled back on the throttle. "I'm going to make this as slow as possible. Get them hidden."

"If they were watching us, they'll know we have five crew." End reached under the pilot's console and felt for a small, magnetic box. He pried it away from the equipment and pulled it free.

"Lucas never went outside, so they shouldn't have seen him." Dareen eased back a bit more and started her turn. "Francine's hair was hidden—maybe they'll believe she was me."

Francine slid a hand over her hip and laughed. "You wish."

Dareen glared over her shoulder. "*You* wish. If they don't buy it, your butt is as much on the line as ours. More, probably. *We* can claim we didn't know who Lucas is. You can't."

Francine's smile slid off her face. "You're right. Sorry."

"Come on, let's get you hidden." End climbed out of his seat. He squeezed between the two jump seats and hurried past the airlock.

"Hold on!" Dareen called. "Starting the turn!"

End pressed his hand against the inner airlock hatch, but the turn was slow and easy. He continued to the back of the ship. "Lucas," he called as they entered the cargo hold. "Unbuckle. Gotta hide."

"Why?" Lucas's face blanched.

"We're being boarded." He crossed to the empty bike charging cabinet.

"That's the first place anyone would look," Lucas protested as he unfastened his safety harness.

End shook his head and rolled his eyes. "Who do you think you're dealing with? Marconi, remember?" He jabbed his thumb at his chest.

"Hide in plain sight?" Francine asked.

"Not quite." End snapped the magnetic box against the back of the cabinet. Across the cargo hold, a panel on the side of the ship popped open. End hurried around the pallets of cargo and pulled the panel away. "Down."

Francine looked through the narrow space. "That's not big enough—"

End cut her off. "It's bigger on the inside." He reached in near the edge and unhooked the latches. That allowed him to lift a floor panel, revealing a narrow shaft. "Sit on the edge and stick your feet down there. You'll feel a rung about half a meter down. The ladder is only three rungs. When you reach the bottom, turn around and crawl. There's plenty of room."

"Cool!" Lucas pushed past Francine and dropped onto his butt.

End held out his hand. "Gimme your comtab."

"But you locked it out." Lucas's hand went to the chest pocket on his coverall.

"It still produces a signal." End made a gimme gesture. "No electronics in the hole."

"Great, you call it the hole," Francine muttered. She pulled a device out of her own pocket and handed it to End.

"Where'd you get that?"

She shrugged. "Lifted it off Kert yesterday. You can't expect a girl to be without communications!"

"I can and do!" End said. "Who have you contacted?"

"No one," Francine said. "Check it. I did a few web searches through your ship's interface. I haven't touched it since we got on the shuttle. Go ahead and check. I know you know how."

"I will." He glared at Francine. Then he turned to Lucas. "Come on, squirt. Give up the device."

Lucas heaved a dramatic sigh and turned over his comtab.

"Thanks. Climb on down. Strap in. If we get through this, we won't let you out until we're in orbit. And stay quiet!" He gestured for Lucas to climb down.

"We'll be at the hold point in ten seconds," Dareen's voice came through the speakers. "Get them stowed!"

End grabbed Francine's shoulder as she moved toward the bolthole. "If you betrayed us, Gramma will hunt you down."

Francine looked him in the eyes. "I did nothing but take a walk around the warehouse. I have no desire to be ransomed to my family or turned over to the Federation."

"Well, maybe the kid did it with his game," End said. "Make sure he stays quiet down there."

Francine winked. "You got it, boss." She climbed onto the ladder.

"You aren't increasing my confidence in you!" End hollered.

"There's a car meeting us on the apron!" Dareen called. "Get back up here, End."

He slammed the hatches shut, raced across the cargo hold, and pulled the magnetic key off the inside of the bike cupboard. A few long strides took him to the tiny bunk behind the cockpit. He slapped the mag-key to the underside of the upper bunk and pushed it flush with the frame, into the space created to hide it. Then he jogged to the front and slid into the co-pilot's seat, flipping the restraints over his shoulders so it looked natural.

"About time," Dareen muttered. "Launch shields opening."

The heavy metal cover split and slid off the forward port, allowing them to look down at the car waiting on the apron. Two men stood beside the car staring up at them. Dareen smiled and gave a finger wave. She turned to End. "You wanna meet them, or should I?"

"I'll go," Stene said.

"Let me and Dareen do it." End grinned at the men and gave a jaunty salute, then climbed out of his chair. "Maybe you should be drunk. Channel your inner Tony."

Stene grunted. "Toss me the booze."

End grabbed a square bottle tucked into the drawer under the bunk and handed it to Stene, holding it low so it wouldn't be visible through the window. "We'll be the stupid kids trying to keep Uncle Stene out of trouble."

Stene gave a thumbs-up and splashed some of the whisky on his shirt. "Alcohol abuse," he muttered before taking a small drink.

End clapped him on the shoulder and followed Dareen to the airlock. They stepped inside. He reached for the release, but Dareen grabbed his arm.

"Cycle the airlock—like we don't know how to open the thing all the way. The dumber we look, the better." She jerked her head toward the inner hatch.

End grinned and pushed it closed.

The system ran, checking internal and external pressure before popping the outer hatch. Two uniformed Federation Customs officers waited on the other side. The shorter one held a tablet; the taller had a long-range blaster slung over his shoulder.

"Cool!" End drawled before anyone could speak. "Is that Brachester 47?!"

The man with blaster blinked and opened his mouth, but the other stopped him. "Officer Pettigrew with the customs department. This is Officer Santiago. We need to inspect your cargo."

"We loaded this cargo a few minutes ago." Dareen pointed across the tarmac. "Right over there. Didn't you inspect it when it was delivered?"

"I'm sure someone did," Pettigrew said with a shrug. He pointed to his tablet. "My instructions are to inspect the cargo."

Dareen shrugged. "Okay, come on in." She turned and headed back inside. "Come on, get in here."

"Pop the airlock, please," Pettigrew said.

"Pop it? I can't do that!" Dareen's eyes went big. "My dad would kill me if I wrecked his shuttle!"

"Popping the airlock doesn't hurt the shuttle, miss," the man with the weapon said.

Dareen looked at End, who shook his head. "Nope, we can't do that. We ain't been trained that way. If you wanna come in, you're gonna have to cycle in like a civilized person."

Pettigrew looked at Santiago. The bigger man shrugged. They climbed up the step into the airlock. With four people inside, the space was claustrophobic. Sweat appeared on Pettigrew's upper lip.

With his back to the men, End winked at his sister. "Close the door, Mister Pettigrew," he called over his shoulder.

"That's officer," the man said. "And it's called a hatch."

"Okay, Mister Officer, close the hatch, please." End grinned.

Dareen snorted and coughed. "Sorry, got a cold, I think. Could be Banian Flu, I suppose. We were on Bania last week. Ugly place."

The men behind him stiffened and one gasped. End almost felt sorry for them. The inner hatch popped to the accompaniment of very loud, very bad, singing.

"*Hütet das Gold! Vater warnte vor solchem Feind.*"

Dareen tripped through the inner hatch, catching the bunk to steady herself.

"What is that noise?" Pettigrew demanded.

"That's Uncle St—Stervin," End stuttered. "He, uh, likes to sing when he drinks."

"Make him stop," Pettigrew commanded, clapping his hand and his tablet to his ears.

"I'll try, but when he gets started on the ancient opera..." Dareen hurried into the cockpit. "Uncle Stervin! It's not singing time."

"IT'S ALWAYS TIME FOR FLOSSHILDE!" Stene roared, before breaking into the same song again.

End grinned uncomfortably. "Let's go into the cargo hold. It'll be quieter in there."

"I need to see the cockpit, too," Pettigrew said belligerently.

"You wanna go there first?" End asked.

"No, let's go to the hold."

End gestured toward the hold, but Santiago stepped back. "Lead the way, please."

With a shrug, End led them into the cargo space. "There's the stuff we picked up." He waved at the pallets stacked side by side, filling most of the hold. Then he did a double take. Someone—it had to have been Stene—had used the cargo arm to move one of the pallets on top of the hole's access panel. The man moved fast.

The customs agents scanned and cataloged the cargo. End lounged against the bulkhead, trying to not look at the pallet atop the hidey-hole.

"*Nicht fürcht' ich den, wie ich ihn erfand—*" Stene bellowed, stumbling into the hold, swinging the square bottle. He draped an arm over End's shoulder. "*Haltet den Räuber!*"

"Enough!" Pettigrew hollered.

Stene took a bow and nearly toppled over. End caught him before his head hit the deck and slowed his slide to the floor. He leaned the older man against the nearest pallet.

The customs agents stalked past them toward the cockpit. As they passed, Pettigrew muttered, "This *cannot* be the shuttle they wanted us to search."

End hid his grin, winked at his uncle, and followed the men to the front of the ship.

CHAPTER 12

BY JUMP DAY, Quinn was bored with a capital B. Even on Fort Sumpter—an asteroid military base—there'd been places to go: the gym, the commissary, the theater. The *Solar Wind* was tiny, and as passengers, they were restricted to the lounge—which was also the mess hall—and their cabin.

"Even the grain hauler was better than this," Quinn grumbled. She hitched herself up against the pillows and closed her e-reader.

Tony looked up from the Sergeant Sinister's bottle in his hand. "A grain hauler? I'd think they'd be dusty and crowded."

She shrugged. "Yeah, but the captain made excellent bread. And, to be honest, I was toasted most of the time."

Tony laughed and sloshed a generous shot into a second glass. "Here's to being toasted." He handed it to her and raised his own in salute.

"Cheers."

Tony picked up his comtab and activated an app. "Okay, it's safe to talk now. I don't want to say something when I'm drunk."

"You don't have the sex noise app on, do you?" Quinn asked. "People don't do that during jump."

"Some people do," Tony wiggled his eyebrows suggestively. "But

I'm sure Charles Anthony is not one of them. It's set to 'quiet beverages' now. Enjoy."

Quinn chuckled. "Quiet beverages is a setting? I'll have one drink, but that's it. I prefer to jump sober. It doesn't have the same effect on me as it does on you."

Tony chugged his shot and grimaced. "I can't believe you drink this stuff!" He poured another and slugged it back.

"Drank." Quinn took an experimental sip. She shivered. "Not something I'd pick up these days."

"If I'd known, I'd have gotten something else." Tony poured himself another shot. "What's that, four?"

"I think it's three, but the effect is more important than the number, right?" She contemplated another sip but changed her mind. "How do you feel?"

Tony lay back and swung his legs up on the bed. "Feelin' pretty good. Oops, no shoes on the bed, Tony!" He tried to kick his ankle-high boots off, but almost toppled off the bed instead.

"You drink. I'll take care of the shoes." With a laugh, Quinn rolled onto her knees and scooched to the end of the bed.

"This is Wingard." The captain's deep voice rumbled through the intercom. "Jump will commence in thirty minutes. Please secure all loose items. Jump restraints are provided in each cabin and the lounge. Report your location at this time."

Quinn jumped off the bed and pressed the intercom panel by the door. "This is Quinn Te—Anthony. Mr. Anthony and I are secure in our cabin. Safe jumping, Captain."

"Acknowledged," Wingard replied. "I'll ask you to check in again after jump."

"Thank you, Captain," Quinn said. She itched to tell him this wasn't her first jump, but caution kept her mouth shut. The less he knew about her, the better.

She turned around and pulled Tony's boots off, stowing them in the drawer under the bunk. Then she dumped the remains of her rum down the sink and rinsed the glass. It snapped into a holder above the basin. "I love how tidy spaceships are," she said. "A place for everything. You about done with that?"

"This?" Tony blinked owlishly at her and waving the bottle. "Jus' one more, I think."

She reached out and pulled the bottle from his grasp. "Let's save the last drink for a bit, okay? We've still got thirty minutes."

Tony nodded. A grin spread over his face, and he continued bouncing his head up and down. "You're jumping!"

Quinn laughed. "You are such a happy drunk. Say, Tony, can you tell me more about your mission?"

He blinked a couple times. "Don' have a mission. I'm tired. Retired. Ha-ha, I got new tires!"

"Tony!" She climbed up onto the bunk and took his face in both hands. Staring into his eyes, she said, "What's your current mission?"

Tony smiled. "To take down Andretti. He's a bad, bad man."

"Yes, I know. But who ordered you to do that?"

"No orders. You got somethin' on your cheek." His hand swung up and slapped against her face. "Oh!" His eyes went wide. "I didn't mean to hit you! I'm so sorry!" He caressed her cheek, then his eyebrows scrunched. "What *is* that?" He rubbed her cheek, harder.

"Stop!" Quinn pulled away with a laugh and sat back against the pillows. "It's a temporary tattoo. You can't rub it off! Tell me about your mission."

"No mission." Tony settled back and closed his eyes. "Gotta take down Andretti. He's bad."

"Yeah, he is," Quinn repeated with a sigh. She took the glass from his limp fingers, debating whether he needed another shot. A soft snore answered that question. With a chuckle, she put away the bottle and glass. Then she pulled the jump webbing down over them. It lay loosely against their bodies but would tighten in the seconds before jump. She lay back and waited for the countdown.

"JUMP COMPLETE. Destination coordinates confirmed. Welcome to Lunesco System. All hands, report."

Quinn flinched as Tony pulled the jump webbing away. Jump made her skin feel raw and sensitive for a few hours.

"Oh, sorry!" he said.

She shrugged. "No big deal. How are you feeling?"

"Great, as always." He folded the webbing back into the slot above the bed. Then he pressed the intercom button. "This is Charles Anthony. All secure in our cabin."

"Acknowledged. Bridge out."

"On the return trip, I'm bringing a different libation."

Quinn grinned. "Not a fan of the sergeant, eh?"

"That stuff is vile." He ran his tongue over his teeth. "I need to brush my teeth." He busied himself at the tiny sink.

Quinn picked up her e-reader.

"Did I tell you anything useful?" Tony reappeared, toothbrush in hand.

"What?"

He looked at her in the mirror. "When I was drunk. Did I tell you anything useful?"

"Only that you're madly in love with me," Quinn joked. His back went stiff. "And that Lou's lifelong ambition is to win an ice-skating championship."

Tony's shoulders relaxed. "Don't tell anyone. Those are both classified."

"My lips are sealed." Quinn heaved a dramatic sigh. "No, you didn't tell me anything. Don't you remember?"

"It's a little fuzzy," Tony admitted.

"How'd you stay undercover for so long if you have to get drunk every time you travel?" Quinn asked.

"Private cabins and prayer." Tony rubbed his chin. "I should ask Maerk who the patron saint of hyperjump is."

Quinn picked up her e-reader again. "What are we going to do for the next seven days?

"More of the same, I guess." He pulled out his comtab. "You ready to be back on the record?"

She shrugged. "Yeah. Maybe if I read this textbook aloud, whoever's listening will fall asleep."

Tony chuckled and flicked the app.

THEY ATE dinner with the rest of the passengers and crew, as always. The captain and crew members ate quickly and returned to their duties, but the other passengers—two crop rotation specialists returning from their university studies and a government census taker—must have been as bored as Quinn. Tony lectured them at length on Charles Anthony's favorite subject: himself.

"I left the university when politics began to interfere with my academic freedom." His audience's eyes had glazed over, but they were too polite to ignore him. "The protocol officer insisted on being present for lectures. He believed he was conversant in the field, but he was a total dilettante."

Quinn sighed and picked up the basket by her feet. The engineer liked to knit in his spare time and had offered her some yarn. She hadn't done any handwork in a while but had learned to crochet as a child. Anything that would help her ignore Tony's yammering!

"Professor Anthony." The census bureau man—Sebi Maarteen—frowned. "The Federation's protocol officers are highly trained." He rolled his eyes around the room, apparently in warning. "While his understanding of the parables may not have matched your own, I'm sure he wasn't a dilettante."

Interesting. A government employee reminding a civilian of possible surveillance. Quinn glanced at Tony. He remained in character, but his eyes flicked briefly to Quinn's.

The two farmers took the interruption as an opportunity to escape. "We must go. We have to…" Ralph's voice trailed off, clearly at a loss for an urgent appointment on the slow boat to Lunesco.

"Study." Lin-tuan nodded at Ralph. "The information we learned in our coursework was difficult. We don't want to forget anything important before we can implement it."

"Yes, difficult." Ralph nodded enthusiastically. "Important."

Tony dismissed them with a regal wave of his hand. They were hardly Charles Anthony's target audience. He turned back to the census taker.

But Sebi had leaped to his feet as well. "Jump has left me a bit, er, under the weather." He barked a fake cough. "I must beg your pardon, Professor, madam." He bowed slightly in Quinn's direction.

"I hope you feel better soon," she called as he hurried out the door. "You've scared them all away, Charles." She gave Tony a mock-glare. "Politics are never a good topic."

"I must have academic freedom!" Tony declared.

"I'm going to see what's in the bar." Quinn thrust the yarn back into the basket. She investigated the tiny shelf against the inside wall for the fiftieth time.

"I don't think they've stocked anything new since we embarked." Tony patted his stomach. "I am going back to our cabin. The stew is wreaking havoc on my delicate system. Come." He herded her into the hall as though the idea that she might stay without him was inconceivable.

"Probably the LaRaine potatoes," Quinn said. "Those have never agreed with you."

Tony shot her a look, his lips clamped together, but his eyes sparkled in appreciation. Quinn's mother-in-law owned the patent on the LaRaine potato, and their last interaction with her had been rather gut-churning.

When they were safely inside their cabin, Tony activated the scrambler. "What do you think about our friend Sebi?"

Quinn shrugged. "Maybe he's a nice guy who doesn't like stupid people to get in trouble?"

"Nice guys don't work for the Federation."

"Hey, we both worked for the Federation," Quinn reminded him.

"There are some nice people. What about your girlfriend, Evelyn Parasite?"

Tony laughed. "Yeah, she was great until she sold me out to the Feds. I don't trust him, though."

"We don't have to trust him," Quinn said. "We just have to stay in character and hope we don't go crazy before we get to Lunesco."

CHAPTER 13

LONG BEFORE THE *Solar Wind* finally achieved orbit around Lunesco Three, Quinn was ready to scream. Two days after jump, she'd asked the captain's permission to use the crew gym. She hated working out but sitting around doing nothing was worse. Wingard had granted permission, as long as she gave crewmembers priority. After that, she escaped the monotony of their cabin every morning. Using the aerobic machines burned off excess energy and pummeling a punching bag in the gym allowed her to play her role of subservient wife in the passenger lounge without strangling Tony.

"This is Wingard," the captain's low voice rolled through the gym. "We have entered our parking orbit. Shuttle to the surface will depart in two hours. All passengers will debark at that time. Thank you for flying on the *Solar Wind*. Live long and properly."

Quinn hopped off the treadmill, wiped it down, and headed to their tiny cabin. When she entered, Tony grinned, although he looked tired, too. "Live long and properly." He raised his hand up with the middle and ring fingers spread apart. "Obviously Wingard hasn't seen the source material."

She raised her eyebrows. "I guess I haven't either. Must be a—"

She bit off the rest of the sentence, remembering the cabin was likely monitored. "Must be more popular where you grew up."

Tony nodded and glanced up at the ceiling, as if looking for the mics hidden there. "Are you packed?"

"Yes. Need to shower and change. I'll be ready in a few minutes."

"Put this in your gear." He held out a stunner. It was a newer model—small enough to hide in a pocket, but strong enough to take down an assailant at twenty meters. "We're going to a fringe world. I want my wife to be able to protect herself."

She grinned and tucked the weapon into her bag. Then she grabbed the clean clothes she'd laid on the bed and escaped into the tiny bath. A quick sonic shower and rubdown removed the sweat, but she never felt completely clean. She'd be happy to return to a planet with plenty of water.

Debarkation was quick and painless. They said farewell to Wingard and his crew and climbed onto the shuttle with Sebi Maarteen and the two farmers. The craft spiraled through the atmosphere to land on a wide, dusty field. They pulled onto a parking pad and the pilot came on over the intercom. "Welcome to Lunesco. The customs building is a half-klick to the north. Exit the shuttle and turn right. You can't miss it. Enjoy your stay." In a quieter voice, as if he'd forgotten he was broadcasting, he muttered, "Or your life. Can't imagine spending the rest of it here."

Maarteen, the census taker, snorted a laugh and glanced at Tony. Their cover story had been relocating to Lunesco, but that conspiratorial glance made it clear Maarteen didn't believe they were staying. Quinn made a mental note to discuss that with Tony.

"Why couldn't they park closer to the terminal?" Tony demanded.

The others ignored him, unfastening their restraints and collecting their belongings. Quinn unlatched the buckle and flipped the straps off her shoulders.

"Come, wife." Tony rose. "We have much to do."

Quinn ducked her head so the other passengers wouldn't see her eyes roll. She grabbed her bag and followed the other passengers into the airlock, where they waited for the hatches to cycle. "I wonder why they don't open both," Quinn said. "I thought that was standard procedure for planetary landings."

"Only when the atmosphere is within Federation standards," Tony said pompously.

"The air quality here is good," Lin-tuan, one of the farmers, said indignantly. He pulled a pair of goggles down over his eyes.

"It's quite dry and dusty." Maarteen took a similar pair of goggles from his bag. "Opening one hatch at a time keeps the shuttle cleaner."

Quinn nodded. Maarteen continued, "Once they get the spaceport built, they'll have accordion tubes that will attach to the shuttle's external hatch and allow passengers to reach customs without trekking across the flight line. But for now, we park where they tell us and walk."

"If you can't make a half-klick walk to the building, you shouldn't be on Lunesco," Lin-tuan muttered from behind the bright green scarf wrapped around his nose and mouth. "This planet demands hearty souls, not whiny cits."

"And you don't have to cross the flight line," Ralph growled. "That would be ridiculous and dangerous."

Maarteen bowed slightly. "My apologies. I misspoke. And you're correct that anyone wishing to stay on Lunesco should be prepared for the conditions. But visitors such as myself will welcome the new building."

"Have you been here before, Mr. Maarteen?" Quinn asked as the outer hatch opened.

A blast of hot air slammed into the airlock, grit-laden wind buffeting them like a sandblaster. Without a glance at their companions, the two farmers leaped out of the shuttle and strode away.

"Let me assist you, Mrs. Anthony." Maarteen jumped to the dusty tarmac and braced his feet widely, then offered his hand.

Quinn took it. "Thank you, Mr. Maarteen." As she stepped

down, Maarteen squeezed her hand, gently. He let go as soon as she reached the ground, leaving a small, flat item in her palm. Then he nodded farewell and struck out for the building in the distance.

Quinn casually slid her hand into her pocket. She dropped whatever Maarteen had passed her and pulled out a handkerchief to protect her nose and mouth from the dry, gritty wind. Maarteen had ignored her for the better part of the flight. Why was he suddenly so helpful? And what had he given her? A data-card?

She stared after the departing passengers. Lunesco was flat. Long, dusty vistas as far as the eye could see. A small, dirt-brown building squatted a few hundred meters away—the only building nearby. Heat waves rose off the dirt, and the blowing dust limited visibility. A small clump of rectangles in the distance might be a town. She squinted, but it didn't help.

"Wife!" Tony called. "Take the baggage!"

Quinn turned and raised an eyebrow. Tony thrust both bags at her. She took one and stepped away. "Careful, that first step is a big one."

With a theatrical glare, Tony jumped the half-meter to the tarmac. Then he turned, leaning into the wind, and strode away.

Quinn rolled her eyes and promptly got a piece of sand in one. She stumbled, one-eyed, in Tony's wake toward the waiting customs building. The sooner they could leave Mr. and Mrs. Anthony in the dust, the better.

THE BORED LUNESCO customs official glanced at their IDs and waved them toward a set of doors marked "Welcome to Lunesco." Without a word, he returned to swiping something on his comtab.

"Is there an auto-cab system on this planet?" Tony asked.

"Nope, but you can call Jessian." The customs man pointed at a sign on the wall without looking up.

The sign read "Ride with Jessian" and listed a contact code. Tony punched it into his comtab as they pushed through the doors into the outer lobby.

Quinn wandered around the small waiting room, peering out the windows. A dusty parking area held three vehicles. One of them pulled out of the space, and Ralph and Lin-tuan drove away. Maarteen stood beside a second one, talking with someone. The other individual wore goggles, gloves, and long robes that covered every inch of his or her body. The driver gestured toward the car door, then loaded Maarteen's bag into the rear compartment. As he opened the vehicle, she caught sight of a sign on the side: "Ride with Jessian."

"Ton— Charles!" She yanked on his sleeve and jerked her head at the window. "Maybe we can get a ride with Mr. Maarteen."

"Does this Jessian have only one car?" Tony demanded.

"How would I know?" Quinn waved to Maarteen as he climbed into the vehicle. "But it's a small planet, and he hasn't answered, so maybe yes?"

Maarteen stopped. He raised his eyebrows, pointed at the vehicle, then back at her. She nodded and turned back to Tony. "He says we can ride with him."

"Does he?" Tony grabbed both bags and strode toward the door. "I wonder why. That isn't standard Federation procedure. In fact, accounting regulations specifically forbid Federation employees from sharing transportation. Unless he's planning to split the cost with us."

"Only a Federation accountant would know that." Quinn hurried to the door Tony now held open. "If it gets us into town faster, that's good, right?"

Tony nodded and followed her onto the enclosed porch. "Might give us a chance to figure out what his game is." He pushed the outer door open, and the hot air blasted in, scrubbing them with grit.

They battled against the wind and handed their bags to the waiting driver. Inside the car, Quinn relaxed against the padded rear seat. "The wind doesn't seem to bother our driver."

"She's dressed for it," Maarteen agreed. "You'll find the locals all wear similar garb. If you're staying, you'll at least want to invest in a pair of goggles."

The driver climbed in and shut the door. "Gonna run the vacuum. Everybody shake!" She gave her head and shoulders a quick, practiced jerk. A cloud of fine dust poofed around her. "Now, hold onta your stuff."

A loud whirring filled the car, and the air whipped around them. Quinn squeezed her eyes shut and shook out her hair. When the whirring stopped, she opened her eyes.

"That gets the worst of the dirt." The driver pulled off her goggles and grinned, showing off slightly crooked teeth. "I'm Jessian. Welcome to my cab. Who are you and where are you headed?"

"Charles Anthony," Tony said. "We have a reservation at the Homestead."

Jessian whistled. "Lots of big spenders today! Let's go!" She pressed the start button and pulled out of the parking lot. "Mr. Maarteen here is goin' the same place, so there's no extra charge. Y'all splittin' the bill?"

In the front seat, Maarteen shook his head. "No need. I can expense it."

Quinn darted a look at Tony and hid a smirk. Not everyone followed the Federation accounting rules. Clearly, Maarteen wasn't worried about being reported. "Thank you, Mr. Maarteen."

"My pleasure," he replied. "If you're staying here long, Jessian can probably suggest a more affordable accommodation."

"Hell, yeah," Jessian said. "The Homestead is nice, but it's for tourists. Mucho credits. My auntie runs a boarding house that's way cheaper."

"I believe I might be interested in that." Maarteen glanced over his shoulder and winked at Quinn. "My lodging rate is the same, wherever I stay. A little extra scratch is always helpful."

"Especially for a government employee," Tony said, his eyes measuring. "The Federation isn't known for its generous salaries."

Maarteen nodded but didn't reply.

"Wanna go there direct?" Jessian asked.

"We will stay at the Homestead," Tony declared. "If you prefer to drop Mr. Maarteen elsewhere first, that is, of course, his prerogative."

Maarteen waved his hands. "I'll spend tonight at the Homestead, too. I have to meet a couple people there. But tomorrow, I'd like to see your auntie's boarding house." He half-turned in his seat. "Here on Lunesco, 'auntie' is any older woman, not necessarily a relative."

Quinn nodded absently. She stared out the window, appalled at the endless flat, brown plains. "This planet is flat."

"Don't be ridiculous, darling," Tony said. "Flat planets aren't possible. They're all spherical. You don't want people to think you're an idiot."

Quinn's head turned slowly toward Tony, and she gave him the stink-eye. "If you're going to be pedantic, it's an oblate spheroid."

Tony's eyes flicked toward the front seat and back to her. She glared harder. He didn't need to make this charade more difficult.

"Yup," Jessian said, missing the interplay between her passengers. "Flat as a pancake. You can see forever."

The car slowed, and the cloud of dust blew away. They pulled to a stop in front of a three-story, gray brick building. Two other vehicles were parked beside it, and a small patch of dusty grass lay before the entrance. A weathered sign hung over the doors indicating The Homestead. No other buildings were visible.

Jessian pulled her goggles over her face and grinned before yanking her scarf up over her mouth and nose. "Ready? I'm going to open the door. Y'all run for the building. I'll bring the bags."

She didn't wait for a reply. The moment she opened the door, gritty heat blasted them. Quinn scrambled for the latch and shoved her own door open. She raced up across the parched grass and up the steps. The doors swung open at her touch, landing her in a wide entry hall.

Tony pushed the door shut and turned to watch the street. Maarteen and Jessian went to the back of the car. "What do you think they're arguing about?"

Quinn peered through the thick glass. "Looks to me like Mr. Maarteen doesn't want Jessian touching his bag. I wonder what he has in there?"

"Dangerous people-counting stuff?" Tony chuckled. "His stash of illegal, chocolate-covered jellybeans?"

"Yuck!" Quinn made a face.

Tony swung the door open to let the other two inside. "Thank you for bringing the luggage, Jessian." He took their bags.

"My pleasure, sir." The driver shoved her goggles up again. "Shake off the dust while the vacuum runs, and then we'll go inside."

They dislodged vast clouds of fine dust, and the excellent air handlers whisked it away. "Come on." Jessian pushed through the second set of doors. "Let's get you registered."

CHAPTER 14

THE *MILLENNIUM PEREGRINE* jumped to the Lunesco System a couple of days behind the *Solar Wind*. Thanks to their faster in-system drive, the long trek to Lunesco Three only took four days instead of seven, getting them to the planet shortly after Tony and Quinn arrived.

End sat in the captain's chair, tapping his fingers against the armrests in a complicated rhythm. He'd taken drum lessons when he was younger, and only the lack of a trap set kept him from pursuing his dream of being an interstellar rock star. That and the lack of bandmates. And being too lazy to practice. He grinned, flipped his hair out of his eyes with a practiced head jerk, and continued pounding the chair.

"End! Stop!" Dareen moaned from the communications station. "You are driving me insane. I can't hear the comm bands over that racket."

"Put on the headphones," End pummeled the armrest. "You can't stop the music! Drum solo!" He pounded harder, working up to a triumphant crescendo and final slap. "Thank you! Thank you very much!" He threw his arms into the air and mimicked the noise of a crowd cheering.

"They don't block the sound that well." She swiveled her chair away, eyes closed. When he started drumming again, she growled and pulled the archaic headphones over her ears.

The door opened, and Francine sauntered onto the bridge, followed by Sashelle. "What's up?"

End stopped playing. "We'll reach parking orbit in about an hour. I don't know what happens then. Gramma hasn't said."

"You ever been to Lunesco?"

He shook his head. "No, our forays into the Federation are usually to the central planets. Quick pickups, and the occasional smuggling operation."

Dareen swung her chair around, yanking the headphones off. "End! Don't tell her that!" Sashelle jumped up into her lap, purring.

"What?" End said. "She already knows what we do. She probably hacked into the Commonwealth databases and pulled our records while she was on N'Avon."

Francine smirked. "Not quite, but I did some research. It's not like your activities are a secret from the Russosken."

"Do you know why Tony is there?" Dareen stabbed a finger toward the floor.

"How would I? I haven't talked to Tony since you left us on N'Avon." Francine wandered to the pilot's chair and picked at a frayed spot on the back. "Good job with the Romara situation, by the way. Thanks for not turning me in."

Dareen grimaced. The caat butted her hand in a command to resume petting. The girl complied. "Turning you over would have drawn too much attention to us. Plus, if we outed you, they'd have found Lucas, too."

"Still, I'm sure you could have figured out a way." Francine spun the chair idly. "I won't tell anyone about your hidey-hole. Not that the Russosken would care. This ship is small potatoes to them."

"Don't tell Gramma that," End laughed. "She thinks we're as big and bad as anyone."

Dareen stared hard at Francine. "I'll bet the Russosken would be happy to make use of us, if they knew."

"Well, they won't. Not from me. You've been better to me than my own family, and I appreciate that." Francine gazed around the bridge, avoiding eye contact. Then she nodded, once, and turned to go.

"I'm surprised Gramma is letting you wander the ship," Dareen said.

Francine grinned over her shoulder. "Who says she did?"

Dareen's eyes went wide, but End laughed.

"Calm down," Francine said to the younger woman. "She didn't bother locking me in. I'm sure she's still watching, though." She looked around the upper corners of the bridge, as if looking for cameras. "I can help you. You're shorthanded, and I can help!"

The grin faded from End's face. "She won't take your help. She's still hoping Mom and Dad will come back."

"No, I'm not," Lou's voice said through the speakers.

The three on the bridge exchanged laughing glances.

"I saw that," Lou said. "Liz and Maerk wanted to go out on their own. Well, they're on their own. We don't need 'em. Francine, come to my office!"

Francine raised her eyebrows.

"She means the lounge," End said.

The caat jumped off Dareen's lap and followed Francine off the bridge.

Dareen shrugged and pulled her headphones back on. "Don't even start."

End slapped the armrest a couple times, to prove he wasn't taking orders from his little sister, then relaxed into the chair and closed his eyes. Time for a nap.

FRANCINE STRAIGHTENED her shirt with a quick jerk to the bottom edge, smoothed down her pants, and strode into the lounge. She was casually dressed—linen slacks, silky T-shirt with a scooped neck, and low heels—perfect for a business meeting with a mafia boss. She ignored Lou, crossing to the mini fridge to grab a bottle of water before turning to lean her butt against the counter. "You requested my presence?"

Lou's eyes narrowed. "Pretty snippy attitude for a girl on the run."

"I have options."

"No, you don't." Lou barked a hard laugh. "If you did, you wouldn't have come to me. But I'm slim on options right now, too. I need someone to negotiate sale of the cargo, and nobody else on this boat has a clue."

"Sounds like you need a cross-training program." Francine took a sip of her water, watching the older woman closely. "I have some sales expertise. I could probably get a good deal on your cargo. I could even take Dareen under my wing and train her. What's your offer?"

"My offer is I don't strand you on Lunesco."

"You'll have to do better than that," Francine said. "I could be a valuable asset. But I'm not going to do my best work for someone who treats me like a nuisance. I want to be a member of the team. A trusted member of the team."

"Trust has to be earned," Lou growled. "What have you done to earn it?"

Francine ticked things off on her fingers. "Helped Tony and Quinn get the kids on Hadriana. Didn't expose your hidey-hole on Romara. Uh." She broke off, unable to come up with a third thing. She needed to beef up her list.

"I'm supposed to trust you because you didn't give yourself away?" Lou looked her up and down. "Self-preservation isn't a great sales claim."

Francine squirmed inside but managed to keep cool on the outside. Or so she hoped. She didn't want to go back to the

Russosken, but civilian life had proven boring. She lifted her chin. If they didn't want her on the *Peregrine*, she'd find somewhere else. "Fine, dump me when we get back to Romara."

"We aren't going back to Romara, girl," Lou said. "Maybe I'll dump you here. After Tony's mission is complete, of course."

"Please, don't leave me here!" Francine's breath caught in her chest. The cool negotiator fled in panic. "I can't live on a dust ball in the fringe. Let me help. You can watch me like a hawk. But please, give me a chance."

Lou's eyes bored into her. "Fine. Dareen or End will shadow you. Every communication will be recorded. If you prove yourself here, we'll keep you on till we get back to civilization. But don't give me a reason to dump you. You double-cross me, and you'll be headed to Lunesco without a shuttle."

Francine nodded. She wasn't sure Lou would throw her out the airlock. The captain's activities on the *Peregrine* didn't always jibe with the rumors about the hard-hearted head of the Marconi family. But Francine wasn't part of that family, and if there was one thing that Lou had made clear, it was that family came first.

"And, no matter what happens—" Lou got to her feet and stomped toward the door. "You still owe me for Hadriana. That debt will be called in later, when I need it."

Francine nodded, but Lou had already left the room.

CHAPTER 15

QUINN TOOK a deep breath of the flower-scented air. Lush, green foliage hung from the walls. Highly-polished planks in a lavender hue stretched across the wide space to a deep purple desk. Behind the desk, water trickled down a stone slab, tinkling softly in the background.

"The wood was harvested in the Darien Valley," Jessian said. "Yes, the purple is natural. Pender! Got some new folks for you."

A dark man with bright green eyes stepped out from behind the vines. He bowed slightly to them and smiled, his teeth glinting with small crystals. "Welcome to the Homestead!"

Tony bustled up to the desk, stepping in front of Maarteen. "I have a reservation under Anthony."

Pender nodded and tapped a screen embedded in the tall, purple desk. "Yes, a suite on the third floor. And this must be Mrs. Antony? May I see some ID, please?"

While Tony handled the paperwork, Quinn turned back to Jessian. "Where's the rest of the town? There's nothing here except this building."

"The town's down yonder." Jessian pointed in the direction they had been heading. "About three more klicks."

"Really? I didn't see anything except this building." Given the flat landscape, a town that close should have been clearly visible.

"The town's in the valley. Much nicer down there." Jessian grinned. "The Homestead is where the first settlers landed. They were dumped here by the Federation a century or so ago. Criminals, they say. Probably political dissidents." The girl shrugged. "They built a shelter here, because they didn't know there was any place better. They obviously didn't have any survey data, because the valley's right over there. When they ran out of food, they started exploring and found the valley. We keep the Homestead for visitors. And to remind ourselves of our roots."

Was Jessian a dissident? Quinn's lips twisted. Likely the whole planet was, with that kind of background. "If someone new moved to Lunesco, would they be in the valley?"

"Most likely," Jessian said. "They might try to settle out on the plains, but they'd figure out fast enough that's suicide. The winds never stop, and there's no water. Plenty of solar, if you can get the panels, but you'd have to bring cash in from off-world to buy 'em. There's a guy way out thatta way who's been here ten years." She waved vaguely toward the rear of the building. "Far side of the shuttle strip. But he had lots of credits and imported a bunch of stuff. Basically off-grid."

"Ten years?" So not Doug Parra then. He'd been with her on Fort Sumpter only four months ago. She didn't want to ask for him by name, since she wasn't sure of Tony's plan. "That's a long time to live alone."

Jessian nodded. "Not something I'd want to do but live and let live. It's kind of a planetary motto."

"Most fringe residents adopt that one," Maarteen said. "It's why they move out here in the first place."

"You've been to a lot of fringe worlds, Mr. Maarteen?" Quinn asked.

"Please, call me Sebi." He smiled. "It's my territory. None of my colleagues want to go this far from civilization, as they call it." He sent an apologetic grimace in Jessian's direction. "So, I rotate between fringe planets. Do my job, report back to Romara, then on to the next."

"And what, exactly, is your job?" Quinn asked. "You don't really count people, do you?"

Maarteen laughed. "Not personally. I train local citizens to administer the census. They analyze the data back at headquarters, and I come back to audit and investigate any anomalies."

"Anomalies?" Jessian's tone was belligerent. "What's that mean? Are the answers suspicious? Is the Federation worried about the attitudes of us fringe-dwellers? Is that why you're back so soon?" She locked eyes with him. "You were here a few months ago."

"No, no, of course not." Maarteen gave an easy laugh. "Well, okay, technically, yes. But the anomalies were in data collection, not the responses, per se. I need to retrain our local team. The answers we received made it clear they are not using the standard questions."

Jessian continued to stare at him, her eyes flat and hard. Maarteen didn't seem to notice. "I can't go into details, as that information is confidential, but it's a fairly minor problem."

Quinn nodded, since he seemed to be waiting for some kind of response, and Jessian wasn't giving one. Confidential census questions sounded like an oxymoron and sending a live person to adjust a minor issue wasn't the Federation's usual method. In her experience, the Federation was more of an "ignore it until you can't, then burn it to the ground" government. That was why she'd always tried to stay between the lines.

"Our suite is finally ready." Tony held up an old-fashioned keycard. "Thank you for the ride, Mr. Maarteen, Jessian. Perhaps we'll see you later. Come, darling." Without waiting for her reply, he swept away.

Quinn nodded to the others, ignoring Jessian's raised eyebrows and Maarteen's sad head shake. The role of long-suffering wife was getting old.

They climbed the staircase wrapped around the side and back of the wide lobby to a balcony on the second floor. From here, the front desk was hidden beneath them, but Jessian waved from the lobby door. Quinn waved back.

"This way." Tony held a door open. A wide, carpeted stairway led up to the third floor. As soon as the door shut behind her, Tony took her bag with a twisted smile. "There doesn't appear to be any surveillance inside this building."

"When did you check that?" Quinn followed him into the third-floor hallway.

"While Pender was setting our card-key. But I've got my jammer running." He set down the bag and pulled a card from his pocket. When he waved it at the access panel, the door clicked open. "I can add this to your comtab, so you can come and go as you please. I didn't ask for a card for you, since that would be out of character."

"How much longer do we have to play these parts?" Quinn stepped into the room.

More of the beautiful wooden floors gleamed under throw rugs in assorted colors. Sleek wooden chairs with thick upholstery stood on either side of a gas fireplace. A small desk and chair sat under the windows. Through a door, the adjoining bedroom held a huge bed with a smooth, white coverlet and a multitude of pillows. Flowers on the bedside tables gave off a light, sweet aroma, like honey and citrus.

Quinn crossed to the window. She pulled aside the thick blue drapes and was rewarded with a view of the flat plains stretching out to infinity. She squinted. There was the barest suggestion of mountains in the far distance. Or maybe that was dust.

"Not much longer." Tony stepped into the other room and tossed the bags on the bed. Then he pulled his comtab out. "One more check." He held the device upright and slowly turned. He disappeared into the bathroom, then returned to the sitting room. "Nope, we're clear."

"Maybe they have something you can't detect?" Quinn whispered.

"I don't think so. Nothing Federation-made." He swiped the

comtab and soothing music poured from the speaker. He set it on a side table. "But I'll leave the jammer running."

"Can you finally tell me what we're doing here?" Quinn dropped into one of the chairs.

"We're here to talk to Doug Parra."

"You said that, but why?" Quinn stood again. "I need some eyedrops. That sand is still smarting."

"Hang on." Tony disappeared into the bedroom and returned with a small basket. "Saw this in the bathroom."

Quinn pawed through the collection of soaps, conditioners, lotions, and toothpaste. She pulled out a small package and held it up. "Good call. We aren't the only visitors without goggles." She placed the sterile mask over her face, and a heavy, cool mist soothed her scratchy eyes. "This is a pretty classy place for a fringe planet like Lunesco."

"It's where the Federation employees stay," Tony said. "And I've heard it's occasionally used for secret, high-level talks between the Feds and the Commonwealth."

Quinn's eyes nearly popped out of her head. She whipped off the mask to stare at him. "They have those? I've never heard a whisper…"

"They're *very* secret. People in the Commonwealth usually hear rumors, after the fact, but the Federation keeps it locked down. Someone like Francine probably knows."

"But Francine isn't a Federation citizen," Quinn protested. "And don't think you've managed to change the subject. We're going back to Doug Parra when we're done with this."

Tony chuckled and acknowledged her point with a nod. "Actually, Francine *is* a Federation citizen. All the Russosken are."

"Why have I never heard of them?"

"Same reason you haven't heard about the secret talks. The Federation likes to keep her citizens in the dark." He got up and took the basket out of the room. When he returned, he went to the mini fridge. "Want something to drink? There's some sparkling water."

"Sure." Quinn waited until he'd returned to his seat and handed her the bottle. "Now spill. What does Doug Parra know that we need to risk arrest and death to ask him about in person?"

"When you say it that way, it sounds so dangerous." Tony chugged some water. "If I knew what he knows, we wouldn't need to talk to him."

Quinn pursed her lips and glared. "You must know something, or we wouldn't have come."

He smiled. "I love yanking your chain." He paused, as if ordering his thoughts. "When we escaped from Fort Sumpter, and I left all of you at Zauras Base, I left the gold too, remember? Well, most of it. I kept a little, to fund this kind of thing."

Quinn looked away, trying to recall that day. Tony had landed his Krimson agent shuttle on the Zauras Base flight line, using all the appropriate codes and call signs. They'd taxied to a parking spot, and all of them, except Tony, had gotten off the shuttle. She vaguely recalled the two crates of gold being unloaded, but she hadn't cared about them—she was anxious to see her kids. As soon as they'd cleared the engine zone, Tony took off. "They took us to debriefing, and that was the last I saw of any of them. I have no idea where the gold went."

"The rest of the group was debriefed and released." Tony rubbed his chin. "From what I've been able to learn, only Cyn and Doug managed to keep any gold. Oh, and Tiffany, of course. I'm sure the Federation took the rest. Except the nuggets that disappeared along the way into random pockets." He paused to down more water.

"Doug took his share and moved here. There was enough to purchase a nice home with more to spare. He's using the rest—" He glanced at the comtab still spinning out smooth instrumental music. "Well, who knows. Maybe he's saving it." As he said these words, he pointed at the comtab, then made a "gimme" gesture.

Quinn handed over her own comtab.

Tony tapped at the screen, then handed it back. He had opened a scratch pad and typed in the words, "I think he's funding a revolution."

CHAPTER 16

FRANCINE SAT ON THE COUCH, her legs and arms crossed, trying to take deep, cleansing breaths. The old woman couldn't hurt her, she told herself. A different voice in the back of her mind begged to differ. Lou could dump Francine—and all the voices in her head—on this or any other fringe world and fly away.

"What do you mean, our cargo is useless?!" Lou bellowed.

Francine held up her hands. "Don't shoot the messenger. Didn't you check what they needed on Lunesco before you bought it?"

"Of course we did!" Lou yelled. "Kert checked." She stomped to the intercom. "KERT! Where's Kert?"

"I'm in engineering." Kert sounded as grumpy as Lou. "Your damn ship is in terrible shape."

"What's wrong with it?" Lou demanded.

"Nothing to worry about, Gramma," Dareen's voice said. "The in-system engine is misbehaving, but I can tweak it. It won't take long."

"Is Kert helping you, or getting in the way?" Lou asked. "Never mind. Get up to the lounge right now, Kert. Dareen can fix whatever's wrong better than you can."

Francine sat very still, hoping Lou would forget about her.

Ellianne skipped into the room. "Can you help me with my math, Francine?"

Lou turned away from the intercom and glared at Francine. "She's helping me now, sweetie." Lou's tone made the hair on Francine's neck stand on end. "She'll come find you when she's done. Why don't you go help Dareen in engineering?"

Ellianne dropped her tablet on the table. "Recess!" she sang as she raced out of the room.

Lou's hard eyes came back to Francine. The younger woman made her face blank and stared back.

Kert paused in the doorway. "What's up, Mother?"

"Come here," Lou said, her eyes still on Francine. "How did you decide what cargo to buy?"

Kert scratched his head and shrugged. "I went on Liz's comm account and read the boards. It said they needed selenium and manganese on Lunesco."

"Which boards did you look at?" Francine tore her eyes away from Lou to focus on Kert.

He tapped the display button on the coffee table and pressed his thumb against the reader. A holographic image appeared over the table, full of open video windows and accompanied by a cacophony of sounds. Kert slapped the mute button. "Here." He poked a finger at an icon and used both hands to stretch it out. "Message board. Here's the one."

Francine and Lou leaned forward to look at the message he opened.

"Kert, you idiot!" Lou stabbed a finger at the message. "This says someone on Lunesco is *selling* selenium and manganese! Not buying!" She slapped the back of his head.

Kert's nostrils flared. "I told you this isn't my thing, Mother! We need Liz back. I'm done with this commerce *futz*!" He stormed out of the room.

Lou's face turned red, and she ground her teeth. "That son of a—"

Francine tried to swallow a laugh and choked.

"What?" Lou growled.

Francine shook her head, her lips pressed firmly together.

Lou glared, but her lips twitched. She growled again, but it turned into a groan. "How do we fix this?"

LATER THAT NIGHT, the crew gathered around the table in the mess hall. Francine stood at the end, trying to hide her smirk. She felt like she was back in the family, but as the boss instead of a lowly underling. From this side of the equation, the whole family thing felt pretty good.

She glanced at Lou. The old woman pinned her with a glare that made it clear she knew exactly what Francine was thinking, and she wouldn't tolerate any attempts to take charge. Francine was here to advise only, not make any decisions. Francine nodded at Lou and looked away, hoping she didn't look as shaken as she now felt.

Lou held up a hand, and the chattering stopped. "We have a problem, and Francine says she has a solution." Lou sounded dubious. Fantastic, they were off to a great start.

"I do have a solution." Francine tapped the table and waved a screen to life. "We jump out and get a new cargo. The stuff we have will sell like nova-cakes on Iraca Five or Daravoo Two. Then we can pick up the cargo they want here on Lunesco."

"That will take days." Dareen leaned in to peer at the data. "We need to be available for Tony."

"We could leave one of the shuttles here." Francine poked a finger at the deck. "Land somewhere in the desert and stay buttoned up until—if—they call. The rest of us go to Iraca and dump this lot. Pick up some—" She swiped through some screens and pulled one up. "We can get some comm gear. That stuff sells here, and it's available for cheap on Iraca. Lunesco will buy that. Or we go to Daravoo and get weapons, those always sell. Look at the stats." She stepped back.

Lou's face twisted in thought. "Who do you propose we leave here? Didn't go so well last time we left Dareen in charge of a shuttle."

The table erupted in protest.

"That's not fair!"

"It wasn't her fault you let her—"

"We managed to save them—"

Francine waited for them to stop yelling. It took longer than she expected.

Finally, Stene bellowed, "ENOUGH! I will start singing if you don't shut up." When they were quiet, he nodded to Francine.

"I propose we land a shuttle with enough supplies to last a week to ten days. You can send whoever you want, but we'll need to keep the appropriate crew on the *Peregrine* to jump in and out." She shrugged. "Whoever you can spare. Maybe Kert or Stene could provide adult supervision."

"I have a better idea." Lou's grin sent a chill down Francine's back. The old woman stabbed a finger at her. "*You* can provide adult supervision. You and End will take the shuttle." She overrode Francine's attempt to protest. "End, you make sure she doesn't contact any Russosken—I've heard they're active in this sector."

Francine's face went pale, and her shoulders seized in panic. "You're leaving me alone on a Russosken-controlled planet with a teenaged boy for protection?"

Lou shook her head. "Don't be ridiculous."

Francine's shoulders relaxed.

Lou's grin widened. "I'm sending *you* to protect End."

THE DOOR of the tiny apartment on N'Avon slammed, and Liz Marconi let out a low growl. Startled, Maerk looked up from the pile of electronic components scattered across the kitchen table.

"Bad day at the office?" he asked his ex-wife.

Her eyes narrowed, and she growled again.

"Sorry." He lifted both hands. "How can I help? Backrub? Hot bath? Target practice?"

She ignored him, stomping across the room to throw her jacket on the couch. "Searching for work is the most soul-sucking activity in the universe!" She flung herself down next to the jacket.

Maerk got up and pulled a bottle from the kitchen cupboard. He poured shots into two glasses, added some ice, and handed one to Liz.

Liz gulped down the amber liquid and handed the glass back to Maerk. "Hit me."

Maerk handed his own glass to Liz, then went to the kitchenette and brought the bottle to the couch. He refilled the glass in his hand. "What's going on?"

Liz sipped from her own glass. "I hate this. I apply for jobs that I'm highly qualified to fill, but never hear back. I get interviews for jobs well below my abilities and expertise, and they hire someone else—because I'm overqualified. Why did you bother interviewing me if I'm overqualified?! You enjoy wasting time? My resume makes my qualifications very clear!" She lifted the glass and emptied it again. "Hit me."

Maerk took the glass. "Let's slow that down a bit, shall we?"

"I think they see 'independent interstellar commerce' and call me because they're curious, not because they want to hire me. Maybe I should go on the talk show circuit. They could pay me to talk about my fascinating experiences in the stars." She said the last bit in a reality show announcer's voice.

Maerk choked back a chuckle—he knew she wouldn't thank him for laughing. Time to change the subject. "Speaking of reality shows, check this out." He snagged his comtab off the side table and flicked a few icons. Then he threw the cast onto the large screen on the wall.

A standard talk-show set appeared: couch, desk, low table with various props and coffee cups scattered about. A supermodel and a sports star bantered about the latter's recent wedding. Behind the desk, the host simpered, throwing in the occasional barbed comment.

"Is that who I think it is?" Liz stared at the screen. "Quinn is going to go supernova!"

"Yup," Maerk said. "Tiffany Andretti, fourth ex-wife of Admiral Pieter Andretti and survivor of the 'Fort Sumpter Scandal.' I think she's the one who coined the name."

"I wonder how much of that gold she managed to hold onto." Liz picked up Maerk's glass and sipped. "Enough to bribe a producer into giving her a talk show?"

"I don't know if Tony ever found out what happened to the crates the survivors took with them. And she's actually pretty good at this. This show is top of the charts in the Federation." He paused the show, shaking his head. "If you like that sort of thing."

Liz smirked. "You watched enough to know she's 'pretty good' at it." She set the glass down and turned to Maerk. "You ever think about going back?"

"Back? Back to the Federation?"

Liz rolled her eyes. "You know that's not what I meant. Back to the *Peregrine*."

"No." He grabbed the glass and drained it, then got up, to pace across the tiny room. "I am not going back to Lou. She put our family in danger for no reason."

"She didn't know how risky that device was," Liz protested.

"If she didn't know, she had no business sending Dareen to get it!" Maerk slammed his hand on the wall.

"Hey, cut it out!" a muffled voice called through the wall.

"Sorry!" Maerk replied. He paced the other way.

"Besides, the kids are still there!" Liz said. "We aren't protecting them by being here."

Maerk froze. "You want to go back? What about my business?" He gestured to the littered kitchen table.

"Fixing electronics for people too cheap to buy new ones isn't much of a business," Liz said. "It pays crap—because, as previously mentioned, your customers are cheap. I know you like doing it, but you can fix things on the ship."

Maerk stood by the table, fiddling with the soldering iron. He dripped solder onto a broken circuit board, creating a little mountain of useless slag. He poked at the slag with the hot iron, saying a quick prayer to Saint Gengulf, the patron of unhappy marriages. He talked to Saint Gengulf a lot—even though he and Liz had been divorced for years. Gengulf had been there for him in the bad times—they were old friends.

With a deep breath, he set the soldering iron carefully on the table and turned back to his ex-wife. "If we go back, we're getting our own ship."

CHAPTER 17

A TAP at the door roused Tony from a light sleep. He froze for a moment, getting his bearings before moving. They'd been on Lunesco for three days and none of his attempts to make contact had been successful.

He lay on the couch in the sitting room of their suite. He'd left the bed to Quinn, claiming the mattress was too soft for him. In reality, sleeping next to her on the ship for ten nights had been excruciating. She clearly viewed him as a friend—just a friend. He had always felt more.

Now that she had severed ties with her idiot husband, he hoped to change their relationship. But not during a mission. He needed to be clear-headed and alert. The couch was comfortable enough, since he wasn't a tall man.

Silently, he folded the blankets back and rolled off his makeshift bed. He pulled his mini blaster from under the pillow. Crouching, he stalked across the room. Another soft tap sounded, and he straightened to peek through the peephole.

Sebi Maarteen. Federation officers visiting in the middle of the night never boded well. Holding the mini blaster behind the door, he swung it halfway open. "It's the middle of the night, Mr. Maarteen. Is there some kind of emergency? Would you like me to call the front desk?"

Maarteen shook his head. "I need to speak with you, Mr. Marconi."

Tony kept his face perfectly still. Then he drew down his eyebrows. "Marconi? My name is Anthony. Have you been drinking?"

Maarteen waved his hand, clearly agitated. "I know who you are, Mr. Marconi, and I need your help. Or rather, you need my help."

Tony let his eyes narrow. "You clearly need some help, Mr. Maarteen, but I'm hardly dressed for it." He gestured to his plaid pants and bare chest and feet.

"We can talk here." Maarteen glanced up and down the hallway. "Please, may I come in?"

"My wife is asleep in the bedroom," Tony said firmly.

"She should probably hear this, too. She's in as much danger as you."

The inner door opened, and Quinn stood on the threshold, yawning. She had a blanket wrapped around her shoulders, and her hair was a mess. Tony pushed down the warm feeling in his belly and yanked his eyes away.

"Who's in danger?" She clutched the blanket in one hand, but the other was hidden in the folds. Tony hoped it held the stunner he'd given her on the ship.

He beckoned Maarteen inside and shut the door. "Mr. Maarteen seems to think we're in danger. He also thinks our last name is Macaroni, so I think some coffee might be in order." He grabbed his T-shirt off the back of the couch and pulled it on as he strode across the room to the coffee maker, never quite turning his back to the "customs agent."

"Ms. Templeton—" Maarteen took a seat in one of the plush chairs. He glanced at the bedding falling off the couch, then back at Quinn. "I know who you are, and I can help you."

Quinn stood in the doorway, frozen. Then her right hand came out of the blankets, stunner pointed directly at Maarteen.

A wash of pride flooded through Tony, followed by a drop of dismay. They might have been able to convince Maarteen he had the wrong people, if she'd kept it hidden. Too late now. He stepped away from the coffee machine and pulled out his blaster.

"How do you know who I am?" Quinn stepped into the room, taking a position with a clear line of sight on the intruder.

"I'm here to speak with Mr. Parra, too." Maarteen smiled gently. "I did my homework. All three of you were involved in the Fort Sumpter Scandal."

"Is that what they're calling it?" Quinn's tone went hard. "A scandal? As if we were holding orgies or something? People nearly died, Mr. Maarteen, left behind by Admiral Andretti. That's not a scandal. It was a tragedy barely averted, no thanks to the military."

"If I have my information correct, one person did die." Maarteen leaned back in his chair. "Colonel Cisneros?"

Quinn's hand jerked, and Tony took a step forward. "Cisneros got what he deserved. He attempted to steal the shuttle and leave without us. And he tried to kill some of us outright. Get on with it. What do you want?"

Maarteen held up his hands in surrender. "As you know, I'm a customs agent. It gives me the opportunity to visit many planets within the Federation. Over time, I've grown—" He paused. "—disgusted with the lack of humanity in our institutions. Did you know the customs department doesn't count some people?" He leaned forward, his voice passionate. "If an individual meets certain criteria, they are labeled *legal residents* rather than *citizens*. People with disabilities, for example. Homosexuals. Religious practitioners. If a planet has a high ratio of residents to citizens, their funding is cut. That means the places that need the most support get the least. Even though their taxes are flowing to the Federation."

He sat back and crossed his arms again. "That was the start. When I learned that, I nearly quit. Then I decided I would work from inside the system to create change." He laughed bitterly. "That didn't pan out. I nearly got myself thrown in prison. My exemplary record convinced my bosses to ship me off to the fringe instead." He laughed again. "Stupid decision. Out here, there are lots of folks looking for someone with an inside connection. I was recruited by an organization that is working to… Let's say they want to repair the damage the Federation has done to our people."

"You work for revolutionaries?" Tony asked. "The Planetary Patriots? The Sendarian Liberation Front? The—"

Maarteen cut him off. "No. NO! Those are terrorist organizations. I am no terrorist. I work with a group attempting to use economics to break free. We're funding increased independence in the fringe worlds. The goal is to become powerful enough to leave the umbrella of the Planetary Societies and form our own federation. A real federation, with strong planetary governments and a weak central government. Not like the UFSP."

"That sounds like treason," Tony said.

"We aren't revolutionaries, Mr. Maarteen." Quinn dropped into the other armchair. She kept the stunner pointed at Maarteen, but clearly had stopped viewing him as a threat. "We aren't fans of Admiral Andretti, but we aren't trying to destabilize the government."

Tony remained vigilant. He wasn't buying Maarteen's story—yet. It could be a ruse, but if so, he couldn't see the goal. If Maarteen wanted to turn in Quinn and Tony for the bounties the Federation must have on them, he wouldn't have come alone. And he wouldn't have needed this story. They were both convicted traitors—there was no need to manufacture evidence. "Who's funding you?"

Maarteen shook his head. "I don't know names. They're wealthy business owners who believe they could do better, financially, without the onerous taxes and regulations the Federation levies."

"Who couldn't?" Tony leaned a hip against the back of the couch and waved the blaster at Maarteen to get his attention. "You still haven't told us why you're here."

Maarteen sighed and looked away. "I'm here, in this room, to warn you. As I mentioned, I believe we both hope to meet with Mr. Parra. Based on your shared experience—" He flicked a smile at Quinn. "—you have a better chance of reaching him than I do. He doesn't receive many visitors. As a customs official, I can force a visit, but that might not be the best approach. I was hoping we could work together."

"You mentioned danger," Quinn said, "to Tony and me. Who besides you knows about us?"

"Those two farmers on the *Solar Wind*," Maarteen said. "Lin-tuan is a local—well known here. His family has been on Lunesco for several generations. But Ralph is an Innie."

"Innie?" Quinn frowned.

"Someone from the interior—the more heavily-settled part of the Federation—who moves to the fringe for unknown reasons." Maarteen nodded, as if he'd imparted great wisdom.

"You mean someone like Doug Parra?" She looked from one man to the other.

Tony shook his head. "Doug's originally from a fringe world. Not here, so they probably watch him pretty closely, but he's not considered an Innie. Innies are highly suspect. Charles Anthony would be an Innie. You're an Innie." He fixed a stare on Maarteen. "If Ralph is an Innie, how'd he get Lin-tuan to bring him here?"

"They met at university. We believe they're, uh, involved. Romantically." His eyes darted from Tony to Quinn, judging their reaction.

Tony shrugged. "Is that it? They're gay? Living out here on the fringe would be safer for them than Romara. Seems like a good reason for an Innie to move out."

"Or a good cover," Maarteen said. "It's a fairly new relationship."

"There must be something else." Quinn stood. With a glance at Maarteen, she crossed behind Tony to get a glass of water, then returned to her seat.

"They were already booked on the flight when I made our reservation," Tony said. "If he's tracking someone, it's not us."

"I think he's watching me," Maarteen said. "Only Lin-tuan was booked when I contacted Captain Wingard. Ralph was added a couple weeks ago. After I booked, but before you did. But you're bigger fish. I'm sure he'd gladly forget about me if it would net him you two. Do you have any idea how big the price on your head is?"

"I don't think I want to know," Quinn said. "That's a good reminder to be careful, though. I've been worried about Federation officers detaining me, but an 'alert citizen' could be all it takes to end up back on death row."

"Or a bounty hunter," Maarteen said.

"Wow, thanks, it gets better and better," Quinn said.

"Let me get this straight," Tony said. "You came to warn us that someone who may, or may not, be following you could recognize us and decide to turn us in, instead. Seems like a flimsy reason to break your cover."

"He also wants us to introduce him to Doug," Quinn reminded him.

"The main reason I came here is to tell you the Federation is on the way." Maarteen looked at the door, as if he expected someone to burst in. "Now."

CHAPTER 18

LIZ FOLLOWED MAERK up the ramp into the old ship. "What a pile of junk!" She slapped the bulkhead. "Is this really the best we can afford?"

"She's not pretty, but she works," Maerk said. "I've checked all the systems, and Porento gave me a test drive. She flies well, she's space-worthy, and she's economical."

"It's kind of small."

"She," Maerk said. "*She's* kind of small. You grew up on spaceships. They're always she."

Liz leveled a look at him. "Until we buy it, it's an it. It can be a she when—if—it's ours."

"Is that some kind of spacer tradition?" Maerk followed her across the cargo hold and into the living quarters.

"No, it's my own rule. Don't get too attached until it's yours. Kind of like naming a puppy at the pound. Bad idea." She turned to look back at the cargo deck. "That's the only cargo deck? It's smaller than the *Peregrine's* shuttle!"

"No, it just looks that way," Maerk said. "You could park Dareen's shuttle inside. If you're careful. Might be tight."

Liz rolled her eyes. "Where's the crew lounge?"

"Through there." Maerk gestured expansively. He led her through a hatch. "Passenger airlock there." He pointed. "And through this hatch, the galley, lounge, meeting room, all in one."

Liz stared at her ex for a few seconds, then let her eyes travel around the room. A table with chairs for eight filled the center of the room. A kitchen—including cold storage, dishes, and an oven—took up the side wall. A large screen filled the other, with lightweight couches and chairs grouped around it. A low bench was built into the back wall on either side of the hatch they'd just come through. Pale yellow covered the walls, with a swirly flower pattern along the top twenty centimeters. "It's a slow boat, isn't it? Lots of transit time to paint pretty flowers."

"She's not as fast as the *Peregrine* when she's going full-out," Maerk admitted. "But she's fast enough for trade. And Dareen and I could soup her up."

"Crew cabins?" Her eyes narrowed. "There are cabins, right?"

"Of course! We'll need a crew, and we aren't going to want a slumber party every night."

"Or ever," Liz muttered.

He crossed the room and stepped onto the low bench that ran across the width of the back wall. Reaching up, he pulled a ring on the ceiling. A trap door opened, and a ladder pulled down from the space. "Right this way."

"You've got to be kidding." Liz folded her arms.

"Not at all." Maerk climbed the ladder. "Extremely efficient use of space. Come on up. There's plenty of room."

With a heavy sigh, Liz climbed the ladder. "I'm getting too old for this." At the top, she stepped into a narrow hallway. Two steps past the access, a door stood open, revealing a small but functional cabin. Cabinets lined one wall, a bunk took up the opposite, and a door led to a tiny head at the far end.

"There are three of these cabins above the lounge." Maerk

pointed. "The other two have bunks, top and bottom, and share a head. The storage cupboards provide sound insulation between."

"Crew of six, then," Liz mused.

He nodded. "Yes. Or the kids could each have their own room. The four of us could run this ship easily." He went back into the hallway. "There's more room back here."

"Back where?"

Maerk pushed aside a panel on the wall opposite the cabin. "It's empty space now. But if we needed to, we could convert it to dormitories. Just bunks, not whole rooms like ours."

"Why would we need to have a dorm?" Liz slid the panel farther open. A grid of meter-square, two-meter-deep shelves filled the space. "I see what you mean—we could slot them in feet first, like memory cards. I wonder what these were built for. You could house a whole sports team up here in individual capsules. But why would we need to? Or want to?" She glanced at Maerk.

He shrugged. "I dunno. Maybe we'll provide transport for a circus? I like that it gives us options. Come back down, I'll show you the flight deck."

END FLIPPED a switch and swiped the screen, releasing Shuttle Two from the *Peregrine*. This shuttle was virtually identical to the one Dareen called *Fluffy Kitten*, but End thought of it as his. He patted the dash. Dareen and Stene had finished overhauling it a few weeks ago, and she still had that new shuttle smell.

"*Peregrine,* this is *Screaming Eagle,*" he announced through the comms. "We are free from dock. Beginning descent now."

"Roger, End," Dareen said. "Remember, you're running silent on this mission, so if you got something to say, now's the time."

"Parcity Flavor sucks. *Eagle* out!" He flicked the comm link closed before she could retort. "Parcity Flavor is her favorite band," he told Francine. "She'll hate that I got the last word."

Francine covered her eyes dramatically. "I can't believe I let myself get railroaded into babysitting you."

"I'm not a baby! I turned twenty this year. And you'd better be nice to me because I'm flying this thing." He yanked the joystick over, throwing them into a roll, then he jerked it straight again. Gramma might not be able to contact him when he was running silent, but that wouldn't stop her from saving up a punishment for misuse of the shuttle.

"Where are we landing?" Francine asked. "Lou kicked me out of the room before they decided."

End swiped open a panel and flicked it to her side of the screen. "Barebones airfield about forty klicks from the official shuttle field. Perfect for a vicious bird of prey like this." He patted the *Screaming Eagle's* dash.

Francine stretched the map bigger. "There's nothing here. Nothing! It's a dry lakebed. There isn't even a landing beacon."

"Don't need one. These shuttles were built to land anywhere. The Marines use them, you know." He pointed at the ceiling where the words "Property of the United Federation of Planetary Societies" were printed in fading letters.

"Federation Marines," Francine grumbled.

"Hey, don't dis the Marines—even the Fed Marines. They're badass."

"Great, I'm babysitting a space Marine wannabe."

"Despite what Gramma told you," End said smugly, "I'm the one babysitting you. She wanted you out of the way."

"That's the smartest thing you've said since we left. She definitely wants me out of the way. I shoulda stayed on N'Avon."

"Nah. That place is dry toast boring. Even this is better. Hang on." He flicked a few switches and set in a landing routine. "We'll be down in a few minutes."

"Fantastic." Francine tightened her straps. "A week to ten days in a tin can with a teenage boy."

"I told you, I'm not a teen anymore. How old are you, anyway?"

"Didn't your mother tell you not to ask a lady her age?" Francine retorted.

"I didn't ask a lady, I asked you." End grinned.

Francine rolled her eyes. "I'm twenty-six."

"Two young people in the prime of life." End winked. "I'm sure we can find something to do for a week. But now, I gotta land the shuttle. Hang onto your bloomers."

While Francine muttered something about her bloomers not being any of his business, End lowered the gear and brought the *Screaming Eagle* down in a perfect landing. They rattled across the rough ground to the far side of the dry lake. He parked in the lee of a low ridge—a spot they'd selected as the least-visible in the area. The ridge should protect them from the worst of the crazy winds but still allow them to launch quickly if necessary.

"This is a new feature." He swiped up a new screen and flicked a pixelated icon. "We got the shuttles resurfaced at N'Avon shipyard. It's called Kamelion. The whole thing is covered in a membrane of tiny scales—like pixels in a comtab. The system uses the cameras to pick up the local coloring, then changes the shuttle surface to blend in."

"Changeable camouflage?" Francine asked. "That's amazing. I wonder if the Russosken have this."

"New tech, super expensive, makes dirty work easier?" End said. "I'm sure they do."

He unlatched his seat restraints and stood, stretching. "Now, let's see if we can find something *interesting* to do." He held out a hand to Francine and wiggled his eyebrows. "I have an idea."

She blinked up at him, surprised. "Maybe you are more mature than I thought."

He led her to the bunk behind the cockpit. "Make yourself comfortable, and I'll be right back."

She tugged on a strand of her hair as she curled up on the bunk with a warm smile. "Bring something to drink, if you have it," she said in a throaty whisper.

End pulled a bottle from the tiny galley cabinet, then ran to his duffle bag and dug through it. He hurried back to the bunk and handed Francine a bottle of Fizzy Pop and a video game controller. "Lock and load!"

CHAPTER 19

QUINN'S HEAD snapped around and she stared at the door, but nothing happened. "You didn't mean 'now' as in this very second?"

"No," Maarteen said. "They'll be here in a couple hours. I picked up transmissions from a Space Force cruiser when it arrived in system."

Tony's brows lowered. "You have equipment to pick up Federation comm chatter?"

"Of course." He gestured at himself. "Customs official, remember? I can save the Federation credits if I travel on scheduled government vessels. Of course, I don't rack up any frequent spacer points that way, so my schedule rarely matches the regular flights."

Tony barked out a laugh. "You're the kind of guy we used to track when I was at headquarters. If you want to avoid an audit, make sure your travel plans are at least three days either side of the regularly scheduled transports."

"Thanks, but I'm not new to this," Maarteen said. "Since I frequently travel to worlds without a heavy government presence, I have a device to alert me to Federation ships entering and leaving a system."

"I've issued those devices," Quinn said. "Back in my comm days.

They don't pick up military vessels unless they're broadcasting. If they're here to arrest you, they wouldn't be. How do you know they're coming?"

"I might have had it, um, upgraded," Maarteen admitted. "Besides, I'm not a big enough target to merit a dedicated mission. They must be coming for some other reason."

"That's not what you said a few minutes ago," Tony said. "I'm feeling less inclined to believe anything you say."

"Yes, you're right. I should have been more transparent. Let me start again." Maarteen cleared his throat. "Can I get a glass of water?"

Quinn rose, but Tony held up a hand. "Quinn, go get dressed and packed." He shook his head to cut off her protest. "No, I'm not trying to get rid of you. You can leave the door open, if you want to hear what we're saying. But we need to leave. Five minutes."

Quinn nodded and ran into the bedroom. As she stripped off her pajamas and threw on her clothes, she listened intently. The men were speaking softly, of course—they didn't want anyone else to hear them—but she caught most of the conversation.

"Which is it?" Tony asked. "Are they after you, or clueless to your existence?"

"I don't know," Maarteen said. "They might be coming for Parra. Or making a random planetary call. They do that out here in the fringe."

"We're going to assume the worst."

For a few moments, the men were silent. Sounds of fabric rubbing against fabric and zippers closing filtered into the bedroom. Quinn shoved her things into her bag. Thankfully, she hadn't unpacked more than necessary. She raced into the bathroom and came out a few minutes later with her toiletry bag in hand.

"You ready?" Tony poked his head through the door.

"Won't it look suspicious that we're leaving in the middle of the night?" Quinn grabbed her shoes and shouldered her bag.

"Don't worry about it. Keep an eye on our friend, will you?" He didn't wait for an answer but darted into the bathroom. Even secret agents had to use the facilities first thing in the morning, she supposed.

She stood in the doorway, watching Maarteen. He sat in the same chair, drinking a glass of water. "You look pretty relaxed for a guy who might be the target of an operation."

Maarteen shrugged. "I've been doing this for many years. If I panicked every time I thought someone might be after me, I'd have been dead a long time ago. Or locked up in a looney bin."

She snickered. "I suppose. What exactly have you been doing all these years? While you run around teaching people to count other people."

"Mostly, I'm a courier," he said. "Passing messages between like-minded people. Smuggling funding in."

"It seems kind of odd that you'd share that with me. I could rob you and leave you here."

"I'm trying to be transparent," Maarteen said, his voice rising a bit.

Quinn shushed him.

"Look, I'm a small cog in a big, slow-moving machine." Maarteen set his glass on the table. "I'm a safe way to pass information and small items, because my travel is sanctioned by the Federation. I need access to Mr. Parra, and I need your help to get that."

Quinn shook her head. Something was not quite adding up, but she couldn't put a finger on exactly what. "Didn't you say you had to meet some folks? That's why you spent the first night here."

He nodded. "That is what I told Jessian. But the folks I wanted to meet were you two. We couldn't talk on the ship—Captain Wingard is about as by-the-book as they come. He would have reported anything suspicious." He blinked. "I wonder if that's why the Feds are coming? Did you two do anything out of character on board?"

Tony came out of the bedroom and handed Quinn a T-shirt. "You left that in the bathroom. Let's go." He grabbed his bag and crossed the room to listen at the door. After a moment, he opened it and looked out. "Clear. Follow me. Quinn, keep an eye on our friend."

They followed Tony out of the room, and Quinn shut the door gently behind her. When they reached the stairway, Tony repeated his listen-and-peek routine before they headed down.

At the deserted front desk, Tony dropped his room card into the checkout box. He swiped the screen. "I'm going to tell him we woke early due to travel lag and didn't want to waste any time." He looked at Maarteen. "What about you?"

The other man dropped his card into the slot. "Not a problem. They're used to me coming and going at odd hours." He crossed to the window and peered into the dark. "I messaged Jessian. She'll be here shortly."

"Does she know about your alternative activities?" Tony asked.

Maarteen wagged his head from side to side. "Yes and no. Jessian usually provides transportation for me."

"And she doesn't mind driving in the middle of the night?" Quinn asked.

"She's here." Maarteen headed to the door. "She doesn't get a lot of business. Lunesco isn't exactly a hotbed of tourism. And I tip well. Ready?" Without waiting for a reply, he pushed the outer doors open and strode into the parking lot.

"It's not windy!" Quinn glanced around. "It's nice here when the gale force winds aren't blowing. Look at the stars!" She stopped on the edge of the parking lot and gazed up at the diamond-strewn sky. "That's amazing!" Quinn had grown up in a city, where light pollution hid the night skies. She'd caught glimpses of the stars through portholes on the many interstellar flights she'd taken during her military career, and later as a dependent. But the flat landscape and total lack of buildings turned the night sky on Lunesco into an enormous, inverted bowl of stars.

Tony stood beside her, silently gazing at the stars with her. "It is amazing."

"Uh, oh." Quinn pointed. "That one is moving—I think it's a shuttle. We'd better get out of here."

They hurried to the car and climbed in.

"Hey, y'all," Jessian said with a yawn. "Headed to town, too?"

Tony grunted, back in Charles Anthony mode.

Quinn glared at him. "Yes," she told the younger woman. "Is there somewhere else we could go? No offense, but there doesn't appear to be a lot of options on this planet."

"None taken," Jessian said. "There ain't much here. We like it that way."

"Let's go," Maarteen said. "By the way, you might get another call this morning, Jessian. There's a Federation ship coming in."

"Cha-ching!" Jessian crowed. She stepped on the accelerator and pulled out onto the ruler-straight road. "Let's get y'all into town so I'm ready!"

Quinn leaned back, looking up through the rear window. The stars glittered overhead, but they'd lost their thrill. A moving light streaked across the sky again, lower and brighter. "Definitely a shuttle. It'll land on the next pass."

Tony nodded but didn't reply.

"Are we running without headlights?" Quinn peered over Maarteen's shoulder out the windshield.

Maarteen flicked a glance back at her and nodded.

"It's more fun that way," Jessian said. "'Sides, plenty o' light from the stars. And as long as you go straight, you can't go wrong."

Tony's eyes flicked from the back of Jessian's head to Quinn. He nodded slightly. Obviously, their driver knew they wanted to stay under the radar and had no problem helping.

"Take us to Auntie B's, please," Maarteen said.

"I figured." Jessian's fingers flexed on the steering wheel. "Hold on!" The car accelerated.

Quinn twisted around to look behind them but could see only a cloud of dust in their wake. She held her breath, hoping that wouldn't be visible from the shuttle when it returned.

They tore across the plains, headed toward a dark gash that ran from side to side as far as Quinn could see. As they got closer, she realized it was a chasm—as if giant hands had picked up the plain and broken it in two. The road disappeared at the edge.

"What happened there?" Quinn asked, her mouth dry.

"That's the valley," Jessian answered. "Where the town is. We'll be there soon."

"I can see that," Quinn replied. "Very soon. Does this car fly?"

Jessian laughed. "No. The road goes down the side of the valley. You can't see it from here."

The closer they got, the wider the chasm appeared. Darkness filled the space—the starlight providing no real illumination beyond the first few meters. Jessian hit the brakes, skidding the car to the left into a tight turn. Quinn's eyes bulged out of her head as a flimsy guardrail swooped toward her window. Then they were around the corner and headed down a steep hill.

"That wasn't terrifying." Quinn's voice shook, and she tried to suck in enough air to slow her racing heart.

Jessian laughed again. "Best part about this job is scaring the tourists."

"We aren't tourists." Maarteen twisted around to grin at Quinn and Tony. "That was Jessian driving carefully."

Quinn swallowed hard. "Thanks?"

"My pleasure." Jessian gunned the engine and squealed into a hairpin turn. "Only ten switchbacks on the way down."

"I'm going to sit here and hyperventilate." Quinn locked her fingers around the door handle in a death grip and closed her eyes. "Remind me to ask Maerk who the patron saint of crazy drivers is."

CHAPTER 20

SIX TERRIFYING TURNS LATER, the car braked, hard. Quinn peeled her eyelids open and peered out the window. On her side of the car, the hillside formed a wall almost close enough to touch. Just above the car roof, the last switchback of the road slanted steeply upward. On Tony's side, the ground fell away, the bottom lost in the dusky light.

They rolled onto a smoother section of road, and the rock next to her was replaced by small, white buildings, seemingly built into the side of the cliff. On the far side, the colorful, domed tops of more buildings crowded the road. Tall lights, carefully pointed downward, lit the narrow street. Thick green vines trailed over most of the buildings, like a lace overlay. Orange spheres hung from the vines, glowing in the light.

"Welcome to Lunesco proper," Jessian said. "Most everybody's asleep now, but it'll be lively in a few hours. Auntie B's is on the next turn."

She eased around another hairpin turn and stopped in front of a two-story building. Light glowed through the fogged glass door, and a sign above it read "Open."

"Auntie B's is a coffee shop?" Quinn asked.

"Coffee shop, boarding house, informal town hall meeting space," Maarteen said. "She even provides rudimentary medical services. Don't ask me how I know."

Jessian laughed. "He fell down the stairs!"

Maarteen gave Jessian a mock-glare.

"Why didn't we come down here three days ago?" Quinn asked.

"They didn't invite us," Tony replied quietly.

They climbed out and carried their bags across the road. "This is the upside." Jessian pointed across the road where the tops of the next row of buildings peeked above the guardrail. "That's the downside. In case anyone gives you directions. There's steps to the next level at the middle of the town." She pointed down the road.

Quinn counted. "There are only five buildings on this street."

Jessian nodded. "Most folks live close to the floor." She pointed toward the valley. "But a few of us like the switchbacks. There's three more before you hit the floor. Me and my pa live on the second one." She pulled open the glass door.

Cinnamon, sugar, and coffee hit them like a warm, cozy blanket. Quinn closed her eyes and took in a deep breath. "That smells wonderful." Her stomach growled in agreement.

"Auntie B makes the best sweet rolls on the planet." Jessian bounded inside. "Auuuuuuntie! Got comp'ny!"

Tony held the door for Quinn and Maarteen, then followed them inside. A plump woman wearing a flour-splashed pink apron came in from a back room. "Jess! And Sebi! So good to see you." She held out a short-fingered hand to Quinn. "I'm Auntie B."

"Quinn." She shook the strong hand. "And this is, uh…"

"Call me Tony."

Maarteen and Jessian exchanged a glance but said nothing.

"Rolls all around, Auntie," Maarteen said. "And coffee. Bring one for yourself, too. Jess, are you staying for breakfast?"

"If you don't have secret stuff to discuss." The girl winked. "But if I get a call, I'll have to run."

The four of them gathered around one of the three small tables crammed into the front of the room. Auntie B bustled around behind the counter, then returned with a tray of coffee cups and plates. She unloaded the tray then slid it onto the table behind her and took a seat.

The next few minutes were silent as everyone ingested calories and caffeine.

Eventually, Martin sat back in his chair. "Auntie B knows everyone in town." He held his cup up in toast. "And she keeps everyone informed."

"Ah, Sebi, you make me sound like an old gossip." Auntie B's twinkling brown eyes moved sharply from one face to the next.

"Definitely not a gossip," Maarteen said. "You know exactly when to keep your mouth shut."

Jessian jumped in her seat. "Speaking of keeping mouths shut…" She raised a finger and pulled her comtab out of the clip on her belt. "This is Jessian." She listened for a moment. "Yes, of course. I'll be there in thirty minutes." She tapped the screen and slid the device back into its clip. "Your Feds are here."

"It only takes twenty minutes to get to the landing field," Auntie B said.

"And ten minutes to hear the rest of the news." Jessian picked up her fork again. She looked at Maarteen. "Go ahead, tell her what's goin' on. I want to know."

Maarteen looked at Tony, who held up his hands in surrender. "You're the expert here."

"I told you before, Tony and Quinn need to talk to Doug Parra," Maarteen said. "They're old friends. I'm hoping they'll introduce me as well." He looked at Tony, measuring, then turned to Auntie B. "I think if you put in a good word for me, it might help."

"Me?" Auntie B said. "They don't know me. What good would my backing do?"

"They know who I work for," Maarteen said. "I think they'd be more inclined to trust a baker than a Federation customs drone."

The corner of Tony's lips twitched. It was the side away from Maarteen, but Auntie B might have noticed.

"Is that so?" Auntie B looked at Quinn. "What's your story?"

"I'm on the run," Quinn said.

"Quinn!" Tony cut in.

Quinn held up her hand. "I'm tired of being on the run. And I'm tired of not trusting people. I realize, if I trust the wrong people, I'm dead. But Auntie B—and Jessian—are the right ones. I feel it. Plus, Doug trusts them enough to let them be his gatekeepers." She raised her brows at Auntie B.

The older woman nodded thoughtfully. "That he does. Did you know his wife was my niece? My actual niece, not a neighbor like Jess."

"Estelle was from Lunesco?" Quinn asked.

"No, my sister moved off-world before she met Estelle's father," Auntie B said. "He was a military man, so they traveled a lot, and stopped by whenever they could. After she died, Doug came to break the news in person. Estelle's parents are long gone. Once he was here, he decided to stay."

"And you recruited him," Quinn said. It wasn't a question.

"And I recruited him," Auntie B agreed. "It wasn't hard, after we dug into the details of Estelle's death."

"What exactly did you recruit him for?" Quinn asked. "What do you hope to achieve?"

"Freedom from the Federation," Auntie B said flatly.

"Hang on a minute." Quinn slapped a hand on the table, alarm building pressure in her chest. She looked at Maarteen. "You said you weren't revolutionaries. I thought—I don't know what I thought. But I'm not a traitor! My family helped found the Federation. I may be angry with the Federation, and I despise Andretti, but I'm not ready to start a revolution."

Tony put a hand on her arm. "I'm not sure there's a difference anymore. Andretti isn't just a symptom of the problems in the Federation—he and his cronies are the cause."

Auntie B jumped in. "Don't think of it as a revolution, think of it as freeing our Federation from those evil men. We—all of the Federation's people—need freedom. The freedom to grow our town, our businesses, without having to ask permission or pay bribes. Freedom from the Russosken and their 'protection fees.' Free—"

"The Russosken are here?" Tony interrupted.

"They own this sector of the Federation," Maarteen said. "Their presence on Lunesco is tiny, but they're here. And anytime the economy is doing well, or the sugar vines are producing heavily, or someone comes up with a new way to get ahead, they're here, demanding a cut. The Federation doesn't *allow* them to operate—they've basically deputized the Russosken to keep the locals down."

"*Futz*," Tony said. "This just got even more complicated."

"The Russosken?" Quinn leaned close to Tony and lowered her voice. "Isn't that…"

He nodded. "Yup. Francine." He raised his voice. "Mr. Maarteen, are they here? As in on the planet at this moment?"

"They have informants here," Auntie B answered for him. "But they don't have a large local presence. We monitor the comms at the jump point. We know when they arrive. Their ships are fast, but they have to jump in at the same place as everyone else. The crappy jump beacons mean we have several days' notice before they show up."

"What triggers them to come?" Quinn asked.

"New residents." Jessian ticked items off on her fingers. "New business starting. Increase in tourism. Not that we're a big draw for vacationers." She laughed without humor. "But a few years ago, my cousin started a farm-cation. Crazy rich people would come on vacation and work his farm. The Russosken sent a representative to 'initiate' my cousin. Then they dropped by at the end of the season to collect their 'premium.' Bastards."

"Language." Auntie B wagged a reproving finger. "They do their homework. They demand enough credits to keep the business operating but not thriving. They'd be better off to invest and promote, but that takes effort, I guess. And risk."

"Typical thug stuff," Tony said. "And no way to keep them away if the government is sanctioning them. Have you tried setting up a local protection force?"

Auntie B looked away, her hands twisting in her lap. Jessian jumped up. "I need to go pick up my fare. They're going to the Homestead. I'll be back after I've dropped them." She kissed Auntie B on the cheek and left, taking her half-drunk coffee with her.

Tony raised an eyebrow at Maarteen.

"They did, years ago. Jessian's mom was on the team." Maarteen's voice was low and angry. "The Russosken came in force and wiped them out. After they eliminated the team, they killed one child from each family, to 'reinforce the lesson.' She was four when she lost her mother and baby brother. People are still too scared to do anything."

"Getting rid of the Federation is the answer!" Auntie B declared. "If we can get rid of them, their trained dogs will have no one feeding them."

"That's a tall order, Auntie," Tony said.

She crossed her arms over her chest. "That's the goal. And Doug Parra is with me. Are you?"

CHAPTER 21

BY THE TIME they'd finished their coffee and breakfast, the sun had started to rise. The winds came up, and the dust, stained orange by the sun, danced in the street in front of the bakery.

"Does the wind blow all day?" Quinn stared out the window at the display.

"Sunrise to sunset," Maarteen confirmed. "But it's not as bad down here. That's why the town starts so deep in the valley." He stood and collected the dishes on the table.

"Give me those." Auntie B snatched them out of his hands. "You have work to do." She put the dishes on the counter and pulled something from her apron pocket, pressing it into Maarteen's palm. "Give this to Doug. He'll talk to you. Oh, and take this, too. He likes 'em." She grabbed a small, aqua green box from the counter and thrust it into his hands.

"Good thing I already ate one, or this might not make it to Doug," Maarteen said with a grin.

"We don't want our revolution scuttled by lack of sweet rolls," Auntie B joked. "Come back when you're done talking. I'll have lunch if you want it."

They thanked Auntie B and clattered out. The wind blew along the street, billowing Quinn's jacket, but it was milder than the gales they'd experienced above. The rest of the town had begun to wake, and a few curtains twitched in the windows of the other "upside" buildings.

"We seem to be gathering some attention," Tony said.

"Visitors do." Maarteen started down the sloping road. "But they're used to me. They'll wonder who you are. Sometimes I bring junior officials on training runs, so they won't be suspicious."

"You bring trainees here?" Quinn fell in beside him. "Isn't that risky?"

"It would be riskier to take them everywhere but here," Tony commented.

Maarteen nodded. "And the folks here know not to discuss certain subjects in front of my trainees." They reached a gap between buildings, and a steep set of stairs led directly down the hillside. "Come on."

The valley ran east to west, giving the roads bright sunlight but leaving the gaps between buildings in dark shadow. Quinn slowed her steps—she didn't need to tumble down and break a leg. Auntie B made excellent sweet rolls, but that didn't guarantee her medical skills.

They stepped out into blinding light on the next street, then plunged into darkness again on the other side. "Where does our friend live?" Quinn asked, her breath coming a little faster. Her couple days of workouts on the ship hadn't prepared her for running stairs. She didn't want to think about going back up.

"He's on the far side of the valley." Maarteen jerked his head toward the east. "The valley turns southward about a klick from here, and he's got a place up on the shelf against the far wall. Nice location, but it gets dark early on that side."

"Are we going to walk all the way?" Quinn asked.

"No, there are solar carts on the floor." Maarteen's breath seemed to be elevated as well, so Quinn didn't feel so bad. Tony, of course, was disgustingly fit and the steps didn't seem to bother him at all.

As they hurried down, Quinn stared out at the valley. She could only see a narrow slice of it from between the buildings, but the visible bit was lush and green. The vines that climbed along the buildings here gave way to fields of grain and plants Quinn couldn't name. A river split the fields, running the length of the valley, with several long bridges spanning it.

"What are these orange globes?" Tony asked as they ducked under a vine draped between the buildings.

"That's one of the crops here. Sugar gourds. All natural, low-calorie sweetener."

Tony whistled. "I'm surprised the Federation hasn't taken a greater interest in this planet. That seems like a huge moneymaker."

"You can't domesticate the vines." Maarteen reached up to tap one of the gourds as they passed beneath another vine. "They grow where they want and produce gourds kind of randomly. No one can predict what kind of yield they'll get, so they've been written off as a cultivated agricultural product. More of a specialty. If it weren't for the—" He looked around as he stepped onto the next brightly-lit street. "Taxes are brutal, so profits are low. Last flight of steps."

They reached the bottom of that stairway and stepped out of the dark alley into a brighter town square. Taller buildings lined two sides, but the opposite side of the square was open to the valley. Vast fields stretched away to the far wall of the chasm. A glint of water marked the river's path. The narrow zigzag of another road climbed to the top of the far wall and disappeared. Tiny white buildings, adorned by lacy green vines, clung to the lower switchbacks.

"The solar carts are over here." Maarteen led them to a stall on the open side of the square. Half a dozen three- and four-wheeled carts were locked into a low metal wall. A roof with solar panels cast a long shadow across the edge of the square. Maarteen fed some coins into the panel at the end of the wall and pressed some buttons. Something clicked, and a restraining arm sprang up.

"There's our ride." Maarteen headed for the freed cart. "Climb aboard." He swung into the single front seat, leaving the wider rear one for Tony and Quinn.

"You know how to drive these things?" Quinn climbed in.

"Easy." Maarteen grinned over his shoulder. "The three-wheeled ones are a little iffy on the switchbacks, but they're fine for the floor. And don't worry, I don't drive as fast as Jessian."

Tony laughed and hopped in, bouncing the cart again. Quinn gave him the stink eye. Tony widened his in mock-fear of her mom-glare.

"You love this stuff, don't you?" Quinn asked.

"Operations?" He bounced the cart again. "Oh, yeah."

"Here we go." Maarteen pushed the joystick, and they pulled away from the parking slot.

The little cart zipped out of the square and onto a long, smooth road. Maarteen turned toward the sun, which now hung low above the horizon, shining down the valley. He flipped his goggles over his eyes. "If you're staying, you need to get some of these," he called over his shoulder. "They're a bit pricey, but the adjustable tint is fantastic."

"We don't expect to stay much longer," Tony said, shielding his eyes with his hand. "I might invest in a billed cap, though."

They sped between buildings on the narrow road. Maarteen waved as they passed other carts, and some of the other drivers returned the greeting. A few klicks on, they left the town, and only the occasional building appeared.

"They keep the arable land for crops, so homes are built against—and up—the cliff." Maarteen waved an arm at the steep, rocky side of the valley. "Smart farming practice. Plus, the sugar vines only grow on the cliffs, and they thrive on occupied buildings. Some local scientists think they feed on human energy."

"They're parasites?" Quinn asked.

"No, no. They don't harm the people." He shrugged. "As far as I know, they haven't quantified it, but empirical evidence shows the vines grow bigger and healthier when there are humans nearby.

When the first settlers discovered this valley, the sugar vines were small, weedy things."

"I'm surprised there aren't scientists all over this place." Quinn peered at the next house they passed. Vines covered most of the home, but the outbuildings were virtually untouched.

"We don't share this information with many people." Maarteen glanced back at them again.

"Why did you mention it to us?" Tony asked. "And why did the locals share with you?"

"I've been here a lot; I noticed the pattern," Maarteen said. "Excellent pattern recognition is one of the reasons I was hired in census. Helps me notice discrepancies in reports."

Now that she'd started looking, it was obvious: homes covered in vines, other buildings clear. Even the cliff-side—with rough natural stone features that appeared perfect for vines to climb—was nearly empty of green. "Don't other people notice?"

"I guess not," Maarteen said. "Until I asked someone about it, I assumed the locals were clearing the vines from other buildings and encouraging growth on their homes as protection from the sun."

"And you told us because…" Tony prompted again.

Maarteen's shoulders twitched, but he was silent.

"I think he's trying to make sure we're invested in the planet," Quinn said softly. "Vines that are responsive to humans? That's either creepy or adorable. He made it sound adorable. And he knows two convicted traitors aren't going to call in a research team."

Tony nodded thoughtfully. "How far to Doug's place?"

"Right over there." Maarteen pointed. The closer wall of the valley curved in front of them. They turned onto a road that crossed the river toward the far wall. The valley made a ninety-degree corner at this point, but it narrowed, and the floor grew rougher. On the far wall, a few switchbacks crawled up to a narrow shelf of land about a third of the way up. A small, vine-clad house sat alone on the ledge. "We'll have to leave the cart at the base and walk up," Maarteen said as they drove closer. "I don't trust this thing on the turns."

The fields ended, and Maarteen parked the cart. He flipped the solar panels on the roof upward, latching them at an angle so they'd catch the most direct sunlight. "That should charge the batteries enough for the return and then some. This way."

They climbed the narrow road, zigzagging up the cliff. At the top, the small house came into view, tucked against the rocky side. A courtyard with a low wall fronted the building, sugar vines providing shade from the morning sun. Afternoons here would be dark and cool, with the cliff blocking the light.

Movement in the shadows caught Quinn's attention. A large dog paced forward, growling. She grabbed Tony's arm, pulling him to a stop. Another growl, this time from behind, sent a shiver up Quinn's spine. She turned her head as slowly as she could. "There's another one behind us."

"I know." Tony's hand eased toward his pocket.

"I don't think shooting Doug's guard dogs is a great way to build trust," she said.

"I don't *want* to shoot the dogs," Tony replied. "But I also don't want to get eaten."

"Mr. Parra?" Maarteen called. "Are you here? Auntie B sent us. I have a sweet roll!" He held the box up over his head, waving it slightly.

"You think I'm a toddler?" A man hidden in the shadows rose from his seat. "To be tempted by a pastry?"

"Doug?" Quinn asked.

The large man stepped out of the shaded courtyard and onto the driveway. Shaggy gray hair grew around the sides of his head and down onto his cheeks and chin, leaving the top of his head shiny and bare. His face was heavily lined. His clothing looked wrinkled and worn. "Quinn? Is that really you?"

"How are you, Doug?" Quinn took a slow step forward.

The dog behind her growled louder.

"Pasha, Enrique, *kemnie!*" Doug commanded in a deep voice. The two dogs ran to their master, sitting at his feet. "Good dogs!"

Doug scratched their heads. "Come on up." He turned and went back into the shade, the two dogs pacing beside him. He dug in his pocket and offered each dog a treat. *"Volno."* The dogs took their treats and settled onto their bellies on either side of the man.

Quinn glanced at the others and followed Doug onto the terrace. "You remember Tony." She took a seat across a small table from Doug.

The big man's eyes narrowed. "What's he doing here? I thought he went back to the Empire."

"Doug, good to see you." Tony extended his hand, then withdrew it when Doug made no move to shake.

"Nice of you to come back," Doug said. "After you abandoned us on Zauras."

"Doug, he tried to stop us, remember?" Quinn laid a hand on the big man's arm. "We wouldn't believe him. And he's the one who got me out of prison. None of that mess was his fault."

"That doesn't stop him from being an enemy agent," Doug said, but his tone was mild, almost conversational.

"True," Quinn said. "But I've spent some time in the Commonwealth. It's not the evil empire we've always believed. Besides, he doesn't work for them anymore."

Doug stared at Tony for a few moments, then slowly reached out to shake his hand. "It's hard to view you as the enemy."

"Likewise." Tony nodded gravely.

"And this is Sebi Maarteen." Quinn indicated the other man. "He's a Federation customs agent."

"And a friend of Auntie B." Maarteen extended his hand. On the palm lay a small gold disk.

Doug glanced at Quinn, then back to Maarteen. He reached out and touched the item in the custom agent's hand. "That—" He took a deep breath and heaved out a sigh. Then he picked up the gold token. It was a coin, about the size of a one-credit piece. He held it up between his finger and thumb, then turned it to look at the back.

"That was Estelle's. Her Federation enlistment coin. I didn't know Auntie B had it."

"I don't know the story behind it." Maarteen spread his hands apologetically. "But Auntie B told me to give it to you as proof that she supported me."

Doug took another deep breath. "Sit down. We'll talk."

CHAPTER 22

"I CAN'T BELIEVE I let you talk me into this." Liz strapped into the pilot seat of the newly christened *Swan of the Night*.

"You don't like her name?" Maerk asked.

"No, that's not it." Liz worked through the pre-launch checklist. "Don't get me wrong—I'd have named it Bob and been done with it, but I've got nothing against *Swan of the Night*. I can't believe you talked me into buying a ship. This ship, in particular. Oh, come on!" She slapped her hand on the console, and the blinking indicator settled to a steady red. "Can you fix that?"

"Of course." Maerk made a note in his comtab. "I'll look at it when we get into orbit." He leaned back in his seat. He knew she'd come around once they were on the move. She'd been miserable on N'Avon. Going back to Lou wasn't in the cards, so getting their own ship was an excellent compromise.

And this ship was perfect. "She's a classic." He slid a loving finger across the dash. "Look at the smooth curves of the console. The line of the engine cowls, the—"

"Yeah, yeah, classic. 'Classic' is another word for 'old and falling apart.' Classic ships need constant tweaking."

"Don't listen to her," Maerk told the ship. "She knows I'm right."

Liz rolled her eyes. "That's it." She flipped the checklist off the screen. "Time to take to the skies."

"You have the ship."

"Don't say that." Liz swiped up the taxi engine screen and pushed the virtual lever up. "That's what you say when you hand control over to another pilot."

"Sorry. It's been a long time since I've flown anything. You'll have to help me get up to speed."

"Start reading those manuals I sent you." She eased the ship out of their parking spot. "N'Avon West Tower, this is MPV delta-six-sigma-two-seven-yellow, *Swan of the Night*, requesting permission to launch."

"*Swan*, Tower. You are number two to launch. Proceed to the waiting point."

"That means—" Liz began.

Maerk cut her off with a laugh. "I know what it means. Just because I haven't piloted in a few years doesn't mean I've forgotten everything. I have been living on a ship, remember?"

"Oh, was that you?" Liz guided the ship to the waiting point. "I've been wondering who the guy sleeping in my cabin was."

Some things never changed. And sometimes reactions to those things changed dramatically. When they'd been married, an exchange like that would have sent one of them off the deep end. Since they'd gotten divorced ten years ago, they'd learned to ignore the imagined undertones. Strange, people said. But it worked for them.

"*Swan*, Tower. You are cleared to launch. Safe travels!"

"Thanks, Tower. We'll see you on the next drop." Liz grinned at Maerk. "Let's see what we've gotten ourselves into!"

AFTER PUTTING the new ship through its paces, Liz landed at the cargo terminal and picked up the load she'd contracted to deliver to

Daravoo Two. Although Daravoo was now part of the Federation, a trickle of trade with the Commonwealth had continued for decades. The system was far from any Federation stronghold and close to N'Avon. The ancient jump beacons meant ships had to enter far from the primary, so only merchants with time to spare bothered with the trip. They were in no rush.

"They'll welcome us with open arms." Liz watched the loaders fill the *Swan's* cargo hold. She'd contracted to deliver some farm equipment to an agricultural commune. That delivery would cover their expenses for this trip. The rest of the hold was filled with luxury foods and textiles—products Daravoo never saw.

Maerk smiled. It was good to see Liz happy again. This was where she belonged—on the deck of her own ship. "I fixed the wonky indicator, checked the scrubbers, and refitted the internal seals. We're good to go."

Liz handed him a tablet. "If you supervise the last of the loading, I'll go start the prechecks. Make sure they put bale 23 on top—I don't want that Fandian silk crushed."

"You got it, boss," Maerk said. When the last load of cargo came aboard, he signed off on the delivery, checked the tie-down straps, and closed the back ramp.

He toggled the intercom. "Cargo to the bridge. We are cleared for departure."

"You mean 'cargo is stowed.'" Liz laughed. "You don't get to clear us for departure. That's up to the tower. Come forward, I'm going to pull us out."

He made his way through the crew lounge, his body swaying easily with the movements of the ship. He made sure the cupboards were locked, and the furniture magnets engaged. It wouldn't do to have a knife or the couch floating around on the way to orbit. That was how people got hurt. One last look, and he nodded to himself and climbed up to the cockpit. "Ready to depart, Captain!"

Liz shook her head, smirking, but didn't say anything. He must have botched it again. That was what made him and Liz a good team.

She flew; he kept the boat running. She knew all the comms lingo; he knew how to load a cargo hold. A good team.

It would be better when they could get Dareen and End to join them. Dareen had become a first-rate mechanic, and End was a wizard with a computer. Dareen had left a drop box message for him—they were headed to Daravoo. All he and Liz had to do was meet the kids and convince them to leave Lou.

CHAPTER 23

MAARTEEN TOOK the chair next to Quinn. She watched Tony prowl around the edge of the terrace, wondering what had him so antsy. She raised a brow.

"I've done too much sitting today."

Doug stared from under his shaggy brows. "You do you, Tony." The dogs looked up at his voice, then settled their heads on their front paws. Pasha closed her eyes, but Enrique watched Tony. At least Tony thought it was Enrique. Whichever dog it was, he wasn't going to turn his back.

"Why are you here?" Doug asked.

Quinn looked at Tony. Tony looked at Maarteen. Maarteen looked at Quinn.

Tony pointed at the census agent. "You first."

Maarteen nodded, resigned. "I represent a group of business owners who would like to see freer commerce on Lunesco."

Doug crossed his arms. "You represent the Federation."

Maarteen wiggled his head, side to side. "Officially, yes, that's my cover. And, to be fair, it's also funding my travel. But my real purpose is to connect my patrons with people on the fringe planets who might be interested in their support."

Doug's lips pressed together. "Say what you mean, bean counter."

Tony laughed. "I'm the bean counter. He's a people counter."

Doug glared at Tony. "I have sensors running scans at all times. It's safe to talk here. You can check."

Tony and Maarteen both pulled out their comtabs and fiddled with them.

"I'm sorry you were blamed," Doug told Quinn while the men checked the terrace. "That was crazy."

"It's not your fault," Quinn said.

"No, it's theirs. Andretti's. The Federation's." The anger in his voice curdled Quinn's stomach. "It was bad enough they abandoned us for profit, but to blame the victim? That's— And then to use murder to cover their tracks—" He broke off and ran his hand over his face.

"But that was one person." Quinn glanced at Maarteen. "Andretti is beyond contempt, but he doesn't represent the whole Federation."

"Yes, he does." Doug glared at her. "He's the second-ranking admiral in the fleet."

"Then we need to go to Admiral Corvair-Addison," Quinn said. "She must not know what he's doing."

Doug laughed harshly. "She knows. A former Federation officer convicted of treason is big news. Even the Admiral of the Fleet is going to hear about that. Do you think she blew it off?" He put on a falsetto voice. "Such a shame Quinn decided to betray the Federation and become a Krimson spy. Oh well, back to business."

"If she trusts Andretti to do his job, she might. She's got a cold war to deal with. And she doesn't know me."

"Clear," Tony said.

Maarteen nodded. "Looks good to me, too. Which is a good thing, considering what you two are discussing. Let me shed some light here. My sources say Andretti and Corvair-Addison are in bed together."

"Not literally," Tony put in. "We all know he goes for much younger women. But my research shows at least part of the gold went directly to her. She has access to an out-system account that accepted a huge deposit after the whole Sumpter thing."

Doug's eyebrows rose.

"I'm a bean counter, remember? I follow the credits." Tony crossed the courtyard, carefully skirting the dogs, then turned to lean against the low wall. "Doug, I'm here to find out what happened after I left you on Zauras. If you don't mind talking about that in front of Maarteen, it might speed things up."

Doug stood. The dogs both alerted, but he put his hand out and they stayed down. He paced around the edge of the courtyard, running his hand along the smooth plaster of the wall. Then he sighed and dusted his hands together. "I don't like to think about it. That's when I— When—"

The others waited, silent.

"We landed at Zauras." Doug stared out over the valley. "Cyn and Marielle and I had talked about it on the flight—we knew those crates of gold would get confiscated when we landed. So, everybody put a couple handfuls of nuggets in our pockets. Not a lot—because that stuff is heavy—but enough to have something, you know." He glanced at Quinn and Tony.

"We should have thought of that." Quinn looked at Tony. "I can't believe we didn't stash some before we landed."

"You trusted the system, even though they'd let you down." Tony's lips twisted.

"Yeah, what an idiot," she muttered. "What happened next, Doug?"

He chuckled. "Cyn was a lot more cynical than you. We loaded a tool chest, too."

"I was wondering why my tools were in a drawer with the towels!" Tony exclaimed.

Doug grinned. "When we parked, we used the antigrav lifters and moved the crates to the apron. Then you left. Smart move." He shook his head. "We all shoulda gone with you. The flight line was busy—no one paid us any attention. Quinn and Tiffany took off, looking for the command center and the brass. Cyn and I hid the tool chest in one of the lockers in the maintenance section. She'd been assigned to Zauras before and knew how to work the personal lockers—where you put your stuff while you're on duty."

He shrugged. "We locked the thing up. Then the MPs came and took us to debriefing. Split us up. They kept trying to get me to say Quinn was in league with the Empire. I don't know what the others told 'em. I told 'em the truth. Eventually, they let us go—without any gold, of course. That all went into 'the evidence locker,' they said. Even the stuff in our pockets." He snorted. "Bastards." He stopped talking, staring out at the valley.

Maarteen opened his mouth, but Tony shook his head.

They waited.

"They didn't tell me about Estelle," Doug finally whispered. "The *Elrond* dropped the other dependents before we got there, of course. But Estelle was on active duty, so she wasn't with them. I didn't expect to see her. I did all the stuff you do—got a temporary apartment, used my 'displaced spouse funds' to buy some new clothes and *futz*. Since they purged Sumpter, the stuff we left behind was gone. I rented a place and got some things out of long-term storage."

He swung around and glared at Quinn. "You know how I found out? Her paycheck stopped. My bank sent me an overdraft alert because there wasn't enough credit to pay the rent. So, I went to finance to straighten it out, and they told me I didn't qualify for a 'surviving dependent stipend' because I was already pulling retirement pay."

He rubbed a hand over his face and his voice thickened. "I told them there was a mistake—I wasn't a 'surviving dependent' but a current one. That she was deployed, and they needed to reinstate her pay. I worked my way up the chain, demanding they fix the error. They finally referred me to Andretti's office. His aide—Marielle's husband—told me she was dead. And that it was her own fault. Arrogant little prick."

He growled, deep in his throat. "*He* has a new sports car. And a vacation home on Balrain. How's he afford that on a lieutenant's salary? I'll tell you how—he got part of the gold."

After a long pause, he continued. "Cyn retrieved the toolbox, and we split the gold. I used it to come here and buy this." He waved at the little house. "End of story."

"Is it?" Tony asked.

"What do you mean?" Doug raised his chin and narrowed his eyes.

Tony wasn't intimidated. "You've been putting out feelers. Even before you moved here. Trying to gauge how far up the chain the corruption goes."

Doug glanced at Maarteen then nodded. "It goes all the way. Like you said. Corvair-Addison got a cut of the gold. And Premier Li got a huge contribution to his political campaign."

"This is why we need your help," Maarteen said. "You know how bad it is. We want to free the Federation from this scourge."

"Scourge?" Doug asked. "That's a big-credit word. I prefer scum. Trash. Dirtbags."

Quinn bit her lip. She glanced at Tony and raised her brows. It seemed like he already knew everything Doug had told them. Surely, they hadn't come all this way and risked their lives for this?

"There's something else you aren't telling us," Tony said. "A tool chest full of gold—even half of it—is way more than enough to buy this. What did you use the rest for?"

CHAPTER 24

FRANCINE PULLED out her earbud and rubbed her ear. Something was beeping—something outside this ridiculous game. "Do you hear that?"

"The orcs are coming!" End yelled. "Get your sword!"

"No, idiot." Francine grabbed his comtab and paused the game.

"Hey!"

"Listen," Francine commanded. "What's that beeping?"

"*Futz.*" End scrambled over her and stumbled into the hall. "We got visitors!"

Francine unfolded her legs and climbed off the bunk. Pins and needles zinged through her nerves, but she shook them off. "What kind of visitors?"

"Federation shuttle." End stared at the readings on the pilot's screen.

"Here?!"

"No, it's landing at the main airfield." He swiped the screen. "I hope Tony saw it. I'll send the info to his drop box, but there's no telling when he'll access it."

"Shouldn't you have that thing set to interrupt the game? I mean, what if they needed an immediate extraction and we missed it because the onks were attacking?"

"It's orcs," he said, disgusted. "But you're right. I thought I had it connected—" He broke off, swiping through screens. "Here's the setting. *Futz*! I turned it off. Good thing you got supersonic hearing."

"Supersonic hearing?" She headed toward the airlock. "Sure, that's a thing. I need a break. I'm going for a walk."

"Are you kidding?" End blocked the exit. "There are gale force winds out there."

"Fine, I'll be doing yoga in the cargo hold." She grabbed a water pack and stomped away. This was going to be a long wait.

THE *SWAN* APPROACHED DARAVOO PRIME. Since it was the only station in the system, the name sounded pretentious, but they hadn't asked Maerk before they named it. He would have come up with something more lyrical, like *Swan of the Night*. He slid his hand over the dash of the ship, admiring the smooth curve again.

"Thank you, Prime." Liz swiped and flicked the controls. "Landing at Columbia Ridge, acknowledged. Have a nice day." She nudged the joystick and pushed the ship into a de-orbit path. "Strap in, Maerk. We're going down."

"Already secured." He thumped his chest strap with his thumb.

"And stop fondling my ride."

"She's a beautiful girl." He stroked the faux hide upholstery.

Liz shook her head. "I worry about you, sometimes. This is why we got divorced, you know. Your weird obsession with inanimate objects."

"You're the only one for me," Maerk whispered to the ship.

Liz mimed throwing something at him. "If we weren't in the process of landing, that would have been something hard and painful."

He grinned. Buying the *Swan* had been the best decision they'd made in years. Liz was happy to be free and flying. He was happy to tinker and travel. Now they had to make a living doing it. "You got a buyer for us?"

She nodded. "Perfect setup. We'll offload the heavy equipment first. The fabric buyer is scheduled to meet us about an hour later. I don't have a buyer for the food yet, but I have no doubt we'll find someone. They don't get a lot of off-world foods out in the sticks."

"You are a genius," Maerk said. "A commerce genius."

"You're a brown noser. First the ship, now the captain. If I didn't know better, I'd think you'd done something. What have you been up to?"

"Nothing. Not this time," Maerk replied. "Storing up good will for the future."

Liz shook her head and replied to the hail from the Columbia Ridge tower. "Roger, Columbia. Landing on runway eight-seven. We'll see you in two more orbits." She looked over the screens. "All systems nominal. You did a good job fixing up this boat."

Maerk's cheeks warmed. Liz's praise was rare and highly valued. "Thanks. I knew you'd like her."

They landed at the small runway, rolling to the end of the long strip. Liz retracted the blast shields and taxied back to the parking apron near a small building. "I'd bet that's our buyer." She pointed to a large truck and trailer parked nearby.

She pulled into their designated parking slot. Before they finished the shutdown sequence, the truck rumbled out to meet them. "You wanna say hello while I finish up here?"

"Yes, ma'am." Maerk unfastened his restraints and made his way to the cargo hold. He unlocked the rear ramp and lowered it, whistling while he waited. It was about halfway open when he noticed the guns.

"Crap!" He slapped the ramp button and ducked. "Liz, we've got hostiles!"

"What?" The reply was muffled by static. Damn intercom wasn't working yet.

He fumbled his comtab and called her on the voice channel. "Liz, we've got guys with guns out there!"

"What?!" This time, the response was clear and shocked. Feet rattled on the deck, and Liz ran in with a blaster in each hand. She ducked to hide behind the ramp as she raced toward him.

"Ahoy, ship!" a voice called. "We here to pick up our cargo!"

Maerk crawled to the side of the ramp and crouched behind the wall of the ship. He flicked the camera on his phone and held it around the corner. On the tiny screen, three heavily-armed men stood beside the massive truck. Two of them wore long, loose coats. The third had a metal shield on his arm. "Does he think he's a medieval knight?" He showed the picture to Liz.

She shrugged. "They aren't aiming at us, so that's a good thing. But who knows what those two have under their coats? I'm going to talk to them."

"No!"

But it was too late. Liz rose, holding her blaster across her body. She peered over the rim of the ramp. "I need some identification."

"Sure." The guy with the shield fiddled behind it.

Liz's comtab pinged and a near-field comm popped up. She clicked something, then nodded. "These are our guys."

"Just because they're our buyers doesn't mean they aren't going to steal our stuff," Maerk whispered.

"Yeah, we might want to reconsider our cargo packing." Liz looked over her shoulder and the load. "Maybe some lockable, moveable walls to section stuff off?"

"Can we get our tractors now?" the guy hollered.

Liz nodded.

"Hang on," Maerk called back. "The ramp is a little hinky sometimes. There it goes." He pressed the open button and allowed the ramp to descend. While it cranked down, he fired up the cargo handlers and started moving the textile bales off the shrink-wrapped tractors. "We need to get Stene to set up some cargo plans for us."

"I'm Boris." The shield man walked up the ramp, followed by his two companions. "This your first run to Daravoo?"

"What makes you think that?" Maerk replied.

"You seem kind of nervous." Boris pointed at the crates stacked beside the first tractor. "And ya got all that fancy food stuff."

"You guys are more heavily armed than our usual customers," Liz said. "That makes me nervous."

Maerk's fingers flew over the control panel as his retractable arm restacked the cargo. "You don't want our fancy food stuff?"

"You won't find much of a market for that here," Boris waved to his assistants. "Boys, unwrap the first one."

"What?" Liz's brows drew down. "We have a buyer for the textiles. Usually fine fabrics and high-end comestibles are highly compatible."

The man by the tractor stopped cutting away the shrink wrap and looked at the markings on the bales Maerk moved away from the second vehicle. "Fandian silk makes good wound dressing." He went back to hacking.

"Wound dressing?" Liz asked. "Those aren't medical textiles. They're specialty fabrics. Dyed and embellished. You know, for fancy clothing."

"I'm a farmer," Boris said. "We don't do fancy clothing. Maybe you'll find someone wanting to make a ball gown and hold a *swah-ray*, but it ain't anyone I know on Daravoo."

Liz stared at the man for a few seconds, then stomped away. Maerk's eyes followed. Were there tears in her eyes? He hoped not—Liz only cried when she was frustrated. And when Liz was frustrated, she was impossible to live with.

"You wanna move that thing, or should I have Yen drive it out?" Boris asked.

Maerk started. "He can drive it. I assume he knows how better than I do."

Boris laughed and clapped him on the shoulder. "Smart man."

He put his fingers in his mouth and blew an ear-piercing whistle. "Take 'er out!"

Yen started up the big machine and eased it out of the cargo hold.

Boris watched his underling guide the tractor down the ramp. "Your woman gonna be mad?"

"At herself." Maerk huffed out a breath. "She's normally very good at judging markets."

Boris held out both hands. "Maybe I'm wrong. Who's the buyer?" He leaned in close and lowered his voice. "The Russosken sometimes want fancy stuff."

"The Russosken?" A chill went down Maerk's spine. "They have a presence here?"

"Who's to say where they have a presence?" Boris made air quotes around the last word. "I know they got a house over yonder. Sometimes there's important people there. Maybe they're havin' a *swah-ray*."

"Maybe. What kind of cargo can I buy here on Daravoo?" Maerk tried to keep his voice casual. Since Lou had come here, she must have discovered a big pay-off cargo. And they needed to locate Lou to find the kids. Dareen hadn't replied to his message. "Grain? Hemp? Weapons?"

Boris went very still. "You looking for weapons?"

"I'm looking for things that'll pay my costs," Maerk said. "We're hitting some other fringe worlds after we leave here. I'd like to have something that sells better than fancy material."

Boris nodded. "You from the Commonwealth." He said it as a statement, not a question. When Maerk opened his mouth, the other man held up a hand. "I ordered these tractors from the Commonwealth, and you brought 'em. I know you got a Federation transponder, or they don't let you land here. For someone like you, there might be a cargo for Lunesco. If you don't ask too many questions."

Maerk eyed the guy. This kind of deal was exactly why he *didn't* want to travel the fringe as a small trader. But after they found the kids, they'd need a cargo to sell. "Who can I talk to?"

Boris pulled out his comtab. "Give me your contact info. I'll pass it on. If you hear from this number, it's my guy."

Maerk's comtab buzzed, and a number appeared on the screen. He saved it. "Thanks. No hard feelings if we find something else first?"

"You don't answer, they call someone else." Boris clapped him on the shoulder again, nearly knocking him to the ground. "Thanks for bringing my tractors. I'll give you a good review on Yup."

CHAPTER 25

DOUG RUBBED his hand over his head, ruffling the fringe of gray hair on the sides as he stared Tony down. "You don't want to know what I spent it on."

Quinn could feel the tension building on the patio.

"You mean you don't want to tell us." Tony crossed his arms.

"Yeah." Doug paced across the terrace again. "You guys know about the Russosken?"

They all nodded.

"Maarteen wants to free the Federation. I think that's too big." He gestured to the others. "The four of us against the Federation? That's insane."

"There are others." Maarteen leaned forward urgently. "Many others."

"Not enough, no matter how many." Doug swiped a hand through the air. "I'm looking at a smaller goal. Don't get me wrong, I'd love to chop off Andretti's balls and feed them to my dogs, but I don't see how I can get there. I *can* protect my little corner of the universe. Come on." He strode across the terrace and into the house.

The dogs lifted their heads when he went inside, then turned to stare at the others as if to say, "Whatever you're thinking, don't try it."

Quinn, her eyes fixed on the dogs, her heart racing, rose slowly and edged toward the building.

Enrique growled.

"Doug?" Quinn called. "Will the dogs let us in?"

A loud whistle shrilled. The two dogs leaped up and charged into the house.

Quinn's hunched shoulders dropped, and she followed the dogs. Tony and Maarteen brought up the rear. They walked through a nearly-empty living room. A couch sat against one wall, with a video screen opposite. Kitchen counters and appliances crowded a corner, and an open door nearby led to a bathroom. Doug stood on the low landing at the base of the stairs that climbed behind the couch. The dogs sat beside him like statues.

"Come on up." He stepped out of the way.

As she walked between the two animals, Quinn could almost feel the menace rolling off them. "These dogs don't like me."

"They don't like anyone except me." Doug barked a humorless laugh. "That's their job. They're trained to keep visitors downstairs. Not that I have a lot of visitors. But they'll let you through, because I'm here. I want to show you what they're guarding. Go on up."

The three of them climbed the steps. Quinn's shoulders tensed again, sensing the dislike of the canines. When Tony and Maarteen stepped between her and them, she felt a little better.

"*Pozor*," Doug said.

Quinn glanced back. The dogs had both risen to their feet. They stood on the small landing at the bottom of the stairs, facing the living room, alert and silent.

Doug squeezed past and led the way. "This is the bedroom, obviously." He stepped through the door at the top of the staircase. The room filled the space over the living room, with a large bed against the back wall, a chest of drawers on the side, and a small chair in the corner opposite the door. Large windows let in bright sunlight. If it weren't for the messy bed and piles of discarded clothing, the room would be lovely.

Doug ignored the mess as he walked around the bed to a closed door in the back corner. After kicking aside a pile of clothing, he pulled it open, revealing a closet. "Over here."

Quinn picked her way through the mess to his side. "You spent your fortune on a new wardrobe?"

Doug barked out a genuine laugh. "Obviously." He gestured to his worn black pants and T-shirt. Then he pushed aside the hanging jackets and pants to reveal narrow lavender planking on the back wall. "Darien wood keeps the bugs away."

He pressed a plank at knee level, and something popped. He slid his fingers into the corner of the tiny space and pulled. The back of the closet hinged open. Ducking to avoid the clothing rail and the top of the door frame, he stepped into the dark space. "Welcome to my secret lair."

"Your secret lair?" Tony's eyes twinkled.

Quinn stepped aside to let Tony follow Doug into the closet. Beyond the low door, lights sprang on, illuminating rough stone walls.

"I always wanted to be a supervillain when I was a kid." Doug disappeared around a corner, his voice filtering back to them. "So that's what I call it. Come on in, there's room for all of us. Shut the door behind you."

Quinn gestured for Maarteen to precede her. She pulled the closet door behind her and rearranged the clothing to fill the space. Then she climbed through the doorway into the secret lair.

The lighting was bright, but not harsh. Screens filled one wall; several closed cabinets ranged along another. A plush couch with soft throws flung over the back stood off to the side. Most of the room was filled with computer equipment. Doug flipped switches on two of the screens. Multiple views of the valley filled them.

A soft beep from Maarteen's pocket drew their attention. He pulled out his comtab. "Auntie B says the Feds are on their way."

"On their way where?" Doug didn't wait for an answer. He strode to the console and pulled up a control panel. The views of the valley closed in quick succession, leaving one. Doug used both hands to stretch the view to fill the screen and zoom in further. "A car is coming down the switchbacks—that must be Jessian."

"They told her to take them to the planetary governor," Maarteen said.

"Who is that? And where is he?" Quinn asked.

"There's an official office in the Homestead," Doug said. "We try to keep off-worlders there. Harim must not be available to run interference."

"I thought you said the Russosken did all the Federation's dirty work here," Quinn said. "Why would they send actual Federation reps here?"

"That's my question, too." Tony raised his eyebrows at the census man. "Maybe Maarteen was right, and they're after him."

"My guess is we're going to find out soon enough." Maarteen pointed at the screen. "They passed Auntie B's."

Onscreen, the car continued down the switchbacks, pulling into the square at the base of the cliff. Three people got out. Jessian swung her arms in large gestures, as if talking animatedly, her robes flapping in the breeze.

"She's signaling." Doug flipped more programs onto his screen. One showed a picture of the planet with orbiting satellites in different colors, and a blinking red ship in high orbit.

"Signaling what?" Tony asked.

"Warning me that we have outsiders nearby." Doug swiped and flipped through more screens.

"Do you have some kind of planetary defense?" Quinn asked.

"I wish. The planet has a laser defense system, but it's controlled remotely by the Federation. If I could hack into that, I wouldn't need these." Doug swiped another screen up.

Quinn glanced at the new screen and gasped. "You have orbit busters?!"

Doug smiled. It wasn't a nice expression. "That's what I spent my gold on."

"The red dot is the Fed's ship?" Maarteen asked. When Doug nodded, he added, "Can your orbit busters take it out?"

"NO!" Quinn and Tony yelled in concert.

"I could, but if I take out a Federation ship, they'll be all over us," Doug drummed his fingers on the table. "Until now, they've basically ignored us. I don't want to bring more attention to my planet than I need to."

"I wasn't suggesting you take it down," Maarteen said. "I was curious how much damage you could do."

"The Fed ship is moving." Quinn pointed at the red dot. "Where are they going?"

They all stared at the screen.

"Why would they come all the way here to drop off two guys and then leave?" Maarteen asked.

"Maybe we should go find out," Tony said. "Let's go meet Jessian."

TONY WAITED while Maarteen pulled the little cart back into the rental kiosk and plugged it in. "Jessian's car is over there." The census man waved across the square. "I wish we had a little more information about these visitors. I don't like walking into a potential ambush."

Tony climbed out of the back seat, his gaze taking in every detail of the seemingly empty square. "That's why we left Quinn and Doug back at the house. They can extract us, if necessary. Let's go bump into the Feds, shall we?"

The two men crossed the square and walked into the squat building on the side. A sign over the door read "City Hall." They passed into a small, empty lobby and pushed through another set of doors. A short hallway led to another set of doors with an exit sign overheard. Four doors, two on either side, lined the hall.

"Harim's office is over here—his actual office, not the show place up above." Maarteen walked to the second door on the left and pushed it open.

"Is everybody incognito?" Tony waved at the blank door.

Maarteen grinned as they stepped into a small room. "If you don't know where to go, they probably don't want to see you." He nodded to an older woman sitting behind a desk, knitting. "Morning, Ro'Sheen."

"It's almost afternoon, Mr. Maarteen." Ro'Sheen barely looked up, her needles clicking evenly. "Who's your friend?"

"This is Charles Anthony," Maarteen said. "He's interested in settling on Lunesco. We met on our transport, and I said I'd introduce him."

"Boss is busy now," Ro'Sheen said. "Visitors."

"Yeah, we saw them arrive. Tell Harim I'm here, will you? He might like some help."

Ro'Sheen gave each of them a brief stare, as if sizing him up, then dropped her knitting in her lap. She picked up a comtab and tapped rapidly, then set it down. "You a farmer?" She gave Tony another hard look as she lifted her needles and wrapped the yarn around her fingers.

Tony blinked. "Me? Uh, no. Retired academic."

Ro'Sheen shrugged. "You'll learn." The needles clicked, tapping out a rapid tempo.

"Most folks who live here assist in the agricultural pursuits," Maarteen explained.

Ro'Sheen's comtab vibrated and she glanced at it. "You can go in." She shifted the yarn on her lap enough to let them see the blaster buried underneath. "I'm here if you need anything."

Tony raised an eyebrow at Maarteen.

"Thanks, Ro'Sheen. We'll call if we need you." Maarteen strode past the desk and pushed open the door at the rear of the room. He waited for Tony to come closer and lowered his voice. "I told you they trust me."

Tony followed him into the office, keeping one eye on Ro'Sheen.

Inside, a man in dusty clothing sat behind a desk littered with tablets and paper. A little plaque said, "Planetary Governor." His gray hair hung over his dark eyes in a shaggy fringe. He stood as they entered. "Ah, Sebi, good to see you."

A man and a woman sat in the chairs in front of the desk. They had turned when the door opened and now got to their feet.

"Glad to see you made it here, Sebi," the male visitor said. "Let's get on with this, shall we?"

The gray-haired governor blanched. "You know Sebi?"

The woman smiled. "You could say we've worked together before."

The door burst open, and Ro'Sheen stormed in, blaster in hand.

CHAPTER 26

LIZ STOMPED across the cargo hold, stopping to kick a bale of Fandian silk. "Damn, stupid, ignorant— Augh! I can't believe I misjudged so badly."

"We'll find a buyer." Maerk lifted the bale and stacked it on top of another. "We don't have to sell this stuff now. Maybe the next planet will want it."

"We're in the fringe," Liz snapped. "They don't do luxury out here!"

"Look, it doesn't do any good to—"

She cut him off with a scream. "I don't need any of your glass half-full crap!" She kicked the next bale and stomped out of the hold.

"Would you like me to come back at a better time?" a voice asked.

Maerk spun around. He'd forgotten they'd left the ramp partially down. He grimaced at the face peering through the opening. "Sorry about that. She's—" He shook his head. "What can I do for you?"

"I've heard you might be looking for a cargo carry?" The man's round face creased in a smile. "I have some things to ship, if you've room for them." His eyes traveled around the hold, taking in the boxes and bales.

"What you see is what I have room for. A couple tractors' worth of space." Mark waved a hand around the empty cargo hold. "Let me put the ramp down so we can talk."

The man stepped back and waited for the ramp to lower, then he stepped aboard. His body was as round as his face. "Rimini Farggaldo." He bowed low with his hands held out to the sides. "I have a cargo that must go to Lunesco, if you're headed that way."

"We'll go wherever the next cargo takes us." Maerk bowed in return. "I'm Maerk Whiting. That was my partner, Liz Mar—Martin. I don't suppose you know anyone who wants to buy fancy fabric or food?"

Farggaldo sighed. "I know plenty who want, but few who can afford. Not many big spenders out here on the fringe. You might want to check in with the big house, though."

"The big house?" Maerk echoed.

Farggaldo pointed across the landing strip, into the foggy distance. "The big house. Where the boss lives. He has a couple daughters. They might want some fancy fabric."

"Does this boss have a name?"

"Allestair Petrov."

"Petrov." Maerk eyes narrowed. "I'm not sure—"

"He's not one of those Petrovs," Farggaldo said. "He's a good man. Very fair. Honest."

"Seems to me that's not how the big boss on a fringe world is usually described." Maerk pulled at his lower lip. "But if he's buying what I'm trying to sell, I'll talk to him. Let's get this hammered out first, though. What are you shipping and where?"

"I have fourteen crates of assorted electronics." The round man turned slowly, looking at the neatly-stacked cargo. "To my cousin on Lunesco. They'd fit in here nicely, even if you can't unload your other items. Maybe my cousin will want some of your luxury goods. Will you break the cases?"

"I'll sell it however I can get rid of it." Maerk swiped his combat. "Fourteen crates of electronics to Lunesco? I think we can manage that. Let me send you a contract." He flicked the document to Farggaldo.

The round man slapped his thumb against the contract, signing it without reading. "You strike me as an honest man," he said with a wink. "Happy to do business with you. Payment is in the escrow account."

Maerk started to wonder what he'd gotten himself into. Too late now, but it was time to locate the kids. "Is there some kind of trade center here? I'd like to make contact with others who fly this area. I have an old friend who said I should look her up when I got here."

"Anyone wanting to buy or sell lands here."

"Oh," Maerk said. "Anyone else been here recently?"

"What's your friend's name?" Farggaldo asked. "Funny you don't have their comm link."

"Lou," Maerk said. "She's kind of paranoid—changes comtabs way too often. She usually sends someone else to do pickups. Might have been Dar or Stene? Maybe End or Kert?"

The man gave him a funny look. "Those names sound familiar," he said slowly. "But no one else has stopped by in the last week or so. Would it have been before that?"

"Nope, Lou said this week." Maerk pulled at his lip again. Had he said too much already? This trader seemed way too interested.

"You should check with Petrov." Farggaldo swiped his comtab. "Drive around to the other side. I'll send him an introduction, so he's expecting you. Soon as my guys get our crates loaded, you can drop by before you head off world."

"Never mind," Maerk said. "You don't need to send any messages on my behalf!"

"Already done!" He flourished the comtab and shoved it in his pocket. "And here're my trucks. We'll get you loaded and off in minutes."

Liz reappeared as Farggaldo's men loaded the cargo. He greeted her effusively, bowing low and exclaiming over her exquisite taste in cargo. "If only I had the cash. Unfortunately, all my profits are currently invested into the business."

"Of course. I should have realized margins would be slim out here." Liz tapped Maerk's arm. "Did you get a lead on our friends?"

Maerk started to answer, but Farggaldo cut him off. "Petrov says you should come over. There are many off-worlders. He messaged me only seconds ago. You are so fortunate!"

Liz pursed her lips. "Yes. So fortunate. Maerk, I'll be ready to go as soon as you get the cargo tied down. Nice to meet you, Mr. Farggaldo." She walked away without waiting for the round man's answer.

"She's still a bit frustrated." Maerk shrugged apologetically. "She didn't mean to be rude, I'm sure."

Farggaldo waved an arm in denial. "Not at all! Such a pleasant woman. I only regret that I can't accompany you to Petrov's house. I have other business to attend, but he is anxious to make your acquaintance and is expecting you momentarily." He beamed at Maerk, then made a quick visual check of the cargo hold. "*Khorosho*, my men are finished. Safe travels, my new friend. Give Petrov my best." He hurried down the ramp and climbed into the flatbed truck idling beside the ship. The truck growled and pulled away, sending up a cloud of dust in its wake.

Maerk closed the loading ramp and secured it. Then he checked the tie-downs. He knew better than to trust someone else's loading team. When he finished, he called the bridge. "Cargo is stowed,"

"He can be taught," Liz marveled in response.

Maerk rolled his eyes and made his way forward.

"I AM SO BORED!" Francine threw the game controller onto the bunk and leaped up. "If we have to spend another day in this tin can, I will—" She let out a sound between a growl and groan.

"Dude, we were in the middle of a game!" End cried. "You got me killed!"

"How will the universe survive?" Francine muttered. "I'm going forward. Maybe a message came in."

"I set it to override the game, remember?" End trailed behind her, stopping by the galley to pick up another piece of freeze-dried or vacuum-packed or stasis-fried something.

Francine ignored him and dropped into the pilot's chair. "Why's this light flashing?" she hollered at End.

"What light?" End scrambled to the front of the shuttle. "*Futz*."

"What is it?"

"Battery." He shoved the rest of whatever he was eating into his mouth and spoke around it. "We're low on juice. Gotta deploy the external solar panels."

"Why didn't we do that when we landed?"

"Didn't need 'em then."

"We knew we'd be here up to ten days." This was the last time she'd get stuck babysitting. Going back to the Russosken would be better than another week of enforced gaming with End.

"Our new Kamelion surface collects power as well as camouflaging us. But apparently it isn't as efficient as the old system. And I might have underestimated the power consumption of the game console." He shrugged. "High-end graphics take lots of power. I'll go set up the panels."

"We should wait until dusk," Francine said. "It's too windy now, and we'd need lights if we do it after sunset. Dusk is perfect. Shadows will be low."

"But they won't start charging until tomorrow, then," End argued.

Why did he always have to argue? Worse, he was right way too often. "Fine, we'll do them now."

"We?"

"If you think I'm staying in here while you get to go outside, you got another thing coming!"

"Fine. You'll need to wear a maintenance coverall. They're closer to the desert coloring." He moved back to the small closet and pulled out the clothing. He tossed her a hat. "Put this on. And some goggles. If someone gets a glimpse of us, we don't want to be identifiable."

They suited up and walked back to the cargo hold. "The external panels are stored near the ramp," End said. He unlatched a section of wall at the back and caught the stack of panels as they fell away from the wall. "Grab the end. They aren't heavy but they're big."

"Fine. What do we do when we get out there?" She took one end and waited for End to lift the other.

"There are brackets on the back of these, and arms that extend from under the shuttle—Never mind, I'll show you when we get out there." He slapped the ramp control, and the back of the shuttle opened wide. The wind rushed past them, stinging bare skin with wave after wave of sand.

"What happens if we have to leave fast?" Francine yelled as they carried the panels down the ramp.

"There's a quick-disconnect in the cockpit," End yelled back. "We'd have to abandon them, so it's only for emergencies. These suckers ain't free."

They leaned the panels against the ramp and End showed her how to pull the arms out of compartments near the landing gear. Then her comtab buzzed.

"How am I getting a call?" She fished it out of her pocket. "Didn't you set this thing to stealth mode?"

"Gimme that." End snatched the device from her hand. "If you got a call, it's from the family." He stared at the screen. "Did you give this number to anyone else?"

"Who would I give it to?" Francine peered over his shoulder, trying to see the screen.

"That's a good question." He tilted the screen. "Someone is trying to call you. Maybe you should answer it."

"Won't that give away our position?" Her finger hovering over the button.

"If they can call us, they already know where we are." He pushed her hand aside and stabbed the screen.

CHAPTER 27

THE COMTAB in Quinn's hand vibrated, indicating a connection had been made. "Finally! Francine, this is Quinn. Where are you?"

A loud rushing poured out of the comtab, Francine's voice tinny and almost impossible to hear. "I'm hiding in a dry lakebed with Tony's cousin, waiting to pull you out. And I'm bored!"

Quinn raised her eyebrows at Doug, and he shrugged.

"Uh, does that mean you're here?" Quinn asked. "In the same place I am?"

A thud boomed through the phone, and the white noise cut out. "Why are you being so cagey? Are you calling from a public place?"

"No, but I wasn't sure if your end was safe." Quinn looked at the screen in front of her. "I'm fully encrypted and bouncing through multiple nodes."

"We are too," End said. "What's going on?"

"End! Perfect," Quinn said. "Are you guys here? Dirtside on Lunesco?"

"Yeah, we're here," Francine said. "Please tell me you have a mission for us. Even if it's just buying groceries."

Quinn laughed. "No groceries—"

Doug cut her off. "If you come past the market, we could use some salsa." Quinn glared at him. "Never mind. That wouldn't be smart."

"I've got salsa," End said. "Was that why you called?"

"Of course not," Quinn said. "We have a little programming problem and could use some out-of-the-box thinkers."

"Great, we'll be right there!" Francine jumped in. "Send me your location."

"We can't leave the shuttle," End argued.

"You stay with the shuttle," Francine said, "but I'm going to help Quinn. That was our mission, wasn't it? To help Tony and Quinn."

"Technically, we're supposed to *extract them* if they need it."

"Then you wait here and extract all three of us if we need it. I'm going to help."

"Wait," Quinn said. "You don't have to come here. I need a—"

"Nope," Francine said firmly. "You want help. You have to tell me where you are, and I will come help you. Otherwise, you're on your own."

"Gramma won't like—" End started, but Francine cut him off again.

"*Gramma* doesn't need to know. Besides, she's not *my* grandmother. Send me your coordinates, Quinn."

Doug grabbed the comtab out of Quinn's hand and poked the screen. "There you go. Stay on the roads. Otherwise, you'll end up in a fireball at the bottom of the canyon."

Francine's gasp was audible on their end of the connection. Then she laughed.

"He's serious," Quinn put in. "We're at the bottom of a chasm that rips through the plains. If you aren't paying attention, you could go over the edge."

The laugh came through again. "Still better than playing another round of onks versus dragons."

"That's *Orcs Rampage VI*," End said.

"Whatever. I'm on my way. See you soon." With a click, the connection died.

"I guess we wait then." Doug laced his fingers behind his head.

"I'm going to keep working on this." Quinn slid an app off the screen and opened a new one.

"I'm going to see if we have any salsa." Doug strolled out of the room, the dogs on his heels.

TONY EASED AWAY FROM MAARTEEN, trying to be inconspicuous.

Ro'Sheen poked her blaster at him. "Don't move."

He held up his hands, freezing in place.

"I've never met these people before," Maarteen said to Harim. "You have to believe me! I wouldn't bring Federation agents to Lunesco! I do my best to keep them away!"

Harim reached under his desk and pulled out a stunner. "You two, move over there with your *friends.*"

"Sebi, Sebi, Sebi." The woman shook her head slowly, as if disappointed with a child. "We're old friends. You just haven't recognized us yet."

"Why did the Krimson spy cross the road?" the man asked.

Tony, Ro'Sheen, and Harim stared at him, speechless.

A grin broke out on Maarteen's face. "To free the Federation!" He pumped his fist. "*Semper Libero!*"

"*Semper Libero,*" both visitors replied.

The woman extended a hand to Tony. "Amanda McLasten. Bruno sent us."

Ro'Sheen waved her blaster. "Stay back, both of you!"

Tony cleared his throat. "I believe these two are from FedFree."

Maarteen nodded enthusiastically. "Yes, they are."

"And FedFree is what?" Harim shook his weapon at them, trying to regain control.

"We're a group of government employees who are trying to fix the Federation." Amanda gestured to her partner. "This is Myung-Dae Petereson. He goes by Pete."

Pete bowed his head. "Pleased to meet you."

"Hey," Ro'Sheen barked. "I still got a gun pointed at your heads!"

They all turned to look at her.

"Ro'Sheen, put that thing away," Harim said. "If Sebi says these people are trustworthy, that's good enough for me."

"It shouldn't be." Amanda quirked a brow. "But we're both armed, so if we'd wanted to kill you, you'd be dead already."

Pete nodded sadly.

Harim blanched.

"Fine." Ro'Sheen lowered the blaster. "But don't come crying to me if they kill you and break your stuff." She backed out of the office, glaring at all of them as she left.

"No more visitors," Harim called as she went. "And no calls."

As the door slammed, Tony heard Ro'Sheen mutter, "Who does he think he is, the premier?"

Harim bowed. "I'm sorry for the interruption. Please, let's continue our discussion. Sebi, pull up a chair for yourself and your friend."

"This is Tony." Maarteen dragged an armchair away from the wall. "He and I were meeting with…a friend of his when we saw you two arrive."

"And you raced back to greet us," Amanda said. "How very welcoming of you."

"I raced back to see who was up to what," Maarteen corrected her. "This planet rarely sees Federation visitors. In fact, your arrival might have drawn unnecessary attention to them."

"We work for the Federation Tax Bureau," Pete said with a shrug. "We're here to review planetary financial data. It's a standard five-year review."

Harim's nose wrinkled. "The Federation has never sent anyone before."

"We're kind of lax in the review department," Amanda agreed.

"Especially in the fringe planets. You don't provide much tax income, so it's hardly worthwhile to do these audits. I mean, sending two people out here for a month? Our per diem alone is likely more than we'll find in miscategorized credits. But the Space Force was doing training maneuvers, so we had a free ride."

"Are they still here?" Tony asked in alarm.

"No, they barely slowed down to drop us," Amanda said. "We'll have to find our own way home."

"We came looking for you," Pete said. "Not you, specifically, but someone who could tell us what's going on. We heard through our contacts within the Russosken that something is up."

Harim's face went red. "You are with the Russosken? They nearly destroyed this planet!"

Amanda held up both hands in a calming gesture. "We don't work with them, but we have some…let's call them sympathetic individuals within their network. They agree that a loosening of the Federation's death grip on planets like yours could improve the bottom line. The more profitable you are, the more the Russosken can benefit."

"The Russosken is the sole reason this planet is so poor!" Harim yelled. "They squeeze every extra credit out of us, crushing enterprise here!"

The door slammed open again, and Ro'Sheen stood on the threshold, holding a blaster in each hand this time.

"Ro'Sheen, I told you no interruptions!" Harim bellowed.

"You yelled 'Russosken'," Ro'Sheen hollered back. "What was I supposed to think?"

Harim walked around the desk and his guests, pushing Ro'Sheen's blasters down as he approached. "I don't care what you think. But unless you hear blaster fire or see blood running under the door, stay out!" He used his body to herd her out, shutting the door in her face. Then he swung back around to glare at all of them. "I don't work with Russosken agents!"

"We aren't Russosken agents." Amanda's voice was low and

soothing. "Our contacts are a *few* sympathetic individuals within their ranks. They disagree with the status quo, but they have no way of affecting change. At least not without risking their fortunes. So, they pass information to us, in hopes we can do it."

"Believe me," Pete said. "The last thing we want is to wrest freedom from the Federation only to hand control over to the Russosken."

"If I may." Tony rose. Being an outsider, maybe he could add a little clarity. "The important thing at this moment is the Russosken think something is going on here. That means they'll send their own investigators. We all know what that looks like."

"The last Russosken 'investigation' was a massacre." Harim stood behind his desk, arms crossed over his chest.

"Exactly." Tony made eye contact with Maarteen. "Now that we have this information, we need to figure out how to stop another massacre."

"We need to keep those devils off our planet," Harim muttered. "We need weapons."

Maarteen leaned back in his chair. "We might be able to help with that."

CHAPTER 28

THE *SWAN of the Night* taxied to a private parking strip on the other side of the runway. As Liz drove them along the taxiway, Maerk focused the external cameras on the shuttles parked on the apron. "Six. Three are painted in matching colors, so they probably belong to the same company. I'd guess whoever owns that." He pointed through the windshield at the massive house beyond the shuttles.

"Petrov," Liz said absently as she focused on the turn. "Wish we knew more about him."

"The other three are older, and I'm pretty sure—" He broke off and fiddled with his comtab. "Yes! The last one is Lou's. Or at least it's showing one of the old transponder codes. They should get some new ones."

"It's not the one we used on Hadriana, is it?" Liz's voice sharpened with alarm.

"No, I made sure that one was permanently red-flagged." Maerk tapped his device and sent a message. "This is an older one—from five or six years ago. But definitely one Lou has used before."

Liz laughed. "She probably sold it to some unsuspecting fool."

"If you're dumb enough to buy used transponder codes from shady dealers..."

Liz glared. "Hey, she's my mother. I can say mean things, you can't."

"Since when? Besides, we aren't married anymore. You're not the boss of me."

"I'm the captain of this ship." Liz glared. "That makes me the boss of you."

"Crap." He tapped his comtab. "I messaged the kids again, but no answer yet."

"You know they only check those drop boxes when they have secure comms," Liz parked the *Swan* next to the *Fuzzy Kitten*. "I'd be worried if she had answered."

"I guess we continue with the plan. Try to sell the cargo and look for the kids. Here's our escort."

A large truck with small windows and a gun emplacement on top pulled into the next parking spot. Maerk refocused the cam to get a closer look. "They've got a rocket launcher on their truck." His face went pale, and cold poured into his gut. "This Petrov is one risk-averse guy."

"You haven't done enough planet-falls." Liz leaned over to glance at the video. "That's pretty standard equipment for the boss of a fringe world. These guys rule through fear. Might not even be loaded."

"I'm not sure that's something I want to test." Maerk swallowed hard. "Let's get this over with."

"Roger. Shutdown is complete. Let's go meet the locals."

They climbed out of their seats and walked to the side airlock. "Get kitted up," Liz said. "These guys respond to power, so we want to look like we're a force to be reckoned with." As she spoke, she pulled open a cupboard and slipped on a bulky overcoat with an ArmorCoat logo. "I'm glad we bought these."

Maerk slipped his arms into the heavy sleeves and fastened the front. He pulled a pair of blast rifles from their clamps and handed one to Liz. She slung it over her shoulder. Gravity-belts with holsters for stunners went over the long split-skirt coat, and No-

Shok hats to protect their heads. "Ready. We look like ancient earth cowboys."

Liz grinned. "Space cowboys are always in style."

They stepped into the airlock and Liz cycled it. "Remember, we have several more crew members aboard. If you need a name, refer to them as Smith or Jones."

"Those don't sound fake at all," Maerk muttered.

"It's kind of a standing joke out here on the fringe. We all go by Smith or Jones at some point in our lives. Plus, it goes with the whole space cowboy vibe."

They stepped out of the lock and down the retractable stairway. That feature had been one of the selling points for Liz—no need to turn your back climbing down a ladder as you exited the ship. They could have lowered the rear ramp, but that gave easy access to the cargo hold—something to avoid in a potentially-hostile location.

A tall, thin woman climbed out of the truck. She wore a short, purple skirt, a low-cut, sparkly blouse, and high-heeled, knee-high boots. A blaster hung on her hip, and she held a comtab in her other hand. Long green hair curled around her face and shoulders, not moving in the breeze. A faint force bubble explained her lack of protective gear. Clearly, their host had credits to burn if he could outfit minor flunkies with force bubbles.

"Hey, I'm Leena." The woman snapped her jaws, popping something loudly as she chewed. The noise and her voice were artificially amplified to carry across the tarmac. "Petrov sent me to get you. Climb in." She turned without waiting for a response. The force bubble melted against the truck as she scrambled into the driver's seat.

Liz and Maerk looked at each other, then at the truck. Liz shrugged. Maerk flicked his comtab to lock the *Swan* and strode across the apron to the massive vehicle. As they approached, the rear door opened. With another glance back at Liz, Maerk grabbed the handle and climbed the rungs into the passenger compartment.

A wide seat filled the space, divided by a folding cup holder. He pushed the thing up into the seat back and slid across to the far side. "Nice vehicle." He ran a hand over the smooth brown seat.

"Hindo hide." Leena turned to lean an elbow on the back of the front seat said. "Native animal. Big, slow, and stupid, easy to kill. Makes excellent shoes." She twisted sideways to raise her leg and show off her boots. "What are your names?"

"I'm Maerk, and this is Liz. Liz Smith, Maerk Jones."

Sitting behind Leena, Liz rolled her eyes.

Oh, right, Smith and Jones were supposed to be aboard. "My wife is still on the ship."

Liz kicked him.

"Too bad. She miss the party. Let's go." Leena twisted to the front and poked the vehicle's screen. The truck rumbled to life and backed out of the parking spot.

"Party?" Liz mouthed at him. He shrugged.

Leena swiveled around to lean against the door, swinging her feet up onto the front seat. She ignored the control panel, letting the truck drive itself. "You ever been to a Petrov's party?" The question was punctuated by another loud pop.

"Uh, no," Liz said. "We've never met Mr. Petrov before."

Leena laughed. "Not Mister, just Petrov. He super casual." She popped again. "He always invite off-worlders to parties. Get super boring if it's just Daravooders."

"Daravooders?" Maerk asked.

She laughed again. "That's what I say. Officially—" She made air quotes. "—we Daravians."

"Daravooders certainly sounds like more fun," Maerk said.

Leena grinned. "Daravians is super stuffy. You are more fun."

Liz leaned forward to catch the woman's eye. "He is fun, but his wife is *super* jealous. Best be careful."

"Thanks, *biyach*!" Leena laughed again and eyed Maerk. "He a little old for me, but if he super fun, I don't mind. But I don't poach. Sorry, honey."

"I'm crushed," Maerk muttered.

Liz ducked her head. "Super crushed," she whispered.

Maerk bit back a snicker, not wanting to upset their guide. "Say, Leena, any other off-worlders coming to this party?"

Leena looked up from inspecting her fingernails. "Yeah. Traders. Always traders. From many systems. Couple Feds. Some guys from Reticon Five. And a chick from—I don't know where she from, but her name is Jones, too. Darla Jones, or Darnee. Something like that. Maybe she related to you?"

Liz sat up straighter.

"Lot of Joneses in the galaxy," Maerk said. "I suppose we could be distant cousins. What's up with the Feds?"

"Friends of Petrov." Leena waved them away, then craned her head around to look at Liz. "But the Reticon guys are cute. I got dibs on the tall one, but you might want the other guy. You a little gal, so he perfect for you. 'Less you got a guy on your ship."

"No." Liz didn't even glance at Maerk. "No guy on the ship. Short sounds good. I wouldn't want to get a crick in my neck."

"Super." Leena popped the gum again. "Here the house. I gotta send the truck back to the garage, so I see you inside. Go on in."

The truck stopped in the circular drive of the huge house they'd seen from the runway. Wide, shallow steps ascended to a portico with tall columns and an angular roof. Dozens of windows stared down from four different levels.

"Thanks, Leena," Maerk said.

She winked. "My pleasure."

Liz used her gravity belt to float to the ground. "What?" she said in reply to Maerk's headshake. "That truck is a long way up for a little gal like me."

He bit his lip to hide the smile and slid down to stand next to her on the drive. They climbed the wide front steps. The front door, hidden in the shadow of the roof, stood open. Music, voices, and laughter drifted out.

They stepped through the door and the sound cut out. A long, empty hallway stretched the depth of the house, ending in large windows. The crowd mingled outside the open glass doors, but the noise of the party was gone. Highly-polished parquet squares covered the floor and the lower part of the walls. Above the wood, brilliant tiles formed pictures of fantastic scenes from classic tales.

Just inside the front door, an android in a shiny black suit stood at attention. "May I take your coat and weapons?"

"No, thanks." Liz shoved her hands into her pockets and pushed past the robot.

The android slid into her path. "Please, allow me to relieve you of your gear. You won't enjoy the party weighed down by unnecessary equipment."

"I'm good." Liz swerved to avoid the robot.

It stuck out an arm and blocked her path. "I must insist. No weapons allowed inside the house."

"But the party is right there," Maerk said. "Outside the house."

"No weapons at the party," the android amended.

Liz heaved a heavy sigh and unslung her blaster rifle. "Take care of that. It was my grandmother's."

The android pressed one of the square panels in the wall. It slid out revealing a long drawer. "You may safely leave it here, sealed with your handprint."

Liz glanced at Maerk and back at the android. "I'll use my comtab, if you don't mind. Don't want to leave handprints on the walls."

"Not at all," the android said. "Many visitors do. However, the handprint is more secure."

"I'm sure it is." Liz slid her rifle into the drawer and added her stunner on top. "Get your own drawer, Maerk." She glared at him, then flicked her eyes to the other side of the room.

"Sure." Maerk stepped back and stumbled a little. His move let him ease closer to the party without looking like he was trying too hard. He hoped. "Can I put mine here?" He pressed one of the rectangles. Nothing happened.

The android slid across the room. "Try this one." It pressed the next panel which popped open.

Maerk slid his rifle strap off his shoulder, fumbling it and nearly dropping the weapon.

"Careful, sir." The android snagged the strap before the gun hit the floor.

He muttered his thanks, although why he was thanking a machine, he wasn't sure. Then he placed his blaster on top of the rifle and used his comtab to seal the drawer.

Across the room, Liz slid her own comtab into a pocket and smiled. "All done!"

"Please remove the stunner from your coat pocket, madam," the android said.

Liz swore under her breath, her eyes narrowed. "Oops." She used her comtab to release the drawer. "My bad."

"Indeed," the robot replied.

Liz stowed her stunner, and the robot bowed then slid back to the corner of the room. "Enjoy your stay."

"Thanks for the distraction," Liz muttered to Maerk. "Too bad the tin man was paying more attention than I expected."

He shrugged. "Should have stashed some other weapons."

Liz shook her head. "That thing scanned us when we came in. It knows exactly how many weapons we had."

They strolled onto the wide steps behind the house. The moment they crossed the threshold, the music and conversation assaulted them.

"Nice noise-baffling." Maerk gazed in admiration at the house behind them. "You can barely see the cancelers." Keeping his hand at waist height, he pointed to the devices above the doors.

"Expensive?"

Maerk nodded. "And pointless, except as a show of wealth. Those glass doors are rated for at least two hundred decibels. They have to be, this close to the shuttle field."

"Do you see Dareen or End?" Liz tucked her hand in Maerk's

arm.

He shook his head as he gazed over the crowd. "I guess we'll have to wade in." He urged her down the three steps to the main terrace.

They wove through the crowd, snagging drinks and snacks from passing waiters.

"Human waitstaff. Also pricey," Liz muttered.

"Maybe not. They might not be getting paid at all. Who knows how this Petrov runs things?"

A hand clamped onto his shoulder and swung him around. Maerk pulled free of Liz's grip as he pivoted, freeing his hands. For what, he wasn't sure. It wasn't like he had any moves, and his weapons were all locked inside. If he was going to go dirtside on the regular, he should probably learn some version of martial arts.

"Hello, my new friends!" A tall man with thick curly hair beamed at them. He wore a shiny silver-green suit with a collarless jacket and pegged pants. An enormous diamond stud poked out of one wild eyebrow. His smile revealed huge, blindingly white teeth. "I am Petrov! Welcome to my humble home."

Liz blinked. "Humble? Huh. I'm Liz. This is Maerk. We're traders. I've heard you might be interested in our cargo."

"No business talk at the party!" Petrov's voice boomed across the terrace, jovial but demanding. Every conversation stopped for the briefest second, then resumed, louder. "We'll talk after lunch." He turned in a slow revolution, his hands outstretched to include everyone. "Come! Time to eat!"

The crowd surged around them, streaming into the house. Maerk grabbed Liz's hand and let the movement pull them away from Petrov. "That guy is terrifying."

Liz shook her head. "He's like a caricature of a Russosken. Looks, attitude, everything. Quite the act."

"You think it's an act?" Maerk lowered his voice and leaned close to her ear. "Stereotypes exist because they're common."

"I wasn't feeling it. Keep watching for the kids."

"Liz," a deep voice said behind them. "Maerk."

They swung around, jamming traffic in the doorway. Liz grabbed Maerk's arm and pulled him out of the flow of people. The other man pushed through the crowds to stay close.

"Stene." Maerk made brief eye contact with his former brother-in-law, then looked away. "Act casual. We don't want these people to know we're connected. Are the kids here?"

"Dareen is over there." Stene nodded at the far side of the terrace. "Chatting up some youngsters. End is on Lunesco."

"What's he doing there?" Maerk demanded. "And where's the *Peregrine*?"

"The *Peregrine* is here, in system." He pointed at the upper stories of the building. "Admire the stonework. As soon as we get this deal negotiated and cargo loaded, we're headed back to Lunesco. That's where Tony and Quinn are. And Francine."

"Francine?!" Liz's voice rose, and heads turned. She froze for a moment, then recovered. "That isn't a name you hear very often. I think it lost popularity last century. How strange we'd both know someone of that name."

Interest dissipated, and the crowd pushed on.

"Some of these people might know our Francine, so keep it down," Maerk whispered.

Liz growled. "I know. I was surprised. Let's find Dareen and get out of here."

"We can't," Stene said. "If they see us leaving, they'll be suspicious. Might lock down the runway. They own this place, so they can do what they want." It was a long speech for Stene—obviously he felt strongly about this.

"You're right," Liz agreed, after a long pause. "I guess we make the most of this. Let's get some lunch. We'll mingle a bit, so no one connects us with you." She pushed into the throngs still clogging the doorway.

Maerk raised his brows.

"Nice to meet you." Stene nodded, his face blank. "I need to find my partner."

CHAPTER 29

DOUG STORMED INTO THE ROOM, waving his comtab. "Have you seen this?"

"Seen what?" Quinn looked up from the screen, taking a moment to rotate her shoulders and stretch her neck.

"Tiffany!" Doug flicked his comtab with more force than strictly necessary, flinging a window onto one of the large screens.

"The Tiffany Andretti Show?" Quinn stared at the screen, mouth open. "I got thrown in prison and she got a talk show?!"

"Wait until you see what she's talking about." Doug paused the screen, then fast forwarded and hit play. The banner behind Tiffany pixelated and cleared, revealing the new topic: The Quest for Quinn's Gold.

"What?!" Quinn squeaked. "Turn up the sound!"

"—crates were empty when the shuttle arrived." Tiffany widened her eyes until the whites were visible all around. "Where did the gold go? My guests today are Marielle LeBlanc, who was with me on Fort Sumpter, and Ejaz Xavier, a special agent with the Federation Investigative Services." She smiled warmly at the camera, then swiveled in her seat.

The view pulled back, revealing the rest of the set. Marielle sat on a couch next to a tall man with broad shoulders, short, military-style hair, and a vid-star-handsome face.

"Where'd they get that guy?" Quinn muttered. "Looks like a recruiting poster model."

"Ejaz, tell me what you've discovered." Tiffany leaned forward, her eyes locked on the poster boy.

"I don't have a lot of new information for you, Tiffany," Ejaz said. He turned smoothly and gazed earnestly at the camera to continue his story. "As your loyal viewers know, Quinn Templeton and Tony Bergen were Krimson spies assigned to Fort Sumpter. They stole several crates of gold from the Federation's Emergency Response Vault." He turned back to Tiffany. "That's gold that has been collected from nefarious actors and is used to help the less fortunate."

Tiffany nodded. "The Federation takes care of all her citizens."

"Bergen and Templeton engineered the evacuation to cover their scheme," Ejaz said. "They even diverted military spouses, such as yourself and Marielle, to cover their escape. After the evacuation ships left, they stole a reserve shuttle and loaded the gold."

"Luckily for us, Tiffany managed to get us aboard," Marielle said, her voice stilted as if she were reading her lines.

Ejaz nodded. "Tiffany outsmarted the Krimson spies and took over the shuttle. But when you landed at Zauras base, the gold didn't stay with you."

"That's right," Tiffany chimed in. "Bergen pushed us off the shuttle but kept the gold."

"That leaves several questions." Ejaz stroked his chin as he leaned toward the Trophany. "Why did Bergen abandon his partner, Quinn Templeton? And what did he do with the gold?"

"There's so much spin on that, I'm getting dizzy," Quinn grumbled.

"As your viewers might also know—" Ejaz gazed soulfully into the camera. "Templeton was later broken out of the Justice Center Prison shortly before her scheduled execution. Did Bergen come back for her? Or are other factions involved?"

He spun back to Tiffany, his face a mask of sympathy. "It must be nerve-wracking, knowing the authors of your horrific experience are on the loose."

"I've been through extensive PTSD treatment," Tiffany acknowledged.

"So, what happened to the gold?" Ejaz swung back to the camera. "The information I've been able to obtain—after weeks of painstaking research—all points in one direction. Templeton and Bergen took that gold to the Krimson Empire."

"That's your big revelation?" Quinn flung up her hands. "Weeks of research tell you the Krimson agents took their ill-gotten gains back to the Empire? Incredible investigative work, Agent Xavier."

"Incredible investigative work, Agent Xavier," Tiffany said. "The Federation is lucky to have you."

The man smiled. "Call me Ejaz."

"Turn that off." Quinn covered her eyes. "Ugh. What a load of crap!"

"Sorry." Doug flicked a remote and the screen went black. "I guess the good news is they don't know anything. They're blowing smoke."

"They talk about the gold as if it's common knowledge. They even came up with a stupid cover story for why it existed." Quinn laughed humorlessly. "Emergency Response Vault. As if the Federation has ever provided emergency relief."

"Someone must have gotten the word out," Doug said. "I mean, they controlled everything. They took the gold as soon as we landed. Plus, they had the crates they took on the original shuttles in our place. No civilians ever saw it—except us. Why admit it existed?"

"You're right, someone must have leaked something. Did they try to gag you?"

Doug shook his head, then nodded. "Yes and no. They appealed to our sense of patriotism. Lots of talk about not inciting terror in the populace and compartmentalized information. 'You don't know all the details, so we can't explain *why* this is secret, but it has to be.'" He shook his head. "By the time they released us, the gold was gone. Cyn and I didn't want to draw attention to the stuff we'd hidden, so we didn't say anything. Other than us, only Marielle, Tiffany, and Cassi knew what was in the crates."

"Marielle and Tiffany are obviously singing out of the Federation songbook," Quinn said. "So, the leak must have been Cassi."

"Or Tony. He *is* a Krimson agent. Maybe the Empire decided it was in their best interest to advertise the gold. Stir up envy, resentment, distrust?"

"Tony doesn't work for the Commonwealth anymore," Quinn said. "He retired to rescue me. But I suppose he had to file a report. And he did keep some of the gold."

Doug waved his hand. "It doesn't matter, does it? We know the Federation has been lying about Sumpter from the get-go. I'm sorry I interrupted you with that drivel."

"It's okay. I needed a break anyway." Quinn stood and stretched. "And I can't finish this until Francine and End get here. There's a tricky bit I can't do myself."

"I can't believe you can do it at all." Doug rose, shaking his head. "If I'd known taking over the planetary defenses was possible, I'd have started looking for a hacker weeks ago, but it's all voodoo to me."

Quinn laughed. "It's not sorcery; it's poor systems management. If you're going to put orbital defenses around a fringe planet, you should upgrade the control system so they can't use it against you. Maybe they thought the tech was too old for anyone to bother with. They didn't count on an out-of-date comm officer getting into the mix."

END ROLLED the bike down the shuttle's cargo ramp and parked it against the arm they'd pulled out to attach the external solar panels. "We should probably put those away," he yelled against the wind. The ridge sheltered them from the worst of the gale but didn't stop the noise. "Without us sucking down power, the Kamelion scales should generate enough to power to recharge the batteries."

Francine dropped her bundle into the cargo pod on the back of the bike and looked up at the shuttle. "Is it going to get enough light with those vines shading it?"

"What vines?" End stared at the vessel. "What the hell? There weren't any vines growing here when we landed. Dry lakebed, remember?"

Francine frowned. "Yeah, I thought it looked different. I wasn't sure *what* was different, though."

Thick green vines protruded from the low ridge they'd parked near. Searching tendrils stretched toward the ship, lacy leaves unfurling.

"Did we drop some water when we landed?" Francine reached up, then thought better of touching an alien plant. "Or maybe it gets moisture from our ship's exhaust?"

"They weren't here when we brought the panels out earlier."

Francine shook her head. "That can't be right. Plants don't grow that fast. We must have not noticed."

"How do you know how fast Lunesco plants grow?" End demanded. "We should move the ship. This is the only green spot on the whole lakebed. We must stick out like a sore thumb from orbit."

Francine wrinkled her nose. "What if whatever caused them to grow here makes them grow wherever we park? Let's reset the Kamelion scales to blend in."

End glared at the waving fronds. "That thing could engulf our shuttle. I've seen videos."

"Were they fictional?"

"Maybe." End crossed his arms over his chest. "But that doesn't mean they aren't true."

"Fine. Let's put the panels away and move the shuttle. But make it fast. Quinn needs our help."

They carried the panels back into the shuttle and folded away the arms. "Good thing we never set this whole rig up," End said. "Takes a lot longer to tear down. You wanna follow on the bike, or bring it back inside?"

"How far are you moving?" Francine tipped the bike vertical and kicked the stand out of the way.

"Over there." End pointed to another ridge about a klick away.

"I'll meet you there." Francine climbed on the bike. "Bet I can beat you!" She peeled out in a cloud of dust and headed across the dry sand.

End raced to the cockpit to start the taxi engines. He hit the rear ramp closure button and as soon as the power came online, he put the ship into motion.

Francine sat on the bike, waiting, when the shuttle pulled up next to the ridge. She smiled and waved, even though she couldn't see End with the blast covers closed over the windshield. For the short move, he hadn't bothered opening them—the cameras worked fine. He ran through the expedited checklist, buttoned up the shuttle, and cycled through the airlock.

"Your ride, sir." Francine poked her thumb over her shoulder.

"No way I'm letting you drive!" End strode to the bike.

"You fly the shuttle. I drive the bike." When he tried to push in front of her, she goosed the accelerator and zipped ahead. "You wanna walk?"

"Fine." End climbed onto the seat behind her, wrapping his fingers around her belt. She leaned forward, and the bike took off, dust boiling up behind them. End's arms clamped around her in a convulsive movement.

Francine laughed. "Hold on tight!"

CHAPTER 30

THE BOISTEROUS CROWD made their way through three buffet lines, loading plates high with tiny, edible works of art. Labels on each dish gave the name and the planet of origin. Maerk counted three types of fish eggs, imported from planets across the sector, seven different meats, and a half-dozen desserts, some gilded with edible glitter.

"What are the odds we'd arrive here just in time for this extravagance?" Maerk asked Liz.

"Higher than you'd think, mate," a man beside him said. The badge on his dark blue coverall identified him as a member of Graint Transport. He loaded item after item onto his already-crowded plate, tucking a couple sturdy-looking morsels into his pockets. "Petrov holds these shindigs every week. Anyone in-system tries to be here on Saturday. Wouldn't want to miss this!"

Liz looked around the room. "How many of these folks are local?"

The man shrugged. "There's a couple—Petrov's inner circle. Some employees." He tipped his head toward the far wall, where a rank of people stood, including Leena. "The employees eat last. Most of us are traders, or enforcers."

"Enforcers?" Liz asked.

The man's eyes narrowed. He leaned across Maerk and dropped his voice to a whisper. "You know Petrov is Russosken?" At her nod, he continued. "Russosken enforcers bring in bounty—like most of this stuff—as well as protection payments. Petrov can't store the perishable stuff, so he throws a party. Different food every week. Best part of doing business on Daravoo." He grabbed two brightly-wrapped cubes and tucked them away. With a nod, he angled across the room.

"Let's find seats and see what else we can learn." Liz lifted her plate and strode away.

"My new friends!" Petrov bellowed. Conversations stopped. Maerk looked around the room, trying to identify the target of Petrov's interest. Then he saw the Russosken staring at *him*, a big grin on his face. "Come! Sit with me! Get your woman!"

Liz froze mid-step. Then she turned smoothly toward their host, a pleasant smile on her face. She made her way through the crowd, nodding at those she passed. Maerk hurried after her. When they reached the large, round table in the center of the room, Petrov gestured to two empty seats.

Liz set her plate down, pulled out the chair, and turned to Petrov as she sat. "I am not his woman. I am his captain." She smiled at the group around the table, shook out her napkin, and placed it in her lap.

Petrov caught Maerk's eye and winked. "Gotta work hard for that one, eh?"

"She is strict, but fair," Maerk said. "And since she authorizes my pay, I don't argue with her."

While Petrov laughed, Maerk pulled out the other empty seat and took note of their table companions. Stene nodded. Dareen's eyes were wide, her face pale. She tore her gaze away from her father and stared at the food. Her hands shook slightly as she picked up a fork. Maerk muttered a prayer to Maria Goretti, patron saint of teen girls.

"Excellent! Meet the others." Petrov waved a hand around the table. "All traders, new to Daravoo. Like you. Networking is good, eh?"

Maerk shoved a huge bite of something into his mouth so he

wouldn't have to answer and nodded. Petrov turned away, clearly not caring if he got a response. He snapped his fingers over his head, and Leena scurried to the table.

"You brought these two in?" Petrov pointed at Maerk and Liz.

"Yes, Petrov." The woman nodded feverishly. Nothing popped—she must have discarded whatever she had been chewing.

"Well done. Get a plate." He smiled at the assembled diners. "I reward good work. You enjoy this food?" He focused on Liz. "I have much, much more. Different dishes every week. You must come back!"

"Actually, I have a cargo hold full of this kind of stuff," she said. "I'm looking for a buyer—"

"No talk of work!" Petrov slammed his hands flat onto the table. Again, conversations stopped as if cut by a knife. "You are new. I will forgive. We talk work *after* lunch." He snapped his fingers again. "Leena! No more food. Back to work."

"Did he punish her because I brought up business?" Liz whispered.

Maerk shrugged. "Dunno. Not gonna test it, though."

"Girl." Petrov turned his attention to Darren. "Do you like the fish?"

Dareen gulped, keeping her eyes on her plate. "It's very good, Petrov."

"You're a nice girl. Sweets for the sweet. Leena! Bring Dareen a plate of dessert!"

DOUG LEANED over Quinn's shoulder, staring at the screen. "What is this gibberish?"

She laughed. "It's system control code. I used a backdoor to download the security code."

"Backdoor?"

"Yeah. Sometimes they're built in to allow maintenance. Sometimes hackers create them. You'd think security software would be set up to find them, but as I said, this is an old system. I was able to find a hack on the net and it worked like a dream."

She pointed to a huge block of text. "That's a copy of the security code. I inserted some new blocks here and here that will allow us to lock out whoever is currently controlling the planetary defenses. Do you know who that is? And where they are?"

"Certainly not local," Doug said. "If I had to guess, I'd say it was Russosken, maybe with Federation oversight?"

"Really? The Feds gave control of planetary defenses to the mob?" Quinn stopped scrolling to stare at him.

Doug rubbed a hand over his head. While Quinn started her hacking, Doug had showered. He shaved his unruly fringe of gray hair and looked more like the recently-retired military man she remembered.

"You clean up pretty good, by the way." She grinned.

He ran his hand over his head again. "Yeah, I got a bit sloppy. New day, new mission, clean head. About the defenses, though. Yes, they gave control to the mob. If I'd known then what I know now, I might not have settled here. They run everything with a free hand. I guess the Feds figure the Russosken can't use this stuff against them."

"It was boobytrapped to prevent them from cannibalizing the system," Quinn said. "Self-destructs if anyone tries to remove the weapons. I'm leaving that in place. But with enough time and patience, they could have gotten around those restrictions. Like I'm trying to do."

"They probably have more powerful weapons," Doug said. "Not worth their time."

"Their loss, our gain. I think Francine will be able to circumvent the last of these fail-safes, and then we'll upload the new code, which will give us complete control of the system. Between this laser system and your orbit busters, you will control all access to this planet."

"The governor might not love that."

"We can give it to him," Quinn said. "Or you can run for office. You'd get my vote."

Doug shook his head. "I don't need to be in charge. I just want to be safe. Who's Francine?"

"She's a friend. Expert hacker." She debated telling him Francine's background, but he probably wouldn't want a former Russosken messing with his computer systems. Quinn wasn't sure it was a great idea, either, but she'd watch Francine carefully to make sure she didn't pull anything.

The dogs barked. "That should be your friends." Doug swiped up a surveillance cam feed. "Unless the Feds got past Tony and Sebi. On a bike?"

Quinn zoomed in to get a closer look at the two of them driving up the zigzag to the house. "Yeah, that's Francine and End."

"You trust Tony?" Doug said suddenly.

"Yes, of course." Quinn turned to look at Doug. "He saved my life. Several times. And yours, remember?"

Doug nodded slowly. "Yeah, but that doesn't mean he's not using us. I mean, having access to our resources is easier if we're alive."

"I don't have any resources," Quinn said sharply.

"That's not true." Doug rose from his stool. "You got him in here. I'd have set the dogs on him if he'd showed up by himself. Speaking of dogs, I'd better let your friends in."

He stopped in the doorway. "I don't trust him, but I trust you. Otherwise, I'd never have let any of you in."

Before she could reply, he left.

Quinn rubbed the back of her neck. Doug's trust felt heavy on her shoulders. She hoped she was doing the right thing.

CHAPTER 31

WHEN TONY RETURNED to Doug's place, he found Quinn, End, and Francine huddled over the computers in the secret room. Doug ushered him in, carrying a bag of chips and a bowl of salsa. "The blonde one brought it." He set the food on the table. "Good stuff."

"Don't blame me," Francine said. "It was in the shuttle. I didn't even check the expiration date. I hope I didn't poison you."

Doug laughed. "I spent a good portion of my active-duty years eating combat rations. And the rest of it eating junk food. I think I'll survive."

Quinn's shoulders twitched. "Combat rats. They called them 'rats' for a reason."

"That salsa was fresh," End complained. "I loaded fresh stuff before we left the *Peregrine*."

"Hush. I need to focus." Francine tapped the screen. "I can get around this bit by adding a distract module, like this." Her fingers flew over the keyboard. "But that part is going to take a bit more finesse."

Tony turned to Doug. "What do you say we leave them to it? I'd like you to meet the friends Maarteen is bringing up."

"More people?" Doug reared back. "My house isn't built for

crowds. And if anyone is watching us, they'll know something is up. I never have guests."

"We aren't too worried about that." Tony climbed through the closet, pausing outside. "The Feds turned out to be good guys. That Ralph character who came in on the *Solar Wind* is the only unknown at this point, and Auntie B says he's out on Lin-tuan's farm. Besides, he didn't ping my agent-meter, so I'm not too worried about him."

Doug followed him down the stairs to the living room and out onto the terrace. Tony crossed to the far edge and turned to look up at the house. He glanced at Doug. "Look, I know you don't trust me. But I believe you and I are on the same side. More so than Quinn and me."

The big man crossed his arms over his chest. "What makes you say that?"

"Quinn still believes in the Federation," Tony said. "She knows there are some bad actors—like Andretti—but she believes the system is good. Fair. Even after seeing how we live in the Commonwealth, she can't give up on her own nation." He tapped his chest. "In here, she's still faithful. You're past that."

Doug glowered at him for a few moments, then rubbed his bald head. "You're right, although admitting it is treason. Estelle's death killed my loyalty. I think the whole thing needs to come down. But that's a big dream—too big. I just want to free my planet from their grip. The rest of the Federation can rot, for all I care."

Doug paced across the terrace and back. "I think Quinn is getting closer to recognizing how bad it is, even if she refuses to admit it to herself. Seeing how much control the Federation has ceded to the Russosken here opened her eyes, at least a little."

Tony's comtab vibrated, and he pulled it out of his pocket. "Well, she might see a bit more. Soon. They're on their way."

AFTER THE LAVISH LUNCH, Petrov's flunkies ushered the guests out, table by table. Many of them returned to the terrace, or the huge swimming pool beyond it, visible from the wide dining room windows. Under the edge of the white-clothed table, Maerk rubbed his stomach, wishing he hadn't indulged quite so recklessly.

Liz caught his eye, and her lips twisted into a quick, mocking grin.

"And now, my new friends, let us talk business," Petrov announced. The room had emptied except for the nine people at Petrov's table. Maerk's eyes flicked to Dareen and Stene, then back to Petrov. Dareen looked ill, and she'd barely eaten. Stene grimly nursed a cup of coffee.

"I have some *items* that require transport," Petrov said. "I would like to contract with all of you."

"All of us?" Warenton, the man on Liz's left, started. "You don't even know where we're going."

"I don't care where you *planned* to go." Petrov put both hands on the table, leaning toward the man. "I care where you *will* go. I need transport to Lunesco. You run ships I have never contracted with. I require transport that is not affiliated with my brand."

"Your brand?" Warenton's first mate, Erin sneered, her voice tight. "You mean Russosken?"

Petrov's face flushed. "I don't appreciate your inflection. Especially after you have partaken of my hospitality. Perhaps I will not contract with you. Oliver!"

A large man, bristling with weapons, stepped into the room. "Yes, Petrov?"

"Escort these good people out." He waved at Warenton and Erin. "Their business here is concluded."

"You got it, Petrov." The man waved a hand toward the door. "This way, if you please."

"Good riddance," Warenton muttered as he stood. "We don't need your patronage."

The three exited. Seconds later, a blaster fired. Twice.

Everyone at the table froze. Maerk's eyes flew to Liz. Hers were wide. Across the table, Dareen looked like she would puke at any second. Stene stared into his coffee mug.

Outside the windows, the party continued. The noise-cancelers on the terrace doors had done their job.

"Now, let us negotiate." Petrov clasped his hands over his rounded belly. "Liz, I believe you mentioned some cargo."

Liz opened her mouth, but for a second, nothing came out. She picked up her water glass, her fingers shaking slightly. After a sip, she nodded. "Yes." Her voice was thin and reedy. She cleared her throat and tried again. "Yes. I have some luxury fabrics and foodstuffs."

"I will take them," Petrov said.

Liz sat back in her seat. "Don't you want to see them, first? I can pull the manifest—"

"Not necessary. Leena!" Petrov yelled again.

Leena rushed through the open door. Did her face look paler than before? Maerk wasn't sure. "Yes, Petrov?"

"Arrange to have Liz's cargo unloaded."

"I would prefer to supervise that myself," Liz said faintly. "I have another contract—"

"Of course. Leena will set it up. Go!" Petrov directed the last word at the tall woman. She scurried out of the room. "Now, you will have room for my cargo. I have ten crates and forty personnel who must be transported to Lunesco."

"Personnel?" Liz squeaked. "We don't have—"

Petrov waved a hand, and she stopped. "You have a Crusador. I know the specs. You have plenty of room. I have comfort pods. It's merely a matter of loading them into your cargo bay. Done."

Petrov looked at Liz' brother. "Stene, I will send my crates with you. I assume you have a larger ship in orbit, since I know that shuttle is not jump-capable. You can transport the crates to your mothership. My crew will send mass requirements and help you load." He pointed at the remaining guests. "Pondir and Elimar will take the remaining twenty passengers."

"I will have to check with my captain," Stene said. "I don't know what cargo space remains. She may have already contracted—"

Petrov cut him off. "Then she can un-contract. This is what I require. Negotiations complete." He rose from his chair, knocking it over as he stood. "If you do well, you will find I am generous. Many more assignments will come your way. You may return to your ships. Thank you for your business." He turned and sailed out the door.

The six of them stared at each other, mouths open. Finally, Pondir said, "He didn't talk about payment."

NO ONE SPOKE as they rode to the shuttle field. Dareen sat between Stene and Maerk, trying to maintain her cover story but unable to resist her father's comforting presence. As they rolled along the smooth roads, she leaned left then right, as if stretching her neck and spine.

"What are we going to do?" she whispered to her father.

Maerk's eyes flicked to Leena in the front seat, then to his daughter. He gave the barest head shake.

Dareen took a deep, shaky breath and closed her eyes.

Beside her, Maerk muttered under his breath, "Saint Drausinus protect us."

In the third row, sandwiched between Pondir and Elimar, Liz reached forward as if to steady herself, grasping the back of the seat. Her warm fingers on Dareen's neck gave a tiny measure of comfort. Darren savored the pressure of her mother's hand.

"We here." Leena consulted her comtab. "Liz, ground crew ready to help unload. Petrov's cargo and the comfort pods waiting on loading dock. We ready to bring it out." She swiped her comtab and tucked it into her pocket. "Let's go."

When they climbed down from the huge truck, Stene offered a hand to Liz. She placed hers on his shoulder, so she could jump the last rung. Dareen thought she said something, but it wasn't audible. She let her father help her out of the truck.

"Dar, start your pre-flight checklist." Stene gestured toward their ship. "I'll open up the rear ramp for the cargo."

Dareen nodded and trudged across the apron, blinking tears out of her eyes. She desperately wanted a hug from her parents, but she knew that was too dangerous. She slapped her hand against the airlock access panel and hit the cycle button, dashing the tears out of her eyes as surreptitiously as possible.

Stene had his comtab out, fiddling with something as he followed her into the airlock. Probably cargo plans. She ran the cycle. After the door sealed, something inside the airlock popped. Dust or smoke puffed out of a corner.

"Gotcha." Stene waved the comtab again, then turned to Dareen. "Fried all their bugs. Liz said we need to run."

"Run? You mean, take off?" Panic pounded in her ears. "Leave Mom and Dad behind?"

"Yes," Stene said. "They don't want you involved with the Russosken, and we need to warn Tony. Forty Russosken headed to Lunesco is not good."

"But we can't leave them!"

"They can handle themselves," Stene shooed her out of the airlock and into the shuttle cockpit. "Petrov doesn't know we're connected. He'll likely come after us, but—"

"Then wouldn't it be better to take his cargo? We could jettison it later, if we need to. Or sell it."

"That would be extremely foolish," Stene said. "Running out on the Russosken is one thing. Double-crossing them is another. We don't want anything of theirs on this ship when we run. Which is why we're doing it now. I've already sent an encrypted message to Lou. Fire up the engines. Emergency protocol."

The inner lock closed again, and Stene pressed a hand against Dareen's back. "Don't turn on the comms. We don't want to hear them or respond. Just go."

"Where are you going?" Dareen asked.

"I'm going to check the cargo bay to make sure we're buttoned up, and then I'll join you."

Dareen hurried past the bunks and storage to climb into the pilot's seat. She flipped the comms off, then began the emergency checklist. From the corner of her eye, she saw someone waving their arms outside the cockpit, but she kept her head down, focused on the list. If they were trying to get her attention because the comms were out, she didn't want to notice.

Stene came forward a few minutes later. She glanced up at him as he stepped into the copilot's position. He stared out the windshield, then waved his arms and pointed at his ear. "Sorry, can't hear you." He held his arm at shoulder height, where they could see it through the window, and twisted his wrist, as if tightening a screw. "Trying to fix it."

"You think they'll buy it?" Dareen asked

"Not for long. Get through that list as fast as you can." He stepped between the seats and moved out of view. Crouching low, so he wouldn't be visible through the windshield, he climbed back into the co-pilot's chair and strapped in. "Ready?"

Dareen took a deep breath. "Not really. But we're safe to launch."

"Get to the end of the runway. Fast as the taxi engines will allow. Don't stop for anyone. Run them down. They'll move."

Dareen took another deep breath and released the parking brakes. "Here we go!" She shoved the taxi engine throttle to full. The shuttle surged forward. Leena, who was still trying to get Dareen's attention, froze. Then her eyes widened, and she dove out of the way. A bright light flashed in the rearview cams—a broken electrical cable.

The shuttle thundered along the taxiway. Dareen hit the brakes and skidded the vehicle into a turn at the end. The end of the broken cable bounced and waved in the rear cams. It must have been wrapped around their landing gear.

"*Futz*, girl, don't roll it!" Stene yelled.

Dareen bared her teeth in a humorless grin. "Don't sweat it, old man! I got this."

She completed the turn and lined up on the runway, then she shoved the taxi engines to full again. A ground vehicle bounced across the apron, headed to the runway. She slapped the blast shield button and pulled up the external cameras. "Not gonna happen," she growled at the screen. She hit the launch sequence button and slid the velocity up to full. "We're going hot!"

Beside her, Stene's fingers bit into the armrests. "We aren't going to make it!"

Dareen shook her head. "Have a little faith, uncle."

The shuttle blasted forward as the engines engaged, slamming them into their seats. They roared down the runway, the individual lights on the sides blurring into a solid line. The ground vehicle reared over the low barriers guarding the taxiway and rolled onto the launch strip.

Blood pounded in Dareen's ears and pressure built up in her chest like a boiler. She let out a long "Yeehaw!" as the front wheel lifted off the ground.

"Take us up!" Stene yelled. "We don't have enough altitude!"

Dareen flicked the pitch control and pushed the engine into the red. "Here we go!"

The rear wheels left the ground, and the shuttle angled up into the sky. In the external cams, the dangling cable snagged on the ground vehicle as they flew over. It pulled tight, then fell away from their landing gear.

Dareen let out a sigh of relief. "We're free."

Stene shook his head. "Only till they launch pursuit. We need to hide."

CHAPTER 32

MAARTEEN, followed by Pete, Harim, and Amanda, trudged up the zigzagging driveway to Doug's home. The cart they'd arrived in turned and sped back to town. "You could have driven up," Doug called as they rounded the last turn.

Maarteen pointed at the corner. "Around that? Are you crazy?"

Doug shrugged. "I do it all the time."

"Jessian wanted to," Maarteen said. "I convinced her time was of the essence and she should go get Auntie B."

"You have a death wish." Harim nodded at Doug. "Thank you for meeting with us."

"Your vines are growing well," Maarteen observed.

Tony frowned, then looked at the thick layer of green wrapped around terrace pergola. "What the hell? That's way more than was here this morning!"

"I told you they feed on human energy," Maarteen said. "More people in the house, more vine growth."

"That would be a problem if you were trying to hide," Tony said. "Say, from the Russosken."

Harim nodded. "If they realized the correlation, that would be true. Instead, they bring flamethrowers and burn everything down.

They know crops, including the sugar vines, are our prime source of income."

"Which is why we're here." Maarteen introduced the visitors to Doug. "Amanda and Pete have intel. They believe a Russosken force may be arriving soon."

"Why would they come here?" Doug asked.

"It might be you," Amanda said, almost apologetically. "A new player, who arrives with credits to spare? Have they tried to shake you down?"

"Of course," Doug said. "I'd barely landed, and they demanded a payment. I grumbled a lot, gave them what they wanted, and they left."

"Then you brought in a bunch of orbit busters," Tony said.

"You brought in what?" Harim demanded.

"You have orbit busters?" Pete asked at the same moment.

"Damn!" Amanda eyes sparkled in appreciation.

"I purchased some equipment to ensure my safety," Doug said. "Our safety. I bought it from some former military friends. The Russosken shouldn't have gotten wind of it."

"We have informers within the Russosken," Amanda said. "And he knew about your purchase. Believe me, they have people here, too."

Doug's eyes narrowed. "How do I know you aren't them?"

"We just got here." Amanda put a hand on Doug's arm. "If we were with the Russosken, we'd have come with the force they're sending. No, someone already here is reporting to them. Who knew about your orbit busters?"

"Too many people" Doug ran a hand over his scalp. "The contractors who helped me install them were from off-planet, but I'm sure someone saw them arrive."

"Too late to worry about that now," Tony said. "The secret is out, and the Russosken are on their way. Hopefully Quinn and Francine will finish their project in time."

"What project?" Harim asked.

Tony shook his head. "A little something that should help. Let's wait to see if they are successful."

"WHAT THE HELL?" Liz yelled as Dareen's shuttle screamed away, her arms waving wildly. "I thought they were taking cargo, too?"

Maerk's lips twitched. Count on Liz to overact. "Guess they decided they didn't want to play."

"They will be sorry," Leena said. "Petrov doesn't like deserters. You saw what happened in the house."

Liz looked around to see if anyone was nearby. "Did he really kill them?"

Leena shrugged. "It's what he do. When you come for lunch, you throwing in with the Russosken."

"Maybe they didn't know that," Maerk said.

Pondir laughed. "Idiots. Everyone knows that."

Leena joined the laughter. "Petrov don't care. You got scruples, you gotta be careful who you hang with. Don't even think about it. You don't wanna be dead."

"I've got cargo to unload, and a business to run. I'm not running away." Liz turned to Maerk, and he could see the pulse beating too fast in her neck. "Open the cargo hold. Let's sell some crap."

"Sell?" Leena laughed again and stuck something in her mouth. She chewed and made the popping sound. "You not gonna sell that cargo. Petrov takin' it in exchange."

"Taking it?" Liz demanded, swinging back to the girl. "In exchange for what? You aren't taking my cargo! I paid hard credits for that stuff. If you don't want to buy it, I'm leaving."

"You ain't been listening," Leena said lazily. "You don't wanna leave. He hunt you down. Like he gonna hunt down those two." She waved a hand at the sky. "Open the boat."

"I told you, I'm not giving away my cargo!" Liz glared at the taller woman.

Leena held up her hands. "Ain't up to me. Petrov say he take it. He didn't say he buy it."

Liz spun on her heel and stomped back to the truck. "Take me back to the house. This is unacceptable."

Leena whistled. Four large soldiers in heavy gear trotted out from behind the nearest truck. Mirrored helmets hid their faces. They closed around Liz.

Maerk held up his hands. "Let me talk to her. We don't want any bloodshed."

"I don't care who your boss is." Liz waved her arms again. "He can't take my cargo! And then demand I work for him? That's not how commerce works."

"It how the Russosken works," Leena said flatly. "You gotta prove your value if you wanna get paid." She turned to Maerk. "Talk to your captain, Maerk Jones. She needs convincing."

"Give us a minute." He hurried to his ex-wife. "Liz, let's go into the ship and discuss this."

Two of the goons blocked Liz with their weapons.

"You talk here," Leena said. "I don't want any more unauthorized launches."

"Fine. Let her come over here, okay?" Maerk took a couple steps away from Leena. "Can we have some privacy?"

Her eyes narrowed. "Don't try anything stupid. We watching you." She waved a quick signal at the goons, and they stepped back. "Guard the ship. Don't let them inside until I say." She pointed to the other two shippers. "You two, open your ship. We load it first."

Pondir and Elimar trotted across the apron to their ship, muttering to each other. More goons arrived, spreading out to encircle the *Swan*. Maerk took Liz's arm and pulled her away from the vehicles and listening ears. "Give them the cargo."

"How are we supposed to make a living if we give everything away?" Liz twisted out of his grasp.

"We'll figure that out later. Right now, we need to stay alive.

Besides, the sooner we get into space, the faster we can find out what happened with..." He twitched his head toward the runway.

"Fine." Liz stomped across the apron to Leena. "Take the stuff. I want to get off this rock."

Leena tapped her comtab, and a truck rumbled out of the warehouse beyond the parked shuttles. "The cargo handlers be here in a minute." She sauntered away to lean against the truck.

Maerk and Liz opened the shuttle's rear ramp, and the flatbed truck rumbled up. Three handlers climbed out of the cab and set to work directing their cargo bots. Soon the cargo hold stood empty.

"Hey, wait!" Maerk said. "I just picked up those cartons of electronics here on Daravoo. I have a contract with Farggaldo!"

"Your contract is canceled," Leena said. "We take care of Farggaldo." She swiped her comtab, and Maerk's buzzed in reply.

When he looked, a notice canceling his contract popped up—already signed by Farggaldo.

Liz gazed at the truck loaded with her expensive fabrics and foods. She heaved a sigh and turned away. "How long do we gotta wait for our passengers?"

"They coming now," Leena said without moving. "Bringing the comfort pod. They no trouble to you."

"I wonder what Petrov is going to do with the cargo he wanted to send with Dareen and Stene?" Maerk muttered.

"Part goes with you." Leena appeared beside him. "Part with them." She pointed at the other shuttle. "They got plenty room. You, too."

"Not with a comfort pod and twenty passengers," Maerk said.

Another truck rumbled up with a huge cube-shaped crate. Magnetic lifters whined, and the crate lifted off the truck. A half-dozen handlers maneuvered the massive thing into the *Swan*, barely clearing the edges of the door. Once inside, they pushed it against a wall and set it down.

"Hey, I need to have a balanced load!" Maerk said. "Put that thing in the middle. I don't want to strain my starboard engines because of bad loading!"

The handlers conferred among themselves, then lifted and moved the crate. "This good?"

Maerk ran an app on his comtab. "It'll do. Not much room for anything else."

"We make it work." Leena waved at the handlers.

Another truck crawled across the apron. Twenty smaller cubes, each barely a meter on a side, were stacked against the massive one and strapped down. One of the handlers approached Leena. "That's it. You sign off?"

Leena nodded and thumb-printed his comtab. "Good work." She flicked her device, and Maerk's' own comtab pinged. "You're good to launch. Straight to Lunesco, you get paid."

"What about the passengers?" Maerk asked.

"They already in the pod." Leena turned away, uninterested.

"What?" Maerk stared at her. "They're already inside? Why would—"

"They're suspended." Leena mimed sleeping with her hands under her cheek. "They wake up when you get to Lunesco. Cheaper that way. People eat a lotta food." She laughed.

"I didn't think food was something you worried about here." Maerk glanced at the truck idling nearby with their cargo.

"Parties are fun," Leena said. "Feeding *soldaty* is expensive."

"*Soldaty*? You mean troops?!" Maerk's stomach clenched. "Wait a minute! We aren't a military transport! Nobody said anything about troops!"

"What kind of passengers you think Petrov has?" Leena rolled her eyes. "They no bother to you. They wake up when you arrive. You land, and they get off. You can keep the pod."

The thought of people in suspended animation made him queasy. The idea of *soldaty*—armed Russosken troops—in his cargo hold made his stomach roll. He swallowed against the nausea. "Do we have to...do anything? To wake them up?"

"Nah, the pod handle it." She laughed again. "They wake up on time. Don't take any side trips, though. You don't want a hold full of hungry, angry *soldaty*."

Maerk breathed in through his nose, clenching his gut muscles. *Get it under control, Maerk*, he told himself. "Got it."

"Oh, yeah, Lima and Saul here gonna ride with you." Leena paused halfway into the vehicle. "Just to make sure you get there." She slammed the door, powered on the truck, and motored away.

Two more goons marched forward carrying duffle bags "Let's go."

The other gestured toward the *Swan* with his weapon. "After you."

CHAPTER 33

DAREEN BLASTED her shuttle out of the atmosphere, spiraling higher and higher. Her uncle held on to his harness, muttering under his breath. She laughed. "That was amazing! Terrifying but amazing!" She glanced at her uncle. "Are you praying?"

"It works for Maerk," he said through gritted teeth. "Where'd you learn to fly like that?"

She grinned. "Mom."

"My sister never flew like that. Lou woulda blistered her hide."

"She's the one who taught me." Dareen swiped through screens and pulled up the comms. She swiped that window to her uncle's side of the screen. "Monitor the comms. We need to know if they launch anything against us. Check Daravoo Prime frequencies. If they're going to intercept us, they'll launch from there."

Stene slid old-fashioned headphones on and fiddled with his screen. "There they are. Got some chatter with the ground. Petrov's people are demanding they stop us. Station is demanding payment." He snorted. "Ground is threatening destruction of the station. These people are crazy."

"Incoming!" Dareen shoved a finger at her monitor. "Torpedoes targeting us! Activate our *chaffin fleurs*."

Stene's hands flew over the screen. "*Chaffin fleurs* activated! Take evasive actions...now!"

Dareen jinked the shuttle over, firing a blast from her attitude rockets to change vectors. She blasted forward and sideways, leaving the electronic *chaffin fleurs* behind to attract the torpedoes.

Two bright flashes left ghosts dancing before their eyes. The cam screens went black to compensate, then came back. On the tactical display, electrical and magnetic signals blossomed and went black. "*Chaffin* worked! Torpedoes are toast." Dareen pumped her fist, then pointed. "I'm going to take us behind that moon."

"No." Stene held up a hand.

Dareen's fingers froze over the screen. "What? Why not?"

"They have a base back there. Lou picked it up when we arrived in system. Take this course." He flicked a file to her.

"Course change entered." Dareen tapped the controls. "Switching to auto-evade in three, two one, now."

"I'm shutting down artificial gravity." Stene tightened his restraints. "Need to conserve power."

"Roger."

The ship zipped around the planet, then spiraled away from the gravity well toward the asteroid belt. Behind them, two more torpedoes launched, but they succumbed to another *chaffin fleur*. They wove deeper into the asteroids.

"Reverse engines." Stene's eyes were locked on his screen. "Now cut. Use attitude adjusters to put us behind that rock." He pointed to the screen, indicating an asteroid not much bigger than their ship. "Then we wait."

Dareen swiped and flicked, matching velocity with the object. "I'm going to have to lock onto it to stay in step. Our rocket wash is pushing it away." She worked in silence for a few minutes. "Grappling....now! We're locked on." She sat back, breathing heavily.

After a while, she tapped the screen. "This asteroid belt is really close to the planet's orbit."

Her uncle nodded. "Daravoo used to be mostly miners. Zip out to the belt and back in a day, with a nice load of ore. It's the only reason this planet has a station—to transfer rocks to the big freighters."

They sat in silence for a while longer. "Do you think we lost them?" Dareen asked.

"I don't see anything on screen, but they might be waiting." He zoomed his display. "The belt makes it hard to see incoming ships. Great place to hide, for everyone. Best way to detect things is to look for mathematical anomalies in trajectory—"

An alert blared from the speakers. "Incoming!"

"*Futz.*" Stene zoomed again. The screen identified a fast-moving target slaloming through the field. The projected path changed by the second as the thing maneuvered.

"Is that another torpedo?" Dareen fired up the engines.

Stene swore again. "They must have installed a tracker on us. That's homing in on something."

Dareen blasted away from the asteroid, sending it spinning in the opposite direction. "With any luck, we'll take out the torpedo with that. See if you can find the tracker. But stay strapped in!"

The shuttle twisted, flipped, and spun, weaving through the field. "We can stay in the belt, or head for deep space. Where's Lou?" Dareen asked.

"She's beyond the second gas giant. Or supposed to be. We haven't had any contact, of course. Second bogey on our tail."

"Roger. Do they have any other ships out here?" Asteroids flew at her. She dodged and swerved, her hands getting slick on the screen and joystick.

"None that are registering. Even the stealth reader is showing nothing. I think if we can get past these two, we're good. But we need to deactivate their tracker before we meet Lou."

"I'm going to run." Dareen swerved close to a huge asteroid, then whipped around it. "We can't get through the belt as fast as they can —torpedos can take way more risks than a manned ship. And more Gs."

"I think you're taking plenty." Stene's hands clamped around the straps securing him to the seat.

Dareen laughed grimly. "We've got two more *chaffins*. Drop them as we leave the belt. If those don't work, we'll have to use the em-cannon, but it means letting them get close. Now *that's* risky." She zipped around another big rock. "Here we go. Drop on my mark."

She slammed the thruster control to red-line and the craft surged forward, pressing them back into their seats. "Three. Two. One. Mark!" Dareen clenched her legs against the Gs. Most shuttle engines had regulators to keep inept pilots from punching too hard and blacking out, but Lou had Maerk remove them every time she bought a new shuttle. The family had been trained to know their limits and work within them, like fighter pilots from the days before artificial gravity. Red-lining the shuttle's engines like this was dangerous, but better than being dead.

"One torpedo took the bait." Stene watched the electronic flowers bloom and die. "Still got one on our tail."

"Did you find the tracker?"

"When did I have time to do that?" Stene slowly raised his arm, fighting the extra Gs, and flicked the screen. "Scans show one in the airlock and one on the nose of the shuttle."

"How do we get rid of an external one?"

"Torpedo closing in," Stene said. "It'll be in em-cannon range in ten seconds."

A proximity alarm blared. Gritting her teeth, Dareen pushed her finger forward, fighting the acceleration, and swiped it off.

"Five…four…" Stene counted down. "Three…two…one…firing! It's a hit! Torpedo has lost tracking. Evade now!"

Dareen yanked the joystick left and down, the G-forces making it easy to move in that direction. She was vaguely surprised she didn't break it off the armrest. The move sent the shuttle tumbling off its previous course. The torpedo blasted past them, heading out of the system. "Yahoo!"

She flicked the thruster control, and the engines cut out. The resulting weightlessness made her float away from the chair. She tightened the restraints and grinned at Stene. "Let's get rid of those trackers."

LOU WAITED for them outside the *Peregrine*'s shuttle dock. "About time."

Dareen looked away so Lou wouldn't see her eyeroll. "We were a little busy. Had to use drones to remove Russosken trackers from the shuttle. Unless you would have preferred we leave them?"

Lou's face reddened. "Russosken trackers? Are you sure you got them all?"

"We shut down all systems and scanned for active and passive signals," Stene said. "Unless they got tech we don't understand, we got 'em all."

Lou barked out a laugh. "The Russosken tech is no match for Commonwealth-trained technicians." She stomped up the corridor toward the bridge. "I want a full report."

"We need to warn Tony," Dareen said. "Mom and Dad are trying to buy some time, but Petrov is sending 'passengers' with them."

"Mom and Dad?" Lou stopped abruptly but didn't turn. "Liz and Maerk were there?"

"They helped us escape," Dareen said. "Mom told us to run and warn Tony. They have a contract to deliver twenty Russosken passengers to Lunesco."

"And twenty crates that look like individual weapons lockers," Stene put in. "Got a glimpse of 'em before we launched."

With a gasp that she tried to disguise as a cough, Lou hurried toward the cockpit. She pushed through the door before it was fully open. "Kert, get us moving! We need to get to Lunesco yesterday!"

"We can jump as soon as we're rigged," Kert said. "There's no one here to fine us for incorrect departure. But it's still going to take us three days to get from the insertion point to the planet. Lunesco's beacons suck."

"Can't we use data from our last visit to narrow the tolerances?" Dareen suggested. "It was only a few days ago. We can calculate planetary movements and satellite drift and use that to adjust the beacon signal. That should let us jump closer to Lunesco."

"That's my girl." Lou slapped Dareen on the back. "Genius! Highly illegal, but genius."

"Who cares? Lunesco is monitored by the Russosken." Kert started swiping screens open. "Since when did the Marconis give a crap what the Russosken think?"

"Do it." Lou dropped into the command chair and activated the all-call intercom. "All hands, rig for jump."

Kert, Stene, and Dareen looked at each other. "Who are you talking to? We're all here," Dareen said. "The four of us *are* 'all hands'."

A little girl's voice piped out of the intercom. "The living room is ready for jump."

"That's not what you say," Lucas's exasperated voice whispered. "You say 'Lounge is secure for jump'."

"Lounge is secure for jump," Ellianne said. "Did I get it right?"

The intercom clicked off.

"I stand corrected," Dareen said. "There are six of us."

CHAPTER 34

TONY'S COMTAB PINGED, and he sat up in bed. "*Futz.*" He grabbed his clothes and pulled them on, hopping to the bathroom with one leg in his pants. After grabbing his socks and shoes, he raced to the door.

Down the hall, he knocked softly on Quinn's door. "Quinn, wake up!"

The door opened. "What is it?" Quinn rubbed her eyes and pushed her hair out of her face. "What's the emergency?"

Tony shoved the comtab at her as he urged her back into the room. He eased the door shut and leaned against it. Her messy hair and sleepy eyes sent a tingly warmth through his chest and down into his stomach. He took a deep breath. That didn't help, because she smelled good, too.

"Lou is on her way?" Quinn looked up from the device. "That's good."

"Did you read the rest?" Tony demanded, pushing down the emotions. He needed to focus.

Quinn shrugged, then hiked her loose T-shirt up over her shoulder. "Yes. Russosken are on their way. That's what we've been preparing for. We can test our modifications." She grinned. "Using the planetary defenses against them will feel good—exactly what they deserve!"

"Yeah, but they're coming *with* Maerk and Liz." Tony pointed at the tiny screen. "We can't blast them out of the sky."

"Oh, crap!" She yawned and looked around the room. "Sorry, I'm not at my best without coffee. I'll get dressed and meet you downstairs. Should we wake everyone?"

"Sebi, definitely." Tony found it harder to ignore Quinn's bare legs now that his message was delivered. He turned to open the door. "We'll see what he says about the others." He left her to get dressed.

"What who says about the others?" Amanda stood in the hallway wearing a loose silk kimono.

"What are you doing up?" Tony asked.

"Visiting the neighbors." She gave a sly grin. Her eyes went from Tony to the door behind him and back.

"What? No. I—" Tony took a deep breath. He was a Commonwealth agent. He wasn't going to let this Fed put him off balance. Besides, for all she knew, he and Quinn were a couple. What they did behind closed doors was none of her business. His cheeks warmed, thinking about Quinn behind closed doors. "I received a message. Get the others. I'll meet you downstairs." He pushed past her and hurried down the stairs.

AUNTIE B POURED out coffee and set a second pot brewing. She'd been in the kitchen when Tony arrived, rolling out the day's sweet rolls.

"They won't be ready for another hour, dear," she said. "If I'd known you'd be up so early..."

"I didn't know, either. Can you join us?"

Auntie B shook her head. "I've got work to do. Leave the door open, I'll listen from here." She tossed a ball of dough onto the metal table and started rolling it out. "There are some day-old rolls in the case, if you're hungry."

He nodded his thanks and took the tray of mugs. After propping the door open, he settled at a table nearby. He'd barely taken a bite of the still-delicious pastry when Amanda arrived, dressed in a brightly-colored, form-fitting bodysuit with high heels.

"Nectar of the gods!" She wrapped her hands around a mug and cradled it under her nose. "I hate the first night in a new bed. Especially if I'm alone." Her half-closed eyes gazed over the steaming mug, drilling into his.

"Yeah, strange bed, bad sleep." Tony stabbed his fork into the roll. "There are more of these if you want one." Maybe if she put some food in her mouth, she'd stop drooling at him.

"Just coffee for me," she purred, sliding her hand over her flat stomach and across her hip.

Relief washed over Tony as Maarteen, Pete, and Quinn clattered into the room. While he didn't usually object to being the target of a woman's attention, Amanda came on way too strong.

Quinn glanced at Amanda, then at her own baggy sweater and leggings. Tony smiled as he handed her a mug and plate. She looked at the empty table in front of Amanda. With a shrug, she grabbed the sweet roll and sat.

"Our ride has arrived in-system," Tony said as soon as everyone had sustenance. "They've sent a warning that a Russosken force is on its way here."

Maarteen rubbed his hands together. "First test of your handiwork?" He grinned at Quinn.

She shook her head. "Friends of ours have been conscripted to transport them. We can't shoot them down."

A round of gasps and exclamations met that statement.

"What do you propose?" Pete asked.

"We need to be ready for anything," Tony said. "You two are Federation agents. They probably know you're here."

"I don't know if tax collectors are important enough for their notice." Amanda pouted.

"If it means less money for the Russosken, believe me, they know!" Auntie B called from the kitchen. "They probably watch you closer than anyone!"

"My point was, when they arrive, they'll make contact with you, won't they?" Tony raised a brow at Maarteen. "Or do they just storm in and start shooting? Seems like a recipe for disaster if they accidentally take out a Fed."

"They might contact these two." Maarteen jerked his chin at Pete then Amanda. "Or they might not. Anyone the Federation sends out here alone is considered disposable. Present company included." Pete nodded in agreement.

Tony grunted. "They may, or may not, contact you. Let's assume they don't. Where would they land a task force? We probably need Harim here."

"Why don't we head over to Doug's?" Quinn suggested. "Harim can meet us there. We can make plans there where we have access to all our assets."

"You okay with that, Auntie B?" Tony called through the door.

"Harim knows better than I do." She stepped into the doorway, dusting her flour-covered hands on her apron. "He's the expert."

"I doubt he knows more than you," Maarteen said. "But we definitely need him in the loop."

"I trust him, and you," Auntie B said. "Let me know if you need my help. And take some of those day-olds with you."

AN HOUR LATER, they gathered in Doug's living room. The sky above the eastern end of the chasm showed a faint glow. Maarteen and Jessie laid out the coffee and more of Auntie B's rolls, while Doug scrambled some eggs in the kitchen corner. "Peppers and onions?"

The others agreed. When they each had a plate and a cup, they gathered around the table.

Harim glared at the others. "We've got a Russosken task force on the way, and we're sitting around, eating breakfast?"

"We have time," Tony said. "They haven't even jumped in yet, and you know how long it takes to get here from the jump point."

"How reliable is your information?" Maarteen asked.

"My contact was present when the deal was made," Tony said.

"And we can trust them?" Doug asked.

"I trust this contact more than anyone outside this room." Tony raised his mug.

"More than some people *in* the room," Quinn muttered under her breath.

"We know my friends were contracted to transport twenty Russosken 'passengers'," Tony said. "An additional twenty are coming on another transport. There were some crates as well that looked like weapons lockers, but we don't know if they're on the two ships or coming separately. That's all we know. We believe they will land at the airfield, but my friend's ship doesn't require a landing field."

"So, they could drop in anywhere?" Doug asked.

"Theoretically." Tony wagged a hand back and forth. "But my friend will insist on the field. We know the pilot is under watch by Russosken enforcers. They will try to get word to us before they reach the planet. The other ship is a complete unknown. Your system will alert us when they jump in, correct?"

"Yes." Doug pushed a few scraps of pepper around his plate. "That will give us almost three days' notice. Unless they do what your other friends did."

"What's he talking about?" Harim asked. "What other friends?"

"You met Francine and End," Tony said. When the others nodded, he continued. "They were dropped here when Quinn and I arrived, and their ship went to Daravoo. Because they'd just been here, they were able to jump in closer to the planet than the beacons normally allow. They shaved twenty-six hours off."

"I didn't know that was possible!" Harim exclaimed. "We've been basing all our planetary defense plans on at least thirty-five hours warning!"

"It's highly illegal." Amanda held her mug out for a refill. "But it can be done if you've been in-system recently."

"You knew?" Tony picked up the coffee pot and poured.

She smiled but didn't answer.

"Nineteen hours is probably the fastest anyone could get to Lunesco." Tony said, noting the panic on Harim's face. "Surely that's enough time to get your defense team together. If you choose to deploy one."

Harim looked at Doug, and both men nodded. "We haven't put a ground defense team together yet—after the last time," Harim said.

"Now is the time to do that." Maarteen set his cup on the table with a loud clink. "You've got access to the global defense systems; having a ground defense is the next step. Once you start repelling the Russosken, you need to keep it up. They don't take kindly to anyone bucking the system."

"Agreed," Doug said.

Harim swallowed noisily. Sweat stood out on his upper lip and forehead. "Agreed. Although, as governor of this planet, I wish you'd checked with me before you precipitated this!"

"Why?" Doug crossed his arms. "So you could say no?"

"What makes you think I'd say no?" Harim asked. "And at least I have a mandate to make decisions for the planet. You're just some new guy who started waving his big guns and baiting the Russosken."

"Come on." Doug pushed his chair back forcefully and stood. "You've been gun-shy for twenty years."

"With good reason!" Jessian exploded out of her chair. "People died last time!"

"People always die," Doug said flatly. "You can die slowly, choked to death by the Russosken, or you can take a stand. The longer you cower under your rock, the more people will die when the break finally happens. And it's coming. There's no doubt about that."

Tony and Maarteen nodded.

"The signs are there," Maarteen said. "This planet is not the only one breaking away. All it will take is a couple successful rebellions, and there will be a deluge."

"*If* the first ones are successful." Doug started stacking plates, clanging the dishes hard enough to chip one. The piece skittered across the table, unnoticed. "And remember, here we're talking about a two-phase process. If—when—the Federation sees we've repelled the Russosken, they will come to crush us. We'll need to fight them off, too."

"That's where we come in." Amanda pointed to herself and Pete. "There are other planets waiting for the signal. You are the flashpoint for the whole revolution."

Quinn jumped up from her seat. She opened her mouth, then closed it again. "I need some air." She strode between the glass doors to the terrace.

Tony glanced at the others. "This is your decision. We've provided the means. Keep talking. I'll go see what's up." He set his fork on the table and followed her.

Quinn stood by the terrace wall, staring down the valley toward the sunrise. Spectacular reds, yellows, and oranges splashed across the sky with a streak of aqua green. High overhead, one of the moons dimmed as the sun outshone it.

She didn't turn when he walked up.

"You okay?" Tony asked.

Quinn sighed. "I don't want to be a traitor. I'm a loyal daughter of the Federation. My grandparents fought to create the Federation as a place of freedom. A place of equality and sacrifice for the good of all. My parents joined the Space Force to protect that way of life. The Federation has given me everything. I don't want to start a revolution. I just want to live in peace."

Tony didn't say anything. What could he say?

"Why did you bring me into this?" Quinn rounded on him. "You knew how I felt! How I've always felt!"

He looked away. "I needed you to get to Doug. He wouldn't have talked to me alone."

"You said you were here to find out about Andretti and punish him," she said. "You didn't retire from the Commonwealth, did you? This is a mission! The Krimson Empire is trying to topple the Federation!"

"NO!" Tony put out a hand. When she flinched, he dropped it and turned to face the valley. "I did retire. This is not an official Commonwealth mission. I retired to rescue you. And to be honest, I wanted revenge. Andretti threw us away like a used tissue when he saw he could make himself wealthy. And all those other officers climbed on board." He took a deep breath. "Don't you see? How they all jumped in with both feet? Reggie, Marielle's husband, the others. Only Estelle said no, and they killed her."

"Are you sure she's the only one who said no?"

"Everyone else is still alive," he said softly. "I think that makes it pretty clear."

"But that's just Andretti," Quinn argued. "He's surrounded himself with yes-men and sycophants. Of course they agreed. They're all as immoral and greedy as he is."

"The thing is, they aren't the only ones. They're the lucky ones who happened on an asteroid full of gold, but they aren't the only corrupt officers in the force. This kind of thing—betraying their own troops for personal gain—it's happening throughout the nation. The Federation you swore to protect doesn't exist anymore."

"Then show me." Quinn lifted her chin, her eyes narrow. "I want to see proof. If you're right, then I'm all in. If you aren't, I'm out. I'll find some fringe world to hide on."

Tony's lips quirked.

"What are you smiling about?"

"You're amazing. Fighting till the end for what you believe—what you committed to—but willing to see both sides of the story and make your own decision. That's what I love about you." He held his breath, wondering what she'd make of that statement.

"You won't love it so much when you see how hard it is to convince me," Quinn said, totally missing the charged comment. "Come on, show me some proof."

CHAPTER 35

MAERK RAN the checklist so The *Swan of the Night* could launch. With Petrov expediting their departure, they would bypass Daravoo Prime station. Their "cargo" was time sensitive, and Petrov didn't want them to be late.

"When they wake up, the boys get a little—" Kertor Lima broke off and turned to Svenka Saul with a questioning look.

"Rambunctious," Saul said. "You don't want that here."

Lima nodded. "This ship is too small for a rambunctious Russo party. We need to get dirtside before they wake."

The two enforcers had made themselves at home on the *Swan*, taking over the two empty cabins above the living space. Saul had made a disappointed face when she saw the narrow bunks, but Lima insisted she would be fine. "Besides, I'm senior, so if we kick them out of the big cabin, it's mine. You'd still be in a little bunk."

Liz started to object, but Maerk kicked her shin. She glared.

Once they'd stowed their things, the four of them made their way to the cockpit.

"There's no jump seat." Maerk waved his arm around the small space.

"We'll take turns," Lima said. "We both have rudimentary piloting skills. You and Saul can ride in the lounge while we launch."

Liz crossed her arms. "Rudimentary? I am not flying with a beginner in the right chair! This ship is old and cranky. I need someone who can nurse her through her tantrums, not an enforcer with a few hours on a simulator!"

Lima pushed her toward the pilot's seat. "This is how it works. You fly. I sit here. Don't crash."

Liz's nostrils flared and her eyes narrowed. "This is my ship. My rules. If you want to fly with me, you follow them. I don't give a *futz* who you are or what you think you know. And don't wave the blaster at me. If you shoot me, who's going to fly your sorry ass to Lunesco?"

Saul coughed. "She's got you there, boss."

Lima growled. "Fine. You fly. He co-pilots. But there's no chatter with your friends. Disable the comms."

"Have you ever flown before? Ever?" Liz flung out her hands. "Comms are kind of important."

"Look." Maerk stepped between them before Liz started throwing things. "I'll connect the comms to the intercom, so you can hear all our interactions back in the lounge. It won't be very interesting."

"I don't care about interesting," Lima said. "I care about control. Don't tell anyone about your cargo. That's all." He shrugged.

"We can do that." Maerk climbed between the front seats and swiped up a screen. "See, here are the external comm channels. I'm linking them to the intercom, so any time I toggle this on, you'll hear what we say."

"Why should he trust you?" Saul demanded.

"We want to get you guys to your destination, so we get paid," Maerk said. "We don't want to cause any trouble. We certainly don't want to have the Russosken breathing down our necks for the rest of our lives. It's in our best interest to get you to Lunesco and get the hell out of there."

Lima stared at Maerk for a few seconds, then nodded. "Works for me. We'll be right back here." He jerked his head at Saul and waited for her to precede him to the lounge. "Remember, we're listening."

Liz flipped a rude gesture at this back.

Lima chuckled and closed the hatch behind him.

Maerk met Liz's eyes. "He saw that," he mouthed. His eyes ranged around the cockpit, looking for the cam Lima must have planted.

"Probably that too," Liz said aloud as she rolled her eyes. "Preparing to depart. Strap in, folks."

THE *SWAN* WOVE through the asteroid belt at a much slower speed than Dareen had used. "No point in risking our necks," Liz said. "We aren't in that much of a hurry."

"Don't take too long," Lima called through the open intercom channel. "The boys—"

"Yeah, they get rambunctious," Liz cut him off. "We know. We'll get to Lunesco with plenty of time to spare. But I'm the pilot, and I'm not risking my ship. This ain't the Kessel run."

Maerk grinned. He'd taught her that one.

They jumped on schedule, sliding into the Lunesco System at the prescribed entry point. "Jump complete," Liz said. "Report."

Maerk checked his screens. "All systems nominal,"

"We're good back here," Lima's voice came through the speakers. "Saul's going back to check on the cargo." The hatch opened, and Lima strolled into the cockpit. "Why don't you two come back here for a little chat. Set the course and let's go."

"Fine," Liz said. "Give me a minute. Where do you want us to land, anyway?"

"Plenty of time for that," Lima said. "I'll give you coordinates when we get closer."

"Whatever. I'll use the main landing field for now." Liz swiped and flicked through the screens before her. With a flourish and a thunk, she tapped the "engage" button. "Locked in. We'll be there in three days." She stood and stretched.

Maerk unstrapped and followed Liz to the lounge. "Can we make this quick? It's been a long day, and we're both wiped. I need a shower and a nap."

Lima pulled out a chair at the large table. "This shouldn't take long. Please, have a seat."

Liz walked around him and chose a seat at the far side of the table. Maerk stood behind her, one hand on the back of her chair.

With a shrug, Lima sat in the chair he'd offered. "I want to make sure we're on the same page. You will deliver us, and the cargo, to the location we specify. You will remain on the ground until we give you clearance to leave. We will likely require transportation back to Daravoo."

"That was not in the original contract!" Liz spluttered. "I have no intention of returning to Daravoo! We have other commitments."

"Change them," Lima said. "You work for Petrov now."

"I agreed to one contract—one transport." Liz leaned forward, glaring. "As soon as I get you off my ship, we're done."

"I'm afraid that's not how it works."

Maerk's eyes darted around the room, looking for a weapon. The thugs had insisted they stow theirs in the locker by the airlock. He should have kept one on his body. He was not cut out for this pirate lifestyle!

A movement caught Maerk's eye. Liz's hand moved slowly from her lap toward her boot. She hadn't returned her mini blaster to the rack when they arrived. Luckily, their store of weapons was meager, so the empty slot had been one of many. But using a mini blaster on a fully-armored enforcer was a recipe for disaster. He slid his hand forward and bumped his fingers against Liz's shoulder. Her hand stopped moving.

"Hold is secure," Saul reported from the hatch behind them. Maerk froze.

"Good." Lima nodded at Saul. "I'm making sure our new crew

know their duties." He turned to Liz and Maerk. "You will stay out of the cargo hold. That space is off limits."

"Wha—" Liz started.

Maerk gripped her shoulder.

"You will confine yourselves to this room, the bunk above, and the cockpit," Lima continued, not acknowledging Liz's outburst. "You will stand alternating watches. If anyone hails us, you will make sure either Lima or I are able to monitor the discussion."

Under his hand, Liz's already-tense shoulder hardened into rock. "Understood," he muttered.

Lima smiled and pushed back his chair. "Wonderful. I'm getting a snack. Anyone want anything?"

Maerk ground his teeth as Lima started opening cupboards, pawing through their stores. At Liz's low growl, his fingers bit into her shoulder. She remained frozen in place.

"I'll take something," Saul said.

Lima held up two packaged meals, one with a red stripe and one with blue. "Chili mac or beef stew?"

"Chili mac, of course," Saul said.

Lima nodded and put the blue package back. "When you're right, you're right." He tossed the packet to her and grabbed another red. "Nothing for you two?" he asked.

Liz growled again, deep in her throat.

"We'll get something later," Maerk said. "I'll keep an eye on the cockpit. Why don't you grab a shower and get some sleep, Liz?"

Liz tore her eyes away from Lima and glanced up at Maerk. Without a word, she shoved away from the table and stalked toward the step at the rear. Halfway there, she changed directions, stomping up to Lima. She ripped the unopened meal package from his hand. Then she climbed up on the bench, pulled down the ladder, and disappeared into the crew space.

"I wonder what's eating her," Saul asked with a smirk.

Maerk ground his teeth, his jaw throbbing from the pressure, and headed to the cockpit.

CHAPTER 36

QUINN SAT WITH TONY, Francine, and End in the cargo hold of the *Screaming Eagle*. The boy had thrown down a rug, blown up a couple of air chairs, and unfolded a table so they had a comfortable meeting space. It looked like the rec room in a frat house to Quinn.

"This stuff doesn't take much space, but it's handy for long waits." End settled into one of the bubble chairs. "There isn't enough room for all four of us in the bunk."

"In the bunk?" Quinn raised a brow at Francine.

"We were playing *Infernal Galaxy*." End made shooting motions. "Me and Francine."

"Incoming message." Francine looked as if she wished End hadn't said anything. "It's from Lou."

"You play *Infernal Galaxy*?" Quinn couldn't resist teasing the younger woman. "Lucas loves that."

"Only when there's nothing better to do," Francine muttered.

Tony tapped Francine's shoulder then pointed at the screen above the hatch to the cockpit. "Put the message on the big screen."

Lou's lined face appeared. She looked and sounded tired. "We received an encrypted message from Liz. They're in-system. They are under constant monitoring by Russosken enforcers. They tried to take out the observers but were unsuccessful. Their cargo hold contains a pod with twenty Russosken *soldaty* in stasis who are scheduled to wake when the ship reaches Lunesco. Another ship jumped in behind Liz and Maerk. This has been identified as the *Torment of Rederine*, an MPV out of Fortescu. Liz says this ship is carrying another pod of *soldaty*. Both ships will reach Lunesco in approximately thirty hours."

"If they're being monitored, how'd they send that much information?" Quinn asked.

"Code," End said. "An encrypted text file sent on the sly. We do it all the time. Russosken enforcers are no match for my dad."

"No, but if they catch him, he's dead," Francine said in alarm.

"Dead?" End's voice cracked.

Tony gripped the boy's shoulder. "What's the comm delay to the *Peregrine*?"

"Currently, it's about ten minutes, but they're getting closer." End took a deep breath, trying to steady his voice. "They'll be close enough to launch a shuttle soon."

"Are you alright?" She shot an admonishing glare at Francine. The younger woman made a face.

"I'm fine," End lied. "Do you want to send a message back?"

"No," Tony said. "When they get closer, we'll call. For now, let's come up with some scenarios. How do we mitigate the potential problem?"

"We could take out that other ship—the Torment." Francine tapped an elegant fingernail on her plastic chair. "Use Doug's orbit busters before they can land."

"It would be better if we don't blast civilian shippers out of the sky." Tony paced across the hold and turned. "Fortescu is one of the worlds Amanda had been working on. If we kill one of their merchants, they'll be less likely to throw in with us."

Francine looked at Tony, then at Quinn. "And by 'us,' who do you mean? Are you on board now?"

Quinn raised her chin. "Yes." It came out too loud. She wrinkled her nose and tried again. "Sorry. Yes, I am. Tony showed me the mess the Federation is in. I'm finally in. We need to do this." She shrugged. "I guess that makes me a traitor, for real."

Tony put a hand on her shoulder. "You aren't betraying the people of the Federation. You're freeing them from the leadership that has already betrayed them."

"To-*may*-to, to-*mah*-to," Francine said. "I'm glad we have that settled."

"You know the Russosken is tied to the Federation?" Quinn asked.

"Why do you think I'm willing to work against them?" Francine shuddered. "They both need to go down."

"Fantastic, we're starting a revolution!' End whooped and made shooting motions again. "Just like in Freedom Call Seven!"

"It's nothing like Freedom Call Seven," Tony said repressively. "In a real revolution, you don't get to respawn if you die."

"I know." End dropped back in his chair.

"Let's get back on task. What are we going to do about these two ships?" Francine asked. "We could get Liz and Maerk to land here instead of the regular landing strip and have some of Harim's guys ready to take them down."

"That's probably a good start." Tony paced the other direction. "But don't forget they have armed Russosken enforcers watching everything. And we have no way to get the *Torment's* crew on our side. We're going to have to be ready to take them all down when they land."

"There's only twenty of them," End said.

"If everyone on Lunesco were armed, then 'only twenty' wouldn't be as big a deal," Tony said. "Unfortunately, that isn't the case."

"And these are trained Russosken soldiers," Francine said. "If you haven't seen them, you won't believe how efficient and coldblooded they can be."

"We heard the story of their last visit here," Quinn said.

End looked from one adult to the next, eyes wide. "What happened."

"They landed at the field, mowed down the local protection force, burned everything in their path, and then rounded up the townspeople. They killed about ten percent of the population." Tony rubbed a hand over his face. "We need to stop them before any of that happens this time." He turned toward the hatch. "Let's get back to Doug's place. You two want to help train the ground force?"

"Teach a bunch of farmers how to use advanced weapons so they can get mowed down by my distant relatives?" Francine followed Tony to the airlock. "Who wouldn't want to do that?"

Quinn snorted. "I'm sure you can come up with some way to defeat them. You've got the most devious mind I've ever met."

Francine smirked. "Devious is my middle name."

They exited the shuttle. "What's the deal with these vines?" End jumped off the ship's extended step and batted at the leaves hanging above his head. "There's nothing when we land, then this stuff grows around the shuttle after we park." A fringe of sugar vine hung from the cliff wall, leaves and tendrils reaching toward the shuttle in a rippling curtain.

"It's attracted to humans." Quinn fingered one of the meter-long leaves.

"That could get ugly." Francine squinted at the plants. "I mean, it identifies our location. If those *soldaty* land here, they're going to notice there's only one patch of vines. Even if they don't know why, they're going to look closer. It's weird."

"I wonder if that's why they burned everything last time?" Quinn ran a finger along the fuzzy upper side of one of the lower leaves. It felt like velvet. "It freaked them out, so they burned it down. I wish there was a way to take advantage of that."

"Move the shuttle again." Tony turned and pointed across the dry lakebed. "Over there, where there's no cliff. Quinn and I are headed back to Doug's place. You two follow as soon as you park it. The vines won't have time to grow."

"Yes, sir." End flapped his hand above his eyebrows.

Tony rolled his eyes. "That was the worst salute I've ever seen."

"I thought that was how Commonwealth soldiers did it." Quinn bit back a grin. She imitated End. "Goofy."

"It's only goofy if you do it wrong," Tony said blandly. "We'll see you back at the headquarters."

Francine and End both did the sloppy salute, then dissolved into giggles.

"Children," Tony muttered.

Quinn felt a pang of homesickness for her own children. Soon, she told herself. First, they'd kick the Russosken off this rock and make it safer for all the children.

QUINN STOOD with Francine and Auntie B, halfway up the first leg of Doug's zig-zag driveway, staring down at the gaggles of people. A mass of Lunesco citizens stood below her, chatting and mingling. Someone had brought jugs and bags, and they happily passed food and drinks around the group.

"This is your local militia?" Francine waved her arm to indicate the rag-tag collection.

"Yup," Auntie B said. "We train every month."

"To do what? Hold a coffee klatch?" Francine mimed drinking from a mug. "They don't look very formidable."

"They aren't pros, but they do pretty good for amateurs. And Auntie B knows what she's doing." Doug put his fingers in his mouth and an ear-piercing whistle cut through the noise. "Form up!"

The crowd spread out into a rough rectangle, people spacing themselves surprisingly evenly over the newly-raked ground. The food and beverages got passed to the edge of the group and placed against the foot of the cliff.

"Warm up, pair off, and spar!" Auntie B called.

The ranks of Lunescans began a series of jumping jacks.

"Spar?" Francine frowned. "Like hand-to-hand combat? That's not going to be very helpful against armed and armored *soldaty*."

"It's the best we can do," Auntie B said. "We don't have access to a lot of weapons, so I taught them unarmed combat. Some of them are good enough to take out your Russosken."

"If they get close enough. But they aren't going to let you get close." Francine pointed at the far wall of the chasm, then mimed firing a weapon. "They're going to come down that cliff-face using gravity belts, firing on automatic. Blasters and flame throwers. And this place is wide open. Nowhere to hide."

"We aren't going to let them get this close." Auntie B crossed her arms. "Last time they came, we weren't prepared. This time, we know what to expect. They'll land at the shuttle field, and we'll take them out as they exit the ship. The ones that get past, we'll take out when they get to the Homestead. Anyone left over, we can pick off from that ledge." She pointed to a narrow ledge about a meter below the lip of the chasm. Workers, barely visible at this distance, strung safety cables between anchors in the stone wall.

"That's great, if they land at the shuttle field," Francine said. "What if they don't? They could land on the dry lakebed. Or out on the plains."

"We're working on that," Tony said as he strode up. "Quinn has rigged some phony beacons that will make the dry lakebed look like a runway. We think we can convince one of the ships to land there. The other we'll send to the regular landing field. Our primary advantage is numbers, so splitting them up will help."

"Auntie B has some tricks up her sleeve." Doug smirked.

Francine looked at the older woman skeptically. "Really? You?"

Doug's grin widened and his eyes closed halfway. "She's got a bit of practical experience."

"Thirty-four years of practical experience," Auntie B said. "I was commander of the One Ninety-Eighth during the Epsiliis Incursion."

Francine's eyes widened. "You're General Beatrix LaGama?"

The old woman's lips quirked in a tiny smile, but she didn't

KRIMSON SPARK

respond. Quinn hid her own smile—she'd figured out Auntie B's secret identity days ago. Of course, she'd had more interactions with the legend.

"Damn." Francine bowed respectfully. "I retract my previous comments. The Russosken are going to wish they'd never landed here."

"Speaking of landing, Dareen should be down in about twenty minutes," Quinn said. "I'm going to meet her at the field. Can you come with me, Francine?"

"I guess. You don't want me to stay here and babysit the computers?"

Quinn shook her head. "I showed Doug and Harim how to run the defense systems. They're built for ease of use—pretty hard to screw up once you've got access. That's the big thing. If the Russosken know how to override my override, we're toast."

Amanda, Maarteen, and Pete joined the group. "There's no way the Federation would trust them with that information," Amanda said. "Pete and I are going to take a team up to the Homestead to see if we can lay in some more delaying tactics."

Auntie B nodded. "Take C Company." She pointed to a group on the far edge of the field. "They're best with boobytraps."

"Can we catch a ride with you?" Quinn asked. "We're headed to the shuttle field."

"Sure," Pete replied. "Jessian is bringing the flatbed. Plenty of room."

They climbed down the steep path and past the groups of sparring civilians. Francine nodded as they passed a woman throwing her opponents over her shoulder in quick succession. "She's good."

Amanda flicked a glance at the woman. "I could take her."

Francine looked the Federation agent up and down. "You think?"

Amanda showed her teeth in a feral grin. "I could take you, too."

Francine held up her hands. "No argument there. I haven't done any hand-to-hand in over a year."

Quinn studied Francine. She had always thought of the willowy blonde as more brains than brawn. "You studied hand-to-hand?"

"Had to," Francine said shortly. "Standard training in the family."

Quinn shot a look at Pete and Amanda, but the pair didn't seem interested in Francine's capabilities.

The truck rumbled over the bridge and stopped beside the sparring troops. Pete and Amanda climbed into the cab with Jessian. Quinn and Francine claimed seats on the flatbed against the cab, and the members of C Company joined them a few minutes later, sprawling across the bed of the truck. Another jug appeared and passed from hand to hand.

When it reached her, Quinn sniffed the earthenware vessel. Cold water laced with tart fruit and warm spices. She downed a gulp, then offered it to Francine. The blonde sipped then handed it on. The truck rumbled across the valley and began to crawl up the switchbacks of the town.

"Will you teach me?" Quinn asked as they rounded the second turn.

Francine's head swiveled from the view to her companion. "Teach you what?"

"Hand-to-hand," Quinn said. "I learned the basics a million years ago, but I want to get better. I want to be able to defend myself."

Francine looked away. "Sure. If Lou lets me stay."

On impulse, Quinn reached out and squeezed Francine's hand. Francine's lips twitched in a pleased little grin that disappeared as quickly as it arrived.

The truck rumbled over the lip of the valley. Wind whipped across the plains as the vehicle accelerated and plowed along the ruler-straight road toward the Homestead. The women leaned against the shelter of the truck's cab.

"What do you think about Amanda?" Francine asked quietly.

"I haven't." Quinn leaned closer to Francine, so their conversation wouldn't be overheard by the others. "What about her?"

"She's making a play for Tony," Francine said. "And she seems weirdly competent for a tax inspector. I mean in non-tax ways."

"Making a play for Tony?" Quinn repeated. She thought about the last few days. Except for their planning meetings, and the little trip out to the shuttle, she hadn't seen much of Tony. Now that she thought about it, Amanda had been nearby almost every time she'd seen him. "Is he— I don't think he's interested in her. She's not his type."

"You never know," Francine said. "She's hot. He's cute."

"But he's never—" Quinn frowned. "He's never been interested in anyone. For as long as I've known him."

"Didn't that seem kind of odd?" Francine asked.

Quinn shrugged. "Not at the time, but now that you mention it…"

"I can't believe you don't know," Francine said.

"Know what?" Quinn asked.

Francine stared at her. "He's in love with you, idiot. How can you not know that?"

CHAPTER 37

"WHAT?!" Quinn stared at Francine. Tony couldn't be in love with her. They were friends. Had been for over a decade.

The truck stopped. "Everyone out for the Homestead!" someone yelled. Quinn hardly noticed as the men and women around them gathered their gear and scrambled off the truck.

A small, mysterious smile played on Francine's lips, but she didn't answer.

Jessian tapped on the window in the rear panel of the cab then opened the glass. "You two want to come up front? It's quieter. And less dusty."

Francine grinned and hopped down from the truck bed. Eyes narrowed in frustration, Quinn slipped off behind her. As she hit the ground, the wind slammed into her, sending her staggering against the vehicle. Francine ripped the door open and scrambled inside, scooting across the wide seat to make room.

With the door shut, the buffeting noise died to a tolerable rumble.

"Hold on to your hats. I'm going to hit the vacuum." Jessian pressed a button. The air handlers buzzed, sucking the extra dust off their clothes, the seat, dash, and floor. "You brought in a lot of dirt!"

"If you're planning on expanding your business," Francine said, "you might want to invest in a bus rather than a flatbed. A bus with an airlock."

Jessian laughed, then sobered. "I have an idea this little skirmish might put an end to my cab-driving days. If we manage to kick out both the Federation and their Russosken guard dogs, there won't be a lot of traffic landing."

"Maybe not at first," Francine said. "But other fringe traders will still come. And maybe Commonwealth. And if Amanda and Pete are correct, there should be a whole lot more free worlds in the next few years. You just have to hang on until then."

"Besides, you're a resourceful woman," Quinn said. "I'm sure you'll come up with other options. If this thing works, Lunesco is going to need a team to monitor the skies full time."

"Watching the computers in Doug's secret room?" Jessian shook her head. "Doesn't sound like much fun. But folks'll need a way to get there. Hmm."

They reached the small building at the side of the shuttle field and Jessian parked the truck. "Do you want me to wait?"

"No, Auntie B might need you," Quinn reached for the door handle. "And I'm not sure how long we'll be. I'll call you if we need another ride." She shoved the door open and hopped down. "Thanks!"

Jessian gave her a thumbs-up. Francine slid across the seat and landed gracefully beside Quinn. She slammed the truck door, and they hurried into the tiny building.

The lobby looked exactly as Quinn remembered from their arrival. She wasn't sure why she expected it to be different—maybe because so many of her ideas had changed over the last few days.

"It's hard to imagine the locals are worried about *less* traffic to their planet." Francine gazed around the utilitarian room. "Less doesn't seem possible."

"They're pretty self-sufficient, so they should be fine." Quinn willed herself to believe it was true. She glanced at the rigid seats bolted to the wall, then crossed to the inner door and knocked against it. "We're expecting a friend to arrive. Can we come through?"

The door clicked and swung ajar. Quinn pushed through, Francine on her heels. They stepped into the empty front room.

"Hey, Quinn." A young man sat inside the customs booth, flicking through his comtab.

Quinn recognized him with surprise. "Pender! I thought you worked at the Homestead."

"Only when we get visitors. Amanda, Pete, and Sebi moved to the valley, so there's no reason to be there. They put me out here instead. Who's your friend? I thought I'd met everyone."

"This is Francine." Quinn grabbed Francine's arm and pulled her to the desk. "You aren't expected to roll out the red carpet for the incoming Russosken?"

"I haven't received any *official* word of their arrival, so I've got no way of knowing if they'll need rooms." Pender lifted both hands, palms out. "Besides, I wanted to stay out of the way of the boobytrap team. Where are you from, Francine? I like to guess visitors' planet of origin, and I'm coming up blank on you. But you look familiar."

"My family moved around a lot," Francine said. "I lived on a dozen different planets before I went off to college."

Pender snapped his fingers and his eyes narrowed. "I got it. I was just looking at these...you look like them." He swiped his comtab and held it up. A picture labeled "Russosken Royalty?" filled the screen.

Francine's face went a little paler, but she laughed. "That's why I dyed my hair this color." She patted her blonde waves. "Nasty as they are, you have to admit the Russosken are attractive."

"Why are you looking them up, anyway?" Quinn took the comtab and squinted at it. She glanced at Francine and zoomed in. "You do look a lot like them."

"I wanted to see who we're up against," Pender said.

"I don't think the *soldaty* coming in the freezer case look anything like these socialites." Francine rolled her eyes. "This is the 'royal family' of the Russosken." She made air quotes with her fingers. "Beautiful but useless socialites. Not who we're expecting."

"Freezer case?" Pender laughed. "That's pretty funny. I'm going to use that."

Quinn swiped through a few more pictures, then typed in a search. She held up the device. "This is what we're expecting."

The picture showed bulky soldiers in faceless helmets. Black armor covered their bodies, with a broad red stripe running diagonally across the chest. The two in the front held blaster rifles with long-distance targeting computers, and the two in the back pushed a rocket launcher on a float panel.

"Yikes!" Pender took his comtab back. "I am not leaving the window open to greet them." He flicked a control inside his booth and a heavy metal panel rolled slowly down over the glass. He stopped it at once, so it covered only the top few centimeters of his window. "Reinforced blast shield. It won't stop that rocket launcher, but it should be good against the blasters."

"I don't think they'll even bother coming inside." Quinn jutted a thumb toward the town. "They'll roll off the ship and head for the Homestead. At least, that's what we hope."

"Maybe I'll close up early, then. When are they landing?"

"Tonight, probably."

Pender flicked the controls and the blast shield started moving again. He ducked to talk to them beneath the closing panel. "I'm headed back to the Homestead. You want a ride?"

"No, we're good," Quinn said.

"Bye!" The panel clanged shut, and something clicked and jangled behind it.

Quinn swung around and pinned a glare on Francine. "You're not just Russosken. You're Russosken royalty!" She did the same air quotes Francine had used earlier.

"Why do you think I ran away?"

"You aren't even going to try denying it?"

"No point." Francine shrugged fatalistically. "Thanks for

distracting him, by the way. I thought I'd managed to purge all the pictures on the net, but you can't get everything."

"You weren't really identifiable in that shot," Quinn said. "It was mostly a guess on my part. Does Lou know?"

"I haven't told her. But I can't believe she doesn't know. Tony does."

"That's what you told him back on Hadriana," Quinn said slowly. "When he said we should trust you but wouldn't say why."

Francine nodded.

"I'm not sure why that information would make him trust you, though." Quinn threw herself down into one of the hard waiting room chairs.

"It gave him leverage over me." Francine perched on the chair next to her. "He could sell me out if I double-crossed him. As you can imagine, *nachal'nik* will pay to get me back. A lot. Plus, Tony has a soft spot for anyone who bucks their family. He remembers what it's like."

"I suppose so," Quinn smiled a little. Tony definitely had a soft spot for the underdog, which both she and Francine were. Which reminded her... "Why did you say he's in love with me? We're friends. We have been for a long time. Since Lucas was a baby."

Francine rolled her eyes. "It's so obvious. Everything he does is for you. I can't believe you haven't seen that."

Quinn opened her mouth to disagree, then closed it. Tony had risked everything for her. Many times. Starting with the rescue from Sumpter—he could have left them behind and gone back to the Commonwealth. Then the prison break. The trip to Hadriana to retrieve her children. Even his desire for revenge on Andretti. Tony didn't usually do revenge.

But that had been a sham. The whole "taking down Andretti" scheme had been a cover for his desire to spark a revolution here on Lunesco. He'd said so himself. Maybe Francine didn't know as much as she thought she did.

Quinn wrinkled her nose. "He's using me to start a war. I don't think that's love."

"When you put it that way—" Francine rolled her eyes again. "You're wrong. He's starting the war *for* you, not despite you. Not many guys would start a war for their gal. That's some big-league, blockbuster-cinema, classic-literature romance."

Quinn laughed and shook her head. "*Cheesy* big-budget romance."

But the thought kept coming back. What if it were true?

CHAPTER 38

DAREEN LANDED the *Fluffy Kitten* at the main Lunesco field. She ignored the automated lights that directed her to a parking space at the end of the ramp and rolled to a stop in front of the only building in sight. Then she ran the "idle for fast departure" procedures as quickly as possible.

Her comtab buzzed. Local call, so it must be Tony or Quinn. Or maybe Francine or End? She swiped the answer button. "Dareen here."

The noise-canceling effect couldn't block out the rush of wind behind Quinn's voice. "Dareen, it's Quinn! Can you let us in? We're outside your airlock."

"I'll pop the lock. But I'm going to need help unloading." She slapped the disconnect, popped the hatch, and went back to her checklist.

By the time they'd cycled through, she'd finished her work. The engines were off, but she could be ready for launch with about thirty seconds' notice. It didn't pay to be stuck dirtside with hostiles inbound. She climbed out of the pilot's seat and met them at the inner hatch. "Quinn! Francine!"

After hugs all around, Quinn asked, "What do we need to unload?"

Dareen grinned. "You got a truck? Come on, I'll show you." She led the way to the cargo hold. A dozen two-meter crates lay secured to the floor. "I brought you some surprises."

"Those are PK-214s!" Francine crossed the hold to read the label on one of the crates. "Where did you get those?"

"PK-214s?" Quinn asked.

"Armor fryers." Francine poked Quinn's arm and made a staticky noise. "Kind of souped-up tasers. Sizzlers. They fire a magnetic projectile that attaches to armor and shorts it out. It won't *stop* well-trained *soldaty*, but it damages their comms, navigation, that kind of thing. Not effective against the newest armor, but I don't think Petrov has the latest models. And if he did, I doubt he'd waste it on Lunesco. They save that stuff for operations where they expect resistance."

"How much do you know about Russosken armor?" Quinn asked.

Francine shrugged. "I don't know much more than the next person."

Dareen laughed. "Uh, yeah, ya do. I'm the next person, and I don't know anything about it."

"Are you looking for something specific?" Francine tapped her fingers on the crate. "I definitely don't have the specs memorized or anything like that. You'll find more on the net than I can tell you."

"Maybe." Quinn pulled her comtab out. "We need to make sure we're using every advantage we can find. In the meantime, I'm going to let Auntie B know about this."

While the older woman made her call, Francine and Dareen unlatched the tie-downs holding the cargo in place. "How's End?" Dareen tried to sound casual.

"He's fine." Francine grimaced. "Probably playing *Evil Zombie 4000* in the shuttle."

Dareen shook her head. "He plays too many games. Shouldn't he be helping you with this little operation?"

"Don't get me wrong." Francine held up a hand. "He's doing his part. But he seems to think this whole thing is a game. Typical teenaged immortality delusion, I guess."

"Don't let him hear you say he's a teen," Dareen pressed her lips together. "You'd think it was the ultimate insult, now that he's twenty."

"Yeah, we had that discussion." Francine leaned down to unsnap a latch. "And no offense. You don't seem to have the same indestructibility thing."

"I'm a girl," Dareen said. "We grow up faster."

Francine nodded. "Amen, sister."

"Jessian is coming with Auntie B and some of the hand-to-hand experts." Quinn crossed the hold, tucking her comtab into her pocket. "She said to plan on leaving half of the crates here. They'll provide cover and give our side a chance to take out the enemy as they leave the ship. The rest we'll split between the Homestead and the town."

"What about the second landing field?" Francine asked. "I thought we were going to get Liz and Maerk to land there."

"We are. But they have other plans for that." Quinn shrugged. "They didn't say what. I guess I don't have the need to know. Where did you get these things, anyway?"

"Lou picked them up on Iraca Five," Dareen said. "While Stene and I were on Daravoo. Weapons always sell."

By the back ramp, Francine pointed at the screen showing the outside cams. "Jessian's here. Wait until she's in place before you open the loading ramp. The dust and wind out there is nasty."

The truck backed into place behind the ship, and Dareen hit the unlock sequence. Wind poured in through the gap as soon as the ramp began to lower. She ran forward and came back with some goggles which she handed out to the others.

With a quizzical look at the eye gear, Francine pulled the strap over her head. "Are these standard issue on your shuttles? End didn't have any."

"That's because End doesn't do his homework." Dareen snapped the strap over her head. "I always check the weather before I leave the house."

"Since you've never lived in a house, that must be a quote." Quinn pulled on the goggles. "Thanks, this will help a lot."

The ramp rotated into place, touching down on the flatbed. A gaggle of Lunescans swarmed into the ship and started moving boxes. Auntie B climbed down from the cab and walked around to the back.

Quinn jumped down to greet her, so Dareen followed suit, leaving Francine to supervise the unloading.

"Auntie B, this is Dareen," Quinn said. "She's Tony's cousin. She's got these— What did you call them, Dar?"

"Francine said they're armor fryers."

The old woman looked her up and down, making Dareen squirm inside. She felt like she was being measured. She lifted her chin. "We have some other gear for End, too. Can you transport it for us?"

"We'll get it to him." Auntie B turned to watch the unloading.

"We can take it for you," Quinn told Dareen. "Francine is headed back to the other shuttle when we're done here. I assume you're going back upstairs?"

"I think Gramma is trying to get on Mom's good side," Dareen said. "She told me to drop this stuff and get back pronto. She's trying to keep me out of trouble. But I want to stay and help."

Quinn shook her head. "You go back up to the ship. Parents need to know their kids are safe."

"What about End?" Dareen demanded. "He's not even a year older than me. Why does he get to help? It better not be because he's a boy. That excuse might fly in the Federation, but we Commonwealth women don't take that."

"I think your grandmother sent him down here to keep him out of the way. And she hasn't been able to make him go back up. Plus, he has Francine watching him." Quinn held up her hands. "If it were up to me, you'd both be back in orbit, and Francine, too. In fact, once we get that equipment set up, you're all headed upstairs. Let's get End's stuff." She climbed onto the ramp.

Dareen glared after Quinn. Normally, she liked the older woman, but sometimes, when she treated Dareen like a child, it was more than she could take. Quinn acted like she and eight-year-old Ellianne were peers. She shook her head. Time to get back to work and show them how mature she could be.

With the shuttle unloaded, Jessian climbed into the truck's cab. "Anyone want a ride back to base?" The team of experts she'd brought had collected their share of the crates and disappeared into the small building.

Auntie B climbed back into the cab while Quinn and Francine scrambled for a place to sit among the remaining crates. "Fly safely, Dareen!" Quinn called. "Give my kids a hug. We'll see you soon."

Dareen took a deep breath, pushing the disappointment down. She smiled and waved, hoping they couldn't tell how unhappy she was.

"DAREEN'S PISSED," Francine said as the truck pulled away from the shuttle field.

"What? Why?" Quinn asked. She twisted around, trying to find a less lumpy part of the crate to lean against. "She didn't look angry."

"Wow, you're pretty clueless for a mom," the blonde said. "That was the phoniest smile I've seen in a long time. I get it. She wants to be a part of this. It seems exciting and fun from her side."

"Fighting off Russosken soldiers using inferior weapons seems fun?"

"We don't know that their weapons are inferior." Francine swallowed a snort of laughter.

"I wasn't talking about *their* weapons," Quinn retorted.

A yowl cut through the roar of the wind. From behind one of the crates, a nose peeked out. Followed by the rest of a caat. "Sassy!" Quinn stared. "What are you doing here?"

Francine reached out to scratch the caat's head. "She must have come with Dareen. I wonder if they know she's here."

Quinn stared at the caat. "Just what I needed. One more thing to keep track of. You are going to be the death of me, Sassy."

"I'll take her to the other shuttle." Francine gathered the caat into her lap.

"If she lets you," Quinn muttered. Ignoring the cat, she turned back to Francine. "You know what to do with the stuff Dareen brought down?"

"Of course. This won't be my first combat diversion."

"Really?" Quinn asked. "It's my first one."

Francine pointed at Quinn. "Communications officer." She pointed at herself. "Russosken. Different."

Quinn laughed. "When we're done with this mission, I want to hear all about that royalty thing. And don't forget, you promised to teach me to defend myself."

Francine reached out a hand, her face serious. "You have my word. And it's worth way more than the average Russosken princess's."

CHAPTER 39

THE DIM LIGHTING in the secret control room made it difficult to see faces, but easy to focus on the displays. Quinn glanced at the others, each intent on their own piece of the puzzle. Harim and Maarteen chatted quietly in the corner. Doug watched the orbital trackers. Amanda spoke quietly through her comtab to the leader of C Company, currently deployed to the Homestead.

Auntie B wasn't here—she sat in the living room, a portable unit beside her, so she could watch over the valley in real time. Quinn wasn't sure what she thought she could do better from that vantage point, since it was dark, but maybe she preferred the windows and fresh air.

A blip on her screen alerted her to activity. "We have an incoming ship! Transponder says it's the *Swan*, spiraling down."

"Lunesco Control, this is MPV delta-six-sigma-two-seven-yellow, the *Swan of the Night,* requesting permission to land." Liz's face appeared on the screen above Doug's head. Her voice sounded strained through the speakers.

"*Swan*, this is Lunesco." They hadn't bothered with a visual from Pender. "We have you on scope. We had some beacon damage in the last windstorm. I'm sending you an updated frequency list and revised control sequence."

"Roger, Lunesco, entering the revised control sequence now." Liz glanced at something off camera, then continued. "Flight plan plotted. Our ETA is ten minutes. *Swan* out." Her face froze, then the screen went black.

On Quinn's screen, a path lit up in blue dashes, showing the *Swan*'s trajectory. "They're on track for the field."

"Perfect," Doug said. "Now we wait for—"

"Lunesco Control, this is MPV four-eight-alpha-kilo-seven-tango, the *Torment of Rederine,* requesting permission to land." A man with pale, almost translucent skin and water-colored eyes appeared on screen.

"It's a busy night," Pender quipped. "If I'd known we had this many inbound tonight, I might not'a had that second beer."

Everyone in the control room groaned. "What is he doing?" Harim rubbed his hand over his head and gripped the back of his neck.

"You suggested him," Maarteen said. "Said he wouldn't crack under the pressure."

"Uh, sorry, didn't copy that, Lunesco." The *Torment* pilot scratched his beard.

"No problem, *Torment*," Pender said. "I see you on the scope. I'm sending an updated frequency list and revised control sequence. We had some damage last week."

"Roger, the revised files are uploading." The pilot stared down for a moment, then looked up at the camera, eyes narrowed. "Lunesco, this looks wrong. We've landed here before, and this sequence appears to be taking us off course."

"*Futz!*" Harim swore. "What did he do?"

"As I said, *Torment*, we've had some damage." Pender's voice sounded shaky. "Hold one, while I confirm the data." A series of clicks, followed by a panicked cry, "What do I do?"

"What coordinates did you give him, Pender?" Doug asked, his tone deep and calming.

"I sent him to the dry lakebed, like you said." Pender's frantic pitch rolled down a few steps. "I didn't know he'd been here before!"

"You were supposed to send the *Swan* to the dry lakebed, and the *Torment* to the regular field." Doug's tone was conversational, but Quinn thought she could see smoke coming out of his ears.

"The beer joke might have been a stroke of unwitting genius. Tell him to send the regular— Never mind, give me the mic." Amanda strode across the room and motioned for Doug to move. "Pender, tell them we have emergency construction at the regular landing field, so we're diverting inbound traffic to the alternate field. Sorry for the inconvenience. If we'd known you were coming, blah, blah, blah. Give 'em a bit of a guilt trip if you want."

"You got it, boss lady." Pender sounded jaunty again. Clicks snapped loudly in the speakers, then Pender said, "*Torment*, Lunesco. I have confirmed. The new data is correct. We've had to do some construction on the main field. We posted a bulletin on the beacon—you should have downloaded it when you jumped in."

Amanda glared at the console. "That is not what I said."

"Why can't he stay on script?" Harim wailed over the voices coming from the comm system. On screen, the *Torment*'s pilot flushed as he argued with Pender.

"You suggested him," Doug and Quinn said in chorus.

"I suggested him because he's good at improv, but I didn't expect him to go wild!"

"You didn't?" Maarteen smoothed his hair. "I'm not surprised at all."

"Hush." Doug flung out both arms. "We need to hear this."

"Thanks, *Torment*, I'll double-check the beacon," Pender was saying. "My cousin posts the bulletins, but sometimes he smokes the wacky tabacky, if you know what I mean."

The pilot froze.

Quinn and the others groaned.

"You still there, *Torment*?" Pender asked. "Your video is frozen."

"Can I speak to your supervisor?" *Torment* finally asked.

"Sure thing, *Torment*," Pender said cheerfully. "Lemme track him down. You might need to move into a parking orbit if you want to chat before you land, though. Last I heard, he was supposed to be on a drum retreat this week."

The pilot rubbed his face with both hands, muttering under his breath about yokels from the fringe. Finally, he looked up. "What kind of disaster are you running down there? When we were through here a few months ago, things weren't this *vertic*."

"It's low-transport season," Pender said. "We don't see a lot of traffic during the spring, so everyone takes their vacation. It's the only time they let me work here."

"I can see why," *Torment* grumbled. "We've input the data you sent and will land at the alternate field on our next pass. *Torment* out."

Amanda flicked the controls on the workstation. "Now contact the *Swan* and divert them to the regular landing field. We don't want them both in the same place."

STANDING on the lowered ramp of the *Screaming Eagle*, Francine stared into the night sky. "I think I can see them. Yes, that light is definitely moving. Captain Herlen, they're inbound."

"We're in place," the Company B commander replied via the comm link.

"I'm closing the ramp, End. Prepare to launch the drone." She stepped inside and hit the controls.

"Roger." End headed across the cargo bay to sync his comtab to the big screen. "I hope this works."

"Our part is easy." Francine flicked her comtab. "MPV four-eight-alpha-kilo-seven-tango, this is Lunesco Alternate. We see you on approach."

"Lunesco Alternate, *Torment*. I'm not getting video from you."

"Video is not available, *Torment*," Francine replied. "We don't get a lot of traffic in the spring, so the alternate field is barebones. The landing beacons function, though. Are you reading them?"

"Yes, we're reading them," *Torment* answered. "Who was the lunatic at the main field?"

"You must mean Pender." She laughed. "He likes to think he's a real ground control operator, but we only let him work the inactive runways. That's why he's over there tonight."

"Pretty shoddy way to run a planet," Torment grumbled.

"I know." Francine grinned and winked at End. "I try to elevate the standard, but it's an uphill battle. You're cleared to land, *Torment*."

"Roger, Lunesco. See you on the ground."

Francine hit the mute button. "No, you won't. Not if my friends out there have anything to say about it."

She hurried to the viewport at the rear of the shuttle and peered out. The *Torment's* lights grew brighter, and the roar of her badly-tuned engines rattled the *Eagle*. "Launch the drone, End."

"Taking it up." The view screen rotated as the drone launched.

The *Torment* rolled down the center of the impromptu landing lights, following the automated beacons Francine and End had installed a few hours earlier. The ship, about double the size of the *Eagle*, turned at the end, taxiing across the dusty plane. Then it stopped.

Francine slapped her comtab. "*Torment*, please proceed to your assigned parking place. The beacons will direct you." She increased the flash frequency on the landing lights. They blinked in series, forming an obvious road for the ship to follow.

"Negative, Lunesco," *Torment* said. "We'll unload here."

"We have another ship inbound." Francine tried to keep the tremor of fear out of her voice. "Please proceed to your assigned parking place."

"That ship is with us," *Torment* said. "They know what we're doing."

"I don't care if they know." Francine let her tone ratchet up—a rightfully angered ground controller. "This is my field, and I'm telling you to move your *vertic* ship!"

"Ooh, feisty." The pilot laughed. "Are you from Fortescu?"

"No," Francine said between gritted teeth. "But I know swear words from all over the galaxy. And if you don't move your *vertic crepin* piece of ship, I will come out there and move it for you!" She snapped off all the temporary lights except the ones leading to the parking place as she glared through the porthole, hoping Company B had time to redeploy.

The voice laughed again. "Come on out and play, honey." The signal cut out.

"They're unloading!" End toggled Company B's link.

"We see that," Herlen said. "Thanks for stalling. We're almost in place."

After a last glance out the porthole, Francine hurried to End's workstation near the internal hatch. The screen showed black, with random lights, both flashing and steady. "Do you have the night vision on?"

End grimaced and slapped a control. "I do now." The screen resolved to a monochromatic view of the airfield.

Francine smirked. Good thing she was here to babysit.

The *Torment* had lowered one of its external ramps, and several people moved up and down, carrying crates.

"Come on, Herlen," Francine muttered under her breath. "Get in there while they're unloading."

Laser fire lanced out of the darkness, hitting the two men on the ramp. They swung around and dropped behind their crates, peeking over to return fire. Flashes zapped from both sides.

"Keep moving, people," Herlen said to his team. "Fire and move. Stay under cover. Borlen, Arhigati, come around the other side and use those armor fryers."

"Roger, Captain," another voice said. "We're on the move."

"Can you see them?" Francine ran back to the porthole.

End shook his head. "The guys with the sizzlers are really good at hiding. I don't see— Hang on, there's one." He zoomed in on the *Torment*. A pair of Lunescans—Borlan and Arhigati, according to the IDs on screen—ran across the lakebed toward the rear of the ship. "Their pilot either doesn't care about the soldiers or he has crappy external cams on his ship. He should be able to see our guys there."

"If our guys were smart, they took down the cameras first," Francine said. "But that captain is getting paid to transport the troops, not to fight. That's the problem with hiring thugs."

"Hey, my parents aren't thugs!"

Francine ignored him.

Lasers flashed. Blaster fire and grunts provided an audio backdrop.

"Damn it!" Herlen yelled. "I told you to use cover! Oroto is down!"

"Jerlis is down, too," another voice moaned.

Arhigati crept around the *Torment*'s tail and took aim. Borlan fired half a second after her partner.

Two men crouched behind the ramp froze, their weapons aimed but not firing.

"Yes!" End pumped his fist.

"Wait!" Francine ran back and grabbed his arm. "Can you zoom in?"

"Sure." End slid a control bar, and the picture zoomed. The two crouched men started firing again.

"*Futz.*" Francine toggled the comtab. "Company B, they've got Mark Fives."

"Mark Five what?" Herlen asked.

"Newest Russosken armor," Francine said. "They have a series of fuse links. You'll have to hit each one several times with a sizzler before you burn out their armor. And even then, they'll still be able to move. Their electronics will be fried, but they're still formidable opponents."

"*Futz,*" Herlen said. "We're screwed!"

CHAPTER 40

LIZ FIRED HER REVERSE THRUSTERS, slowing the *Swan* to landing speed. She lined up on the runway beacons and double-checked her gear. A burly woman named Bykov sat in the co-pilot's chair, gripping the armrests. The chair creaked in protest.

"What's wrong?" Liz added a little wobble to the descent. "Don't like flying?"

"Don't like landing." Bykov breathed hard through gritted teeth. "Not when someone I don't trust is holding the stick. But don't try anything stupid. I know enough about landing to know if you're doing it right. And I can take you out and do it myself, if I need to."

"I'm sure you could."

After arriving in-system at Lunesco, she and Maerk had tried to take out the enforcers. Maerk's homemade sleep gas hadn't been powerful enough, and Saul had taken Maerk down. Lima had woken two additional soldaty early, and now they kept Liz under constant observation. She'd seen Maerk only once since then. He'd been alive, but badly battered.

The shuttle touched down, hurtling along the runway. Liz fired the reverse thrusters again and rode out the speed. They flashed past a small, lighted building, racing down the narrow path formed by blue, blinking lights.

At the far end, they slowed enough to turn. Liz pointed the nose at the little building. "Where do you want to park?"

"I got it from here," Bykov said.

"What?" Liz turned just in time to see Bykov's armored elbow slam into her nose. Pain exploded in her head, and everything went black.

"WHERE DO WE UNLOAD?" Bykov's voice came through the speakers in the lounge.

"Get us close to the building," Lima said. "We might need to neutralize the idiot in there. Did you take care of the pilot?"

"She won't cause us any trouble." Bykov snickered.

Fear gripped Maerk's lungs, squeezing them. His vision started to darken around the edges. What had they done to Liz? He took a deep breath, and his broken rib sawed at his chest. With a gasp, he pressed his ear against the floor, but couldn't hear anything else.

"Don't worry." Saul stood halfway up the ladder from the lounge, staring into the cubby hole where she'd imprisoned him. "She'll live. So will you. We need pilots."

Whimpering against the pain, Maerk tried to squirm deeper into the coffin-like shelf. Saul had beaten him senseless so she wouldn't need to watch him. He'd woken to pain, darkness, and the rough wood of his prison. If he and Liz got out of this alive, he would rip these cubbies out of the *Swan* with his bare hands and burn them.

So much for transporting a circus.

Saul laughed. "Maybe you learn? You wanna live, don't mess with the Russosken."

She reached down and ripped away the plant she'd nailed across the end. Grabbing the neck of his shirt, she hauled him out of the cubicle like a sack of broken parts. He groaned. She dumped him on the floor, then stepped back and pointed her blaster at him. "Move. Downstairs, now."

Maerk crawled to the ladder and slid down, falling the last two steps to land in a heap. Pain lanced through his chest, and he screamed. Saul grinned from the upper level and flexed her knees to jump. With a loud moan, he rolled away from the ladder. "Saint Margaret the Barefooted, protect us."

"Stop torturing the prisoner," Lima said. "Stick him in the med pod, and let's go. We have a mission to complete."

"The med pod?" Saul asked. "You gonna fix him up?"

"It locks from the outside. I don't want to kill him. We might need him later."

Someone grabbed him by the back of his collar again. He tried to get his feet under him, so the shirt wouldn't choke him, but he couldn't get his legs to work. Heavy boots thumped against the ship's deck as his captor dragged him across the lounge to the med pod in the corner. He was dropped, then lifted. Pain fogged his vision, and he gasped for air. Then there was silence.

TONY CROUCHED on the apron at the landing field, concealed behind a generator. The *Swan* had touched down as expected, but now pulled up close to the small airfield management building. Tony signaled to Kelen, his team leader. "Is someone inside to protect Pender?"

"Pender left," Kelen said. "He's back at the Homestead where he won't get in the way. Team, are we ready?"

A round of affirmatives sounded through the comms. "Tony, you're up."

Tony flicked his comtab and sent a signal to the *Swan*. It was a longshot, but he hoped Liz had used the family protocol for setting their locks. His comtab hummed, then the screen turned green. "Yes! Good job, Liz! Airlock is open."

Kelen led the team across the tarmac, counting on their Kamelion-covered suits to hide them from the occupants of the ship. The hatch opened at Kelen's touch, and they climbed inside. Tony pulled the outer hatch shut and sent another signal. "Go!"

Two teammates burst out of the airlock and into the corridor. According to the specs on this ship, the hatch to the right led to the lounge while the one on the left accessed the cargo hold. Two of the team went to the lounge, while Tony and the rest headed aft. If the *Swan* had *soldaty* on ice, as Lou had reported, the enforcers would be waking them up now.

Kelen waved for the others to stay in place and ducked his head around the edge of the open hatch. "Three bogies." His voice was barely audible over the comms. "They're opening the big crate—that's gotta be our freezer. Let's take them out before they wake their friends. The door must be on the far end."

Tony crawled to the hatch and propped his blaster on the lower lip. A huge cube took up most of the hold, with stacks of smaller crates tied against it. No people in sight. He jumped to a crouch and ran across the space on quiet feet, stopping behind the last stack of crates. Without turning, he felt the rest of the team arrive at his back.

"We're in place." Kelen held up three fingers. "On my mark. Three, two, one, mark!"

Tony lunged around the edge of the cube, weapon ready, eyes searching for potential targets. But there was nothing. A person-sized door stood open in the end of the cube, and light gleamed from inside.

Kelen blinked at him from the opposite side of the cube.

Surely it couldn't be that easy? Tony stepped forward, shoved the door shut, and slammed the latch into place. A muffled shout leaked out, but he ignored it.

Kelen leaned against the door. "We need a way to lock it. Are we sure they're all in there?"

Tony shook his head. "Still need to clear the ship."

"Boss, I got prisoners," a voice reported through the comms.

"Where are you, Murphy?"

"In the lounge with Aris."

Kelen pointed at two of the team. "Find some way to lock that thing. Weld it if you have to. Then stay here and keep an eye on it. The rest of you, move out."

They hurried through the ship, clearing each space as they went. In the lounge, a woman with "Saul" printed on her back lay face-down on the carpet, hands secured behind her back, armor powered down. A smaller woman lay on the floor nearby.

"Liz!" Tony dove across the room to check her pulse. "Is she alive? Where's Maerk?"

"They're alive," said Murphy. "We found them crammed into the med pod. I left the guy there and turned it on. He looked like he needed it more."

CHAPTER 41

"FRANCINE, I can't understand what you're saying. Slow down." Quinn listened, hands holding the old-fashioned earphones over her ears. "Their armor is too advanced for the sizzlers?"

Auntie B's voice cut through. "All unit commanders. Threat at the landing field has been neutralized. Company C, secure your prisoners and leave skeleton teams to monitor the field and drop back to the Homestead. And for Titan's sake, get someone into field traffic control who knows how to follow the script! The rest of you, fall back to the village." As she spoke, she strode into the control room, pulling off her headset. "How are we going to take down the group at the lake?"

"I can target the ship with one of the orbit busters." Doug pulled a screen to the front of his display. Dotted lines showed the proposed trajectory. "They aren't as effective or precise in the atmosphere, but they can make a big boom."

"Hold that in reserve," Auntie B said. "We have people at that field."

Quinn pulled one earphone away from her head. "End has an em-cannon on the shuttle. He can disable the ship. That won't stop the Russosken, but it takes away a retreat option."

Auntie B nodded. "Our team is falling back, so they can do that as soon as the firing line is clear. What else?"

Quinn listened with half an ear while she tried to think of something—anything—that would help. Most of these options had been discussed and built into contingency plans in the days leading up to the attack. The projected outcomes weren't as optimistic as if the sizzlers had been effective, but such was war.

On a hunch, she searched the net for specs on the Russosken armor. Maybe there was a way to turn up the gain on the sizzlers.

The Mark Five was a version of the latest Federation armor. Even though she knew the Federation was supporting the Russosken, seeing those words on the screen sent an arrow to her heart. Despite the pages of proof Tony had revealed, some small piece of her still wanted to believe in the high ideals the Federation claimed to support. But it was all propaganda to cover the greed.

She read through the specs. They were probably inflated to make potential enemies fear the Federation. If she knew which were lies, she might be able to find a weakness. She needed an inside source.

With a grin, she activated a private comm to the *Screaming Eagle*. "Francine," Quinn whispered.

"We're a little busy here, Quinn," End replied.

"What are you doing?" Quinn asked. "I thought you were just monitoring the field until you could get a clear shot with the em-cannon."

"We are," End said. "It's not as easy as it sounds. The—"

She cut him off. "I need to talk to Francine."

"Fine. Francie!"

"I told you not to call me that," Francine growled. "Hey, Quinn. You got something for me? Why did you switch comms?"

"I don't want to clutter up the command feed. Plus, I have an idea that probably won't work, and I don't want to get hopes up."

From the speakers over her head, laser fire blared. Herlen's voice cut in. "We've lost half the team. We need to fall back."

"Draw them away from the village," Auntie B said. "When you're clear, we're going to hit that ship and take it out. Move fast. Maybe we'll get some of those *soldaty*, too."

Quinn leaned closer to her mic. "Are you guys safe?"

"Safe enough," Francine said. "Tell me your idea."

"I'm looking at the Mark Five specs. How much do you know about the comm channels?"

"End, you're clear to fire the em-cannon!" Quinn wasn't sure who said it, but the voice cut through the chatter.

"Target is locked." End's voice was calm and only a little higher than usual. "Firing. *Futz*! It fell short!"

"Can you increase the range?"

"I'll try. The wind is coming up— That must have—" End broke off into muttered curses.

On the screen overhead, the red circles representing enemy fighters stopped. Then they coalesced into two distinct groups. One continued exchanging fire with Herlen's blue team, scattered across the eastern edge of the lake. The other group headed for the *Screaming Eagle*.

"They're coming your way, End," Quinn yelled.

"Firing again!" End said. "No go. With the wind, that ship is out of range."

"Doug, lock and fire," Auntie B said calmly.

"Ma'am?" Doug sounded shocked. "That will kill our team and probably End and Francine, too."

"But it will take out the enemy soldiers," Auntie B said. When Doug didn't respond, she prodded him. "Won't it?"

"I believe so," Doug said. "Even the Mark Five can't withstand that blast at that range."

"Then do it."

"Wait!" Quinn cried. "Please, I have an idea. If it doesn't work, you can use the orbit blaster."

On the screen, a red circle went dark, but two blue icons went down at the same time.

"Our people are dying," Auntie B said.

"And you think killing them faster is the answer?" Quinn asked.

Auntie B studied Quinn for a moment, then turned to the screen. "You have until the red team reaches this line." She dragged her finger across the display leaving a green line. "End, get out of there. Emergency launch."

"Wait!" As she yelled, Quinn's fingers flew on the keyboard and screen, sliding chunks of code from one program to another. "I need the *Screaming Eagle* to send this."

"Quinn, those bogies are getting close," End said. "There's nothing to stop them!"

A view from End's drone popped up on one of the side screens. The *soldaty* loped across the dry lake, their powered armor allowing them to make long, flowing strides. Behind them, pink colored the eastern sky as the sun rose.

It would be beautiful if they weren't killers, Quinn thought. They stopped a hundred meters from the shuttle and began setting up, pulling pieces of gear from their backs.

"Quinn." Francine's voice sounded shrill in her ear. "I can't let them catch me."

"Francine, focus!" Quinn said. "Look at the code I'm sending you. You're the only one who knows this stuff."

"Enemy closing," Auntie B said. "Doug, on my mark."

"Give me a few more seconds," Quinn begged. "End, you can start moving, but don't launch until my signal goes through."

"Belay that!" Doug called. "Moving is going to put them into the blast zone!"

"Quinn, I can see them!" Francine's voice shook.

The soldiers had pieced together a tripod supporting a huge barrel pointed at the shuttle.

"Damn it, Francine," Quinn barked. "Check. The. Code."

Time seemed to stretch. Quinn watched her screen as Francine flipped through the code modules, adding a line here, tweaking a call there. She must be moving at lightning speed, but it felt like hours. Finally, the code windows flicked closed, one by one.

A voice echoed through the speakers. "Enemy shuttle, you have five seconds to open your rear hatch, or we will fire."

"Hit it!" Quinn cried. "Francine, send the signal!" Nothing happened.

"Francine?" A window opened on her screen, then closed again.

"Sassy, no!" Francine cried.

"Ignore the caat!" Quinn cried. "Send the signal!"

No response.

Then her screen flashed and the words "signal sent" appeared.

"Francine?" Quinn asked.

"They've stopped!" Doug thrust his pointing finger at the battlefield display. The blue dots continued to move east, but the red circles had frozen. "What did you do?"

Quinn ignored the cheering around her. "Francine?"

"I'm here." Her voice was raspy. "I can't believe that worked."

"We've got incoming!" Tony's voice came through the speakers. "A private yacht. It must have jumped in with the *Torment*. We weren't looking for a second ship, and their transponder is off."

"Have you identified it?" Auntie B demanded.

"Lou caught it," Tony said. "It's been lurking behind the larger moon. Lou says the drive signature matches a ship called *Vengeance of Omsk*."

Auntie B's face froze. "That's Petrov of Daravoo's ship."

"Exactly," Tony said. "He's on a landing trajectory."

"That vermin will not land on my planet." Auntie B swung around to Doug. "Take it out."

"Locking on target now." Doug spoke with deadly precision. "Planetary defenses locked on. Orbit blaster online. Firing. Target is splashed."

Silence fell. Then a loud whoop went up, other voices joining in until the room rang with celebration.

Auntie B let the cheers continue for a few seconds, then she held up a hand. "We've got cleanup to run. Teams, check in."

As the various teams called in their status, Quinn toggled her comm link to the *Screaming Eagle*. "You okay, Francine?"

"I— The weirdest things happened here." Her voice shook. "Can you see the drone vid?"

"Hang on." Quinn pulled up End's drone feed. The rocket launcher and the fallen *soldaty* were hidden by masses of green vines. *Growing* green vines.

Quinn stared at the screen. "Did that plant *attack* them?"

Francine's shaky voice replied. "I think so."

CHAPTER 42

THE COMMAND TEAM gathered around Doug's dining table. It was a tight fit, but they didn't mind. Auntie B had Jessian bring food from the village. Across the valley, the citizens of Lunesco celebrated while the planetary leaders gathered to review the mission and make plans for the future.

"I'm still not clear on how you stopped them," Doug said.

"We turned off their armor," Quinn replied. "The Mark Five has a maintenance mode that freezes the armor. With Francine's inside knowledge, we were able to trigger that remotely."

"Who would build such a stupid command into battle armor?" Doug asked. "I mean, I know the Federation buys from the lowest bidder, but that's ridiculous."

"This isn't standard Mark Five armor." Francine poked at her noodles. "It's the version sold to the Russosken. The Federation doesn't trust the Russosken, but they use them. I believe this back-door was built to do exactly what we did if the Russosken ever tried something the Federation didn't like. It was too easy."

Quinn nodded in agreement.

"And what about the vines?" Tony poured more wine into the

glasses he could reach. "Has that ever happened before? It was like the plant decided to help."

"I've never heard of the sugar vines attacking anyone." Auntie B took her glass with a nod of thanks. "But we don't normally lie around in deactivated armor. Maybe that maintenance setting emits a frequency that stimulated vine growth. We'll have someone look into that." She waved dismissively. "But the more pressing matter is what are we going to do with our prisoners?"

"No one is worried about attack vines?" Francine whispered into Quinn's ear.

Quinn shrugged. "I thought the fact that they grow only on human settlements was kind of creepy, but this is terrifying. I'm glad I'm not staying here."

"If we ship *soldaty* home, they'll report back to the Russosken," Tony said. "That will make all of us targets."

"This action is going to make us targets regardless." Auntie B looked around the table. "All of us."

"They don't know some of us were involved," Maarteen said apologetically.

"You forget, they have an informant on this planet." Auntie B thrust a finger at him. "We took out a local warlord. The Russosken are going to target us, individually and collectively."

Tony nodded. "I agree." He turned to Amanda and Pete. "That's why we need to spread the rebellion. You have contacts on other planets. Now's the time to get them into motion. While the Russosken are weakened."

"Killing Petrov was probably a huge mistake," Francine whispered. "The *nachal'nik* will read it as a direct attack on the Russosken."

"Unless they have the backing of the Federation's fleet," Doug said, "our planetary defenses and my orbit busters should be enough. And if you stir up trouble elsewhere, that will help."

"Good enough for me." Auntie B rose. "We will need to train a crew to monitor inbound ships. Quinn and Francine's upgrades have given us a fairly robust monitoring system. I have some contacts who can help us buy newer equipment."

She made eye contact with each person in the room. "We are in your debt. We could not have attempted such an undertaking without you. Most of you have no stake in Lunesco. I realize you're working toward something bigger, but to us, you freed our planet." She lifted her glass. "To freedom!"

"Sempre Libero!" Amanda replied.

"Sempre LIbero!" Maarteen echoed.

MAERK STOOD in the lounge of the *Swan*. The med pod had set his broken ribs and injected him with a bone-knitter. He still moved slowly, but at least knives didn't stab through his lungs anymore. The yellow and green bruises on his face had faded, too.

"The Lunescans did a pretty good job cleaning it up." Liz wandered in from the cockpit.

Maerk nodded. "I guess they aren't holding the Russosken invasion against us."

"Not like we had much of a choice. We should have spaced the cargo."

"That wouldn't have eliminated Saul and Lima," Maerk said. "And it would have killed those twenty people."

"Russosken *soldaty*. Invaders. Criminals." With each word, Liz's tone got harder. "Not people."

Maerk shook his head. "Even criminals are people. We don't know why they joined the Russosken. Maybe they didn't have any choice. Like us."

"Ugh. Don't try to make me feel sorry for them. You are way more compassionate than I am."

"Hazards of upbringing." Maerk's comtab vibrated. "They're here."

Liz followed him to the cargo hold. Tony, Quinn, Francine, and

End walked up the extended back ramp. Liz surged forward to throw her arms around her son. "Are you okay? I've missed you so much! Where's your sister? Have you grown?"

A grin split Maerk's face as he strode to End. He pulled his son away from Liz and hugged him tightly. They thumped each other on the back in a manly fashion, then End pulled away.

"It's all good." End's voice cracked, and he coughed to cover it. "We're vine. I mean fine."

"Tony!" Liz hugged him, then pulled back and punched him in the arm. "What the hell, Tony! I thought leaving the kids with Lou was risky, but she didn't bring them into a mafia battle!"

"Good to see you, too, cousin," Tony said.

The two women stood back, watching the family reunion. Maerk made eye contact with Quinn, then pulled her into a bear hug. "Come here, you two!" He reached out and dragged Francine into the group hug. "It's good to see all of you."

"Let's get comfortable." Liz slapped the ramp control then led the group back to the crew lounge.

End dropped onto the couch. "Ouch! Mom, this thing is like a metal slab. If I'm coming with you, you're gonna need a better sofa."

Liz stared at End, tears in her eyes. "Does this mean you're joining us on the *Swan*?"

End squirmed. "Maybe. Depends."

She sniffed and smacked his shoulder. "You'll take what you get and stop complaining."

"Fine." He rubbed his arm. "I'll bring my blow-up furniture."

"Done."

"What's next for you three?" Maerk asked the others.

"I made arrangements with Amanda and Maarteen to help get things moving elsewhere in the fringe," Tony said.

"Mother will have your head if she learns you're starting a revolution," Liz said. "Her livelihood depends on the Federation. If it goes under, she'll have to start over again."

Francine shrugged one elegant shoulder. "Maybe not. If she

knows what he's stirring up and where, it could improve her bottom line."

Tony grinned at Francine. "Excellent reasoning. Remind me to put you on my PR staff." He turned back to his aunt. "I was hoping you would be able to provide transport for me—maybe for all three of us."

"You and Quinn and Francine?" Maerk asked.

"Me, Amanda, and Maarteen," Tony said.

"That's not a great idea," Quinn said quickly. "You can't put all your potatoes in one basket. Too risky."

"Potatoes?" Francine mocked.

"Hadriana thing." Quinn gave Francine a hard stare. "You know I'm right."

"She's right." Francine's eyes glimmered with suppressed laughter. "If you're all on one ship and it gets stopped by the Federation, that would be the end of your rebellion. Besides, you don't want to travel with Amanda. Flying with her would be like traveling with a tiger in heat."

Tony's face turned bright red. Maerk burst out laughing. He rolled back in his chair, fighting for breath. "You should see your face!" He gasped, pointing at the younger man.

"Amanda would be hot if she weren't so old," End said thoughtfully. "Watching her slink around Tony is kind of yeesh. Like seeing your parents kissing."

Maerk leaned over and kissed Liz, soundly.

"Ew," End said. "Exactly."

The others laughed.

"If their cover hasn't been blown, Maarteen and Amanda should continue to travel on the Federation's credit," Liz said. "No point in paying for it themselves. And staying away from each other adds redundancy."

Tony nodded. "You're right. Amanda suggested traveling with you..."

"She wanted some time alone with Tony." Francine wiggled her brows suggestively.

Tony's face flamed again.

"She doesn't know Liz is your aunt, does she?" Quinn asked.

"No, I haven't told anyone that," Tony admitted. "No need to know."

"I propose you four come with us." Maerk swept a finger at the group. "You can share the crew bunks for now. If we decide on a long-term commitment, we can convert that storage space into a couple more crew spaces."

"What about the *Screaming Eagle*?" End asked. "I have to take it back to Gramma. And you don't have a shuttle, do you?"

"No," Maerk admitted. "I think we can retrofit a skiff."

"Ugh." End reared back in his seat. "Skiffs suck. I want to fly a real shuttle."

"You can fly the *Swan*," Liz suggested.

"I don't want to be a long-haul shipper," End said. "Flying the shuttle is almost as good as flying a fighter plane—without all that order-following."

Quinn suppressed a smile.

Maerk looked at his ex-wife. "Maybe End should go back to Lou. He'd be happier there. And we can fly together, so we'll see each other more regularly."

Liz's eyes narrowed. "I'm not sure—"

"Yes," End said. "I'll go back, and Dareen can come over here."

"Look, we don't need to decide any of the details now," Maerk said. "Just the basic plan. We'll work with Lou to set up some transport contracts. Tony can hitch a ride to wherever he needs one. As long as the family is together, we'll be fine."

"What about us?" Francine asked quietly.

"You saved End's life," Liz said. "You're family now."

QUINN WALKED with End and Francine down the ramp to Jessian's waiting car. They had decided Quinn and End would fly back to the *Peregrine* on the *Eagle*, and Francine would stay with Liz and Maerk until they could meet at their next stop.

The wind had died at sunset, as always. The moonlight glinted off the "freezer cases" that had carried the *soldaty* to Lunesco. Those Russosken who had survived the battle—nearly all of them—were awaiting trial inside

"I wonder what they're going to do with them?" Quinn asked without much curiosity.

"Some folks were talking about leaving them there forever," End said. "Kind of a warning."

"That's horrible!" Quinn said.

"Better than what will happen to them if they go back to the Russosken," Francine said.

"Why? What will happen to them?"

The blonde slid a finger across her throat. "Failure is not tolerated. No one cares why you fail, only if you have. They'd be dead."

"Auntie B said they'll be given a fair trial, then shipped off-world." End shook his head. "She didn't say where."

"I'm glad that decision is above my paygrade," Quinn said.

"Hey, Jess!" End waved at the car parked in the lot and jogged over to chat up the driver.

Quinn turned to Francine. "Thanks."

"For what?"

"For derailing the Amanda plan."

Francine laughed. "While it *might* have been fun to watch, too much of Amanda would drive me to violence. Hey, that reminds me. Sashelle is on the shuttle."

"Yeah, I know," Quinn said. "End and I will take her back to the *Swan*."

"Yeah, but—" Francine looked around. Liz and Maerk had stayed inside the *Swan*. End was busy flirting with Jessian. "She fixed the program."

"What?"

"Sassy. During the battle. I went through all that code you sent and tweaked it. There was one block I wasn't sure about. I opened it back up to check. Sassy jumped up on the console and hit something. She *changed* something. I hit send before I realized she'd changed it. And it worked."

"The caat hit the launch button?" Quinn stared at her friend.

Francine stared back, eyes wide. "Afterwards, I looked at the automatic change file. I made a mistake. Sassy *fixed* it."

"You're saying the caat fixed your program and saved our lives."

"I'm telling you what happened. I'm not ascribing intent to the caat." Francine dusted her hands together and held them up. "But she is the Eliminator of Vermin."

THE STORY ISN'T OVER. Did Sashelle save the day, or was it a weird accident? Will Francine stay with the crew of the Peregrine? And what about that data card Quinn got from Sebi Maarteen? Read Quinn and Tony's next adventure in Krimson Surge.

AUTHOR NOTES

August 25, 2023

Thank you for reading the second book in the *Krimson Empire*. I first wrote this book in January and February, 2020, and it was published in April of 2020.

In this book, Quinn starts to come to terms with the idea that the Federation isn't the idealistic place she thought it was. She always knew that, of course, but part of her didn't want to believe it. It's never mentioned in the books, but Quinn's parents and grandparents helped found the Federation as a place of freedom and equality. Then the wrong people took charge, and things changed. But even when her life began to go horribly wrong, it was hard for her to let go of that vision. She'll finally make a clean break in book three, but for now, she's conflicted.

I'd like to take a moment to thank my original publisher, Craig Martelle. He believed in this project when it was just *The Trophany*, and he published the entire series under his imprint when I had very few fans. He gave it a much larger audience than I could have at that time, and I will always be grateful.

I'm also grateful he was willing to return the rights to me now, so

AUTHOR NOTES

I can weave the Krimson Empire into the larger *Huniverse* and introduce it to even more people. I've started working on a cross-over novel, in which the Colonial Explorer Corps "finds" the Federation and the Commonwealth. It could be a bumpy ride.

Thanks so much to my amazing Kickstarter backers. I've listed your names on the next page. Without you, this relaunch would have been so much harder!

I'll be republishing the entire series soon, distributing it through all of the ebook retailers. I also plan to make the books available for sale on my website. If you know anyone who'd like a copy of the series, please send them to juliahuni.com. And if you enjoy hopeful science fiction with heart and humor, check out my other series, listed on the last page of this book (unless the printer adds a few blanks, which they sometimes do in printing.)

You can find me all over the inter webs.

Email: julia@juliahuni.com
Amazon https://www.amazon.com/stores/author/B07FMNHLK3
Bookbub https://www.bookbub.com/authors/julia-huni
Facebook https://www.facebook.com/Julia.Huni.Author/
Instagram https://www.instagram.com/Julia.Huni.Author/

If you'd like to keep up to date on what's going on with my writing, sign up here. Plus, you can download a short story about Sashelle.

Thanks to my fabulous Kickstarter supporters:

Alice Hickcox
AM Scott
Andy fytczyk
Angelica Quiggle

AUTHOR NOTES

B. Plaga
Barb Collishaw
Brenton Held
Bridget Horn
Buzz
C. Gockel
Carl Blakemore
Carl Walter
Carol Van Natta
Cate Dean
Chicomedallas123
Christian Meyer
Clark 'the dragon' Willis
Clive Green
Craig Shapcott
Daniel Nicholls
Danielle Menon
Dave Arrington
David Haskins
Debbie Adler
Diana Dupre
Don Bartenstein
Donna J. Berkley
E. C. Eklund
Edgar Middel
Elizabeth Chaldekas
Erudessa Gentian
fred oelrich
Gary Olsen
GhostCat
Ginger Booth
Giovanni Colina
Greg Levick
Heiko Koenig

AUTHOR NOTES

Hope Terrell
Ian Bannon
Isaac 'Will It Work' Dansicker
Jack Green
Jacquelin Baumann
Jade Paterson
James Parks
James Vink
Jane
Jeff
Jim Gotaas
John Idlor
John Listorti
John Wollenbecker
K. R. Stone
Karl Hakimian
Kate Harvey
Kate Sheeran Swed
Katy Board
Kevin Black
Klint Demetrio
Laura Rainbow Dragon
Laura Waggoner
Laury Hutt
Liliana E.
Luke Italiano
M. E. Grauel
Mandy
Marc Sangalli
Marie Devey
Mark Parish
Martin
Mel
Michael Carter

AUTHOR NOTES

Michael Ditlefsen
Michael L. Whitt
Michelle Ackerman
Michelle Hughes
Mick Buckley
Mike W.
Moe Naguib
Niall Gordon
Nik W
Norm Coots
Patrick Dempsey
Patrick Hay
Paul
Pauline Baird Jones
Peggy Hall
Peter Foote
Peter J.
Peter Warnock
Ranel Stephenson Capron
Regina Dowling
Rich Trieu
Robert D. Stewart
Robert Parker
Rodney Johnson
Roger M
Rosheen Halstead
Ross Bernheim
Sarah Heile
Sheryl A Knowles
Stephen Ballentine
Steve Huth
Steven Whysong
Susan Nakaba
Sven Lugar

AUTHOR NOTES

Ted
(The other) Ted
Ted M. Young
Terry Twyford
The Creative Fund by BackerKit
Thomas Monaghan
Timothy Greenshields
Tom Kam
Trent
Tricia Babinski
Valerie Fetsch
Vic Tapscott
walshjk
wayne
werelord
Wesley Dawes
William Andrew Campbell (WAC)
Wolf Pack Entertainment
Yvette

ALSO BY JULIA HUNI

Krimson Empire
Krimson Run
Krimson Spark
Krimson Surge
Krimson Flare

Colonial Explorer Corps
The Earth Concurrence
The Grissom Contention
The Saha Declination
The Darenti Paradox

Recycled World
Recycled World
Reduced World

Space Janitor
The Vacuum of Space
The Dust of Kaku
The Trouble with Tinsel
Glitter in the Stars
Sweeping S'Ride
Orbital Operations (a prequel)

Galactic Junk Drawer

(contains Orbital Operations
The Trouble with Tinsel
and Christmas on Kaku)

Tales of a Former Space Janitor
The Rings of Grissom
Planetary Spin Cycle
Waxing the Moon of Lewei
Changing the Speed of Light Bulbs

Friends of a Former Space Janitor
Dark Quasar Rising

Julia also writes sweet, Earth-bound romantic comedy that won't steam your glasses under the name Lia Huni.